To Be Honest With You

To Be Honest With You

LINFORD CHRISTIE

Michael Joseph

LONDON

MICHAEL JOSEPH LTD
Published by the Penguin Group
27 Wrights Lane, London w8 5TZ
Viking Penguin Inc., 375 Hudson Street, New York, New York 10014, USA
Penguin Books Australia Ltd, Ringwood, Victoria, Australia
Penguin Books Canada Ltd, 10 Alcorn Avenue, Toronto, Ontario, Canada M4V 3B2
Penguin Books (NZ) Ltd, 182–190 Wairau Road, Auckland 10, New Zealand

Penguin Books Ltd, Registered Offices: Harmondsworth, Middlesex, England

First published 1995
3 5 7 9 10 8 6 4 2

Set in 12/15.75 pt Bembo Monotype
Typeset by Datix International Limited, Bungay, Suffolk
Printed in England by Clays Ltd, St Ives plc

A CIP catalogue record for this book is available from the British Library

ISBN 0 7181 4063 X

The moral right of the author has been asserted

Photographic Acknowledgements
Photographs 1–12 are from Linford Christie's collection
Photographs 29–34 and 43 are taken by Mark Shearman
All the remaining photographs are taken by Jon Nicholson

CONTENTS

In loving memory of
My mother Mabel A Christie
and my grandmother Lillian A Morrison

When men on earth have
Done their best
Angels in heaven can't
Do better

ACKNOWLEDGEMENTS

To all who have helped
Cheered
Laughed and shed many tears
In support over my many years
    Thank You

To all my fans
Who have jumped and screamed
Both at home and in the stands
Biting nail, clapping hands
    Thank You

To my mother, father, family
Friends
On whose guidance and never
Ending support I depend
    Thank You

To Ron, physios, my training crew
Without you all what would I do
When I was down you helped me
Through
    Thank You

To Mandy, what can I say
You've helped and supported
Me all the way
In my heart you'll always stay
Thank you

To Ali, Sue and the 'Nuff Respect crew
Maurice, Diane, Stan, Mark & Jon too
Respect and thanks to you is due
Thank You

INTRODUCTION

The title for this autobiography was chosen for two reasons. 'To be honest with you' is a phrase which I use frequently and, half the time, without realizing it. But it does sum up how I try to be; certainly, it says everything about what follows.

I felt the time had come to tell my story exactly as I see it. There has been plenty written about me and I often wonder who they are talking about; where the details have come from. I can only recount the facts as they happened. I can only be honest with you, for I know no other way. Now you can make up your own mind.

Writing this book has brought me a lot of pleasure mainly because it has allowed me to focus on a past which has brought good and bad – but mainly good. And sometimes brilliant.

I can't complain. I've had a really good time. I have been fortunate enough to compete in a golden era. I've met so many people, and now I can introduce them to you. It has been a great pleasure to compete against the likes of Carl Lewis, Don

Quarrie and Hasely Crawford. I've run at White City and I've been all round the world. I've seen it and I've done it; it's been good.

This is a record of fond memories which I hope you will share, starting with a wonderful childhood in Jamaica, a place where my values were formed, a place where I learned respect. I have tried to stick with those principles ever since. I find it very sad that fewer and fewer people have respect for their elders, respect for others and for their property. I am not trying to deliver any messages in this book but if the account of my life and career so far brings an awareness to others – particularly the adults of tomorrow – then I will be really pleased.

Whatever the interpretation, I hope you enjoy sharing my memories and meeting my friends. Unfortunately, there have been one or two enemies as well, but they are a small minority.

The truth is that, looking back on my life, I wouldn't change any of it and, hopefully, this book will reflect that. I think if you honestly make that claim, then you have achieved a lot.

This book is for athletics fans as well as casual followers of the sport, and anyone who has cheered to see British athletes triumphant. I've talked about drugs; I've had my say about the way the sport is run; I've touched on religion and racism; I have described technique and training. I have painted the picture of an athlete's world while telling my story. I have tried to put into words the answers to questions such as 'What's it like?' and 'How's it done?'. You can judge whether or not I have succeeded.

It's been fun although I must admit that there have been times when I didn't want to do the book because telling tales on people is not my idea of enjoyment. I don't like saying that a certain person has been a right so-and-so, even though that is the undoubted truth. There were moments when I thought that maybe I shouldn't. But, since that was the way it was, I have not held back. This is my only chance to tell the full story; my best opportunity to be honest with you.

Chapter 1

'HEY! I'M BLACK!'

I was always in trouble over my shoes. No matter what my parents bought me — hobnail boots, shoes with steel toe caps, anything — I would somehow manage to destroy them. I had been living in England for about five years when my mum gave me a pair of Tuf shoes. These were the business; very expensive and, according to my mum, definitely not for playing football in.

I started off with the very best of intentions but you know how it is. What else is a twelve-year-old going to do in the school playground? We were only allowed to play soccer with a tennis ball which, of course, was hopeless. I went to kick the ball, missed — and kicked the ground. In one terrible moment I had managed to scuff my shoes very badly. I panicked. I went up to the art room and painted my shoes black! I don't know what I hoped to achieve because, of course, it didn't work on leather. It never occurred to me to buy a tin of polish.

Now I was really terrified. When I got home, I went straight upstairs to my room. Kids can be so stupid. The normal procedure on arrival was to parade in front of my parents so that they could see how smartly dressed I was coming home from school. I was usually no different from any other kid; shirt hanging out, tie halfway round my neck, that kind of thing. But still I had to go on parade each afternoon and it was asking for trouble when I ran straight upstairs. Then I made things worse by getting changed immediately, something which usually took a lot of powerful persuasion as my mother became increasingly annoyed by the sight of me hanging around in my school clothes.

My mum called me down. She asked to see my uniform. That was okay. Then she said 'Where are your shoes?' That's what I did *not* want to hear. I tried to get out of it by doing other things, like making cups of tea to take her mind off the subject, but she kept asking to see the shoes. Eventually, there was no alternative.

I cried from the top stair, all the way down. I knew I was going to get a smacking and, of course, the punishment would be even worse because I had tried to be clever.

My mum had said 'you're not playing football because you are going to kick your shoes out'. But I just wanted to be a footballer above everything else. I'll never forget the first time my dad bought me a pair of Puma football boots. Georgie Best wore Puma and now I had all the skills of Georgie Best. I had his boots on, laced up at the side, so I automatically felt I played much better. I could play in games at school during the week, that was fine. But on Saturdays, when I was supposed to play for a school team against other schools, my parents would not allow me to go because there was work to be done at home. There was no argument about it, that was life. That was the way it had been ever since I had started to grow up in the West Indies.

★

My first memories are of living in Kingston, Jamaica, in a really big house. At least that's the way it seemed to me. I lived there until I was seven and I have been back since. I now realize that the house was not as large as I thought it was. In fact, I'm a bit disillusioned because many of the things which were around when I was a boy have changed a great deal. But none of that can take away the wonderful memories I have of life in Jamaica.

Unity was everything. My mum and dad moved to England very early in my life and I lived with my grandmother (my dad's mother), my two elder sisters, my uncle, his girlfriend and my three cousins. We did everything as one. There was discipline and yet, at the same time, everything was quite relaxed.

My grandmother gave orders to my cousin because he was the eldest. It was his duty to dish out the chores all the way down. I may have been the youngest but I still had to do my bit and muck in with everyone else. The idea (I realize now) was to help us learn what it is like to share the workload. For example, water came from a communal pipe near our house and we had a big barrel which had to be filled each morning before we went to school. Everyone had a container according to their size. I had a tiny bucket and, by the time I got home, there was no water left in it. But that didn't matter. The act of fetching the water every morning was part of the learning process and the acceptance of a sense of responsibility.

Discipline such as that would play a significant role in my athletics because the most important part of being an athlete – or partaking in any sport, come to that – is the discipline. If you haven't got it, then you're not going to be able to do the work. It's as simple as that.

We lived right in Kingston and I remember it as a very happy place. Everyone knew each other. From a child's point of view, it was almost as if everyone was related to you. If you were doing something wrong while walking down the road, then anybody who saw you – and I mean just about anybody – would be liable to give you a good smack and send you home. Then you would be scared of telling anyone in the house because the next question would be 'Why did they do that? It must have been because you were rude or naughty.' And then you would get a second smack. The community was that closely knit. You knew everyone and the underlying rule was that you had to respect your elders. If you didn't, there would be serious trouble at home.

Our house was detached with a garden. There was plenty of room. Mango, coconut, almond and palm trees were all around, so we were never short of fresh fruit. In particular, I liked the soursop tree with its fruit; green and spiky on the outside with black seeds contained in the white inside. We used to squeeze the fruit to make a milk drink. I can remember it well. We had no real need to buy sweets – not that we had that much money. We did receive pocket money, but not as a matter of course. You had to earn it by being good. If you were naughty – no pocket money.

I loved my granny so much. As far as I was concerned, she was the greatest. Even though my parents were not there, it was a typical grandmother–grandchild relationship in that I could do no wrong. If I was about to get a smack from someone else, I'd scream 'Grannyyyy!' and run to her side. She was tough but fair and called me 'Linford'. In fact, rather than shortening my name, she would sometimes call me anything which came into her head. But you always knew exactly who she wanted . . .

Granny played a big part in making sure, by the time I was four and ready to go to school, that I could read and write and recite my times-tables to twelve. That was compulsory and typical of any Jamaican child. You would have received a good smacking if you did not pay attention and learn. It was important to reach that level by the time you went to school. In Jamaica, if you failed to learn, it wasn't because you didn't want to. It was because you couldn't. Liberal use of the cane at school made sure of that. In maths, you were allowed one wrong answer. Any more than that and it was the cane. We learned by repetition – repeat and memorize, repeat and memorize. Each day, we had to take turns at the front of the class. There was a blackboard with A B C and so on written out and you had to get a class of perhaps twenty-five children to repeat it. We had to learn a different verse of the Bible every day which we would recite when we got to school.

Despite all that, I really did enjoy my two or three years of school in Jamaica. If you weren't well behaved you would be punished twice; once at school and, when the teacher told your parent or guardian, there would be another dose at home. 'What did you do to make your teacher cane you?' they would ask. Then they would say: 'You're embarrassing us because we send you to school with a good background and discipline at home, and you've let us down.' And it would be smack, smack, smack – again!

At nine o'clock, the school gate would be shut and anyone still outside would have to line up. That meant more trouble. A lot of emphasis was placed on hygiene. They would check your ears and fingernails to make sure they weren't dirty, then run a pencil through your hair. If it stuck – or if anything was wrong – you had to go home. That meant more smacks because you had given the teacher a reason to send you home. And when you returned to school, you would be late. So you would get it again. And again when you got home! Family honour was a very, very strong thing.

We stuck together. If you messed with me, you messed with

my whole family; that's how it was. I think that attitude played its part when I eventually became captain of the British athletics team. When I make a noise, it is for the whole team and not just for myself. There is no question in my mind about operating any other way.

Perhaps that's why my being British team captain seems to mean a great deal to the older generation of West Indians. They've got this thing about being British. They call the Queen 'Mrs Queen'; it is a mark of warmth and respect. To the West Indians, it is the highest honour to be captain of the British team. The younger generation perhaps do not see it that way but their elders understand the true value. When they meet you in the street, they say with touching sincerity, 'Yesss!! I wish you were my son.' There is a lot of pride, a lot of pride.

England has played a major role for West Indians mainly because those who moved to Britain came to make a better life. From what I've been told, my father came to England a few months after I was born on 2 April 1960; my mother, when I was two years old. She wanted to take me with her but my grandmother would not allow it. In those days, it was common-place to have grandmother look after the kids.

I was told that my parents, James and Mabel, went to England to make provision for us. The popular conception was that the pavements were paved with gold. I didn't know what gold was but I had this mental image of wonderful, shining streets. The path to England was a kind of Yellow Brick Road leading to a land where we were told the houses actually had paper on the walls! When I arrived in September 1967, the sense of anticlimax for a seven-year-old can be imagined. It was – uuggh!

I flew over on BOAC (British Overseas Airways Corporation, as it was then) with my eldest sister, Lucia. My disappointment at not finding gold the minute I stepped off the plane was quickly forgotten. I had a younger brother and two sisters, all born in England, and I was looking forward to meeting them. I had heard all about them from my dad when he came back to Jamaica to organize our trip. And, of course, I would in effect be meeting my mother for the first time. That was special even though, at the time, I regarded my grandmother as my mother.

My parents lived in west London but my cousins, when they arrived a couple of months later, went off to live with their parents, who had settled in Nottingham. The trouble was, my grandmother went to Nottingham as well. I don't think she ever got over that until the day she died. It was very hard for both of us but I think you learn not to show it. It was very, very difficult and I missed her terribly. As a result, I was a little bit withdrawn from my parents. To me, it was like living with two total strangers and I had to get used to them again, gain their trust. I trusted my grandmother implicitly and I had to transfer that trust to my parents. I don't think you get over something like that. I know my parents did what they did for the best but I found myself wishing they had either brought me over with them in the first place when I was very young or that they had left me in Jamaica. I really began to favour the latter when the winter of 1967–8 set in.

The first time it started to snow, I ran outside and opened my mouth to catch it. I had never seen snow before and knew nothing about it. Eventually my fingers went numb, then my toes. The lowest temperatures in Jamaica were usually in the sixties. I'd never felt the cold before and this was a big shock to my system. I really cried. I just didn't understand what was happening.

It is tempting to ask, on reflection, whether or not the life in Britain really was that much better. Would it not have been preferable to stay in Jamaica? The answer is, I really don't

7

know. My parents were in England and my dad was sending money across, providing for us. We never really wanted for anything, so I can say I never realized how difficult life might have been in Jamaica. It must have been hard in some ways but, at seven years old, you don't notice it. Things must have been much harder for my parents.

The first place my father worked was the British Bath Works where they made the big cast-iron baths. He wasn't earning a great deal and yet he had to pay rent, buy food and have enough money to send to Jamaica. How on earth he managed, God only knows. He worked long hours – even when I was there, he would leave at seven o'clock in the morning and I would not see him until seven o'clock at night. He had to send money to us and also pay for our fares; I have no idea how much the flight cost but it must have been a heck of a lot of money for my father to find. Life can't have been easy.

In any case, as a child, you simply accept what is happening. What else could I have done? By December 1967 my entire family was in England. There was no way of going back. Occasionally I wish that I had stayed in Jamaica and finished my education. Maybe I would have been a better person as a result. But maybe I would never have become an athlete. I have no regrets.

I was never aware of athletics as such when running around as a small boy in Kingston. We played marbles a lot and I was the 'Marble King'. We used the traditional glass marbles which I could flick twenty metres and more. I won most of the time and had a big bag of marbles to show for it. I played with a distant cousin who lived next door and we would go into the garden of his house, pitch marbles and challenge the kids in the neighbourhood. Marbles was the main game, although we did play a bit of cricket and rounders. The yard was big enough for games like that and we spent a lot of time in there. They were great days because we were together so much and we made the most of each other. There was very little temptation to play in the street.

It was exactly the opposite in London. We lived in Loftus Road, a few doors away from the Queen's Park Rangers football ground, and the house had no garden at all. There was my mother and father and six children sharing a two-roomed flat in an old terraced house. That was hard. People look at how things are for me now, at what I have achieved, but I don't think they realize just how difficult things were in the early days for all my family.

My dad and my mum both went out to work. They were not earning very much and yet they had to pay the rent and feed their children. There were three rooms on the top floor and we had the two biggest ones, the third was occupied by someone else. We shared a bathroom with other families and the cooker was by our front door, out on the landing. I really don't remember much about the house except that there was a red front door and lots of stairs. But I do remember that those were the days of tying the front door key around your neck, days when you came home from school and let yourself in. They were rough times. It is true that they played a large part in building my character. But, to be honest, they were days I would much rather forget.

My parents had hoped that I would stay at home for a while rather than go straight to school. But I was very keen and went back to lessons not long after I had arrived. I did it because I wanted to and, looking back, school was to play a great part in my learning process when it came to living in Britain. For a start, it gave me my first contact with racism.

The fact that I was a black kid really meant nothing to me. I never knew the difference between being black or anything else until I went to school which, ironically, backed on to the old White City athletics track. Children can be so vicious. A group of them were messing around, chasing one another, when I decided to join in. I caught this girl and she said I couldn't play. When I asked why not, she replied, 'My mummy said I shouldn't play with blackies.'

I thought, 'I'm black!' I was only about eight years old but to this day, I can still hear her voice and remember exactly what she said.

I went back to my mum and dad and said 'Hey! I'm black!' I didn't even realize I was coloured. I can say, hand on heart, that my parents never ever told me to dislike anybody because of their colour – their attitude has always been, treat people as you would like them to treat you. At school, kids started to shout 'Nigger, Nigger, pull your trigger, bang, bang, bang.' My parents never told me to go back and be horrible to them, or anything like that.

Children tell the truth and the white kids picked up these things from their parents, as was evident when that girl claimed 'My mummy said . . .' My parents must have known this moment was going to occur but they didn't tell me me how to prepare for it. I suppose they felt the best thing was to let me find out for myself and work out a way of handling it. My dad once told me that, when he came to England, he didn't realize white people went to jail. He said in Jamaica, all you ever knew was black people going to prison. When he saw the police arresting white people in England, he started to realize what it was all about.

I learned from my experiences, too. I had to grow up very quickly. It helped being smart – which I think I was – because I adapted quite easily and it never really bothered me after that. We had lots of fights at school. At first, I would cry and run away. But once I realized that was a weakness, something which would prompt the kids to really have a go at beating me up, I knew I had to stand up for myself. One day, I had had enough and I threw a stone at one of the leaders of the gang who used to pick all the fights. It hit him clean between the shoulder blades. The trouble stopped after that. In any case, I preferred not to get into a punch-up. In Jamaica, we didn't fight a lot. The kids in the house would argue – as children do – and, as far as I was concerned, they would beat me up anyway because I was the youngest. But fighting was not permitted at school. If you were caught, out came the cane . . .

In England, I found there was quite a bit of fighting in the schools but the great thing about it was that you would be friends later on. The fight would be finished and that was that. Before the start, you would ask, 'What d'you want? Everything?' Usually the answer was 'No, just fists. No kicking or anything like that.' And that's the way it would be. You would go in, fist to fist. You could guarantee, no matter how badly you were beating up the other guy or being beaten up yourself, the code of honour would be observed; just fists, no kicking.

Because the school was predominantly white, my friends were white and there was no problem with that. It stayed that way, going to each other's homes after school and so on, even when more and more black kids came to the school. Kids were kids; as far as we were concerned, it didn't matter about colour. It was only the influence of the adults which would decide otherwise.

We used to play football, blacks against whites. It was always that way and the interesting thing was that the mixed-race kids could decide which team they wanted to play for. But we had no choice. Even if there were perhaps only eight blacks lining up against twelve whites, that was the way it had to be. There was no mixing of teams and you had to play even if the sides were mismatched. Eventually, I learned to cope with that, along with everything else.

The most difficult thing to come to terms with in the English schools was the lack of discipline and respect. I found that really hard to deal with. In Jamaica, when a teacher asked a question, you had to raise your hand and then stand up if you were asked to answer. We would never dream of just sitting there. Standing up showed respect for the teacher. Naturally, I followed that rule when I came to England. I was very keen and eventually the teachers became fed up with me. At first they would say 'Give someone else a chance to answer.' Then it became 'Shut up Christie!' The other kids would pick up on that and call me a 'brain box' or whatever. After a while, I drifted to the back of the class and began to shy away. I found that really strange.

I also couldn't believe it when the kids start arguing with the teacher. I could never do that. I had been taught to say 'Yes Sir' or 'No Miss' and use the teacher's name. And if you dared to argue . . . just don't think about it, that's all.

That aside, Jamaican kids were no different from others. They could be really bad while playing on the street but, as soon as an adult appeared, suddenly they were angels. Even the most notorious bad guy would have respect for his elders. That is the way we were brought up. In England, I might find myself hanging around with one of the boys and his mother would ask him to do something. Quite often, he would swear in reply and my immediate reaction would be to become quite scared – not because of the dispute which would erupt between that boy and his mother, but because I would be afraid of my dad hearing one of my friends swearing at his parents. I knew I would be in trouble for keeping company with someone like that.

I don't think my parents would have been too pleased to know that we used to play 'Knocking Dollies Out of Bed' – knocking on doors and running away! But, when in the street, it would be more common to play 'Knock Outs' which involved kicking a ball between two marks on a wall. It was like playing tennis with your foot; you had to hit the ball between the marks and then the next person would kick the ball on the rebound, and so on. If the ball went outside the marks, you were out.

Cricket was popular too, although it caused the obvious problems on the street when the ball went all over the place. The bat would be chipped out of a piece of wood. Kids don't improvise any more. When I was in Jamaica, we would make scooters out of ball-bearing wheels with pieces of wood on top. We had to make everything – even balls. The technique was to scrunch up newspapers, wrap them tightly in elastic bands and shove them into the end of a stocking, and keep on doing it, fashioning the ball until it was round and really hard.

In London, we would play in a big park at the end of our road. It was quite safe in there and in a nearby cul-de-sac where we played football. I really enjoyed soccer. It was only a matter of a year or two after joining school – it seemed longer than that at the time – that I was playing football in the playground. I must have been running about with my usual enthusiasm when a teacher, Mr Wright, came along and said 'You look nippy. I'd like you to try out for the school athletics team.'

I was game for anything. But I obviously had no idea about the long-term consequences of that moment in the playground of Canberra Primary School in White City.

Chapter 2

SPIKES ON MY FEET

I won my first race – such as it was. The so-called track was marked out on the asphalt of the school playground. There was no atmosphere as such because, apart from the pupils taking part in the trial, there was no one else there.

I can't remember much about the event except to say that I was later accused of cheating by one of my two competitors! He claimed I had been given a head's start but, in fact, it was just the lane stagger. I was about eight years old and neither of us understood what the staggers really meant. All I knew was that I had won and that it was good enough to have me selected for the school team. It made no difference to my standing within the school; kids could see no big deal in being able to run. It was the norm.

The schools in the Shepherd's Bush and Hammersmith areas used to run at the old White City Stadium. It was the first stadium I had ever been inside. The kids were screaming for each other and it was something of a surprise to be running in such a big place. I did not fully appreciate the significance of competing in an arena which seated something like 40,000 people, until the White City was pulled down years later. Now we haven't got anything like that. Maybe football grounds – such as Old Trafford or Wembley – could be used but, as far as athletics is concerned, we've only got Crystal Palace, which holds around 20,000 spectators.

I take great pleasure from the fact that I must be one of the very few runners today who has competed at White City. It's strange, but that sort of thing gives a small psychological edge even though I hardly set the world alight. It's pretty difficult when you don't have a decent pair of running shoes.

Money was too tight to mention at home. There would be various school trips and so on, but I used to throw the letters away. I didn't want to ask mum and dad if I could have spikes and football boots or if I could go away with the school, because I just knew it would put my parents in a difficult position. Of course, there would be trouble eventually when the teachers asked why my parents had not replied. Then mum and dad would find out and I would be told off for not giving them the letter. I think they would have found the money, even if it meant having one less meal, but I didn't want to put them through that kind of pressure.

When I made the school team, my parents were supposed to buy me new plimsolls. It was popular to go to Curtess, a shoe shop on the Uxbridge Road, but I just could not mention it. One of the teachers eventually took me out and bought me a pair – but I didn't want to tell my parents because then I knew I would be in trouble! Having people buying you things was just not acceptable. I went out to race wearing the plimsolls, little ones with black elastic across the front. I ran at the White City Stadium – and I was beaten. I got smoked! I think I must have finished third or fourth. All the kids had spikes and there I was with my little plimsolls and Stanley Matthews nylon shorts, the wind blowing around and making them flap. I may have been beaten but the teachers said 'You did really well; that was good', and I took encouragement from that.

Just before the start, I had been talking to one of the boys and he asked how I was going to run the race. I said I was going to start slow and build up. The race must have been all of sixty metres! Those were definitely the days when it wasn't the winning, it was the taking part, which mattered most. It was fun, and I enjoyed it.

There were seven of us in my family and we all moved to Stowe Road, which was still west London but it meant a change of school for me. Athletics was not on the curriculum at Brackenbury School in Hammersmith; they were very much into football, which put athletics to rest until I went to secondary school in Fulham at the age of eleven. Once there, I made the school team. We had to buy the school uniform – and running shoes were on the list.

My father bought me my first pair of spikes in a sports shop run by Ron Springett, the QPR goalkeeper. Dad made it clear that I would have to buy the next pair myself. Despite my poor record with shoes, I kept those blue leather spikes for years. I wanted to take care of them so much. The first time I wore the spikes I didn't want to practise on the school playground, so I ran across the wooden floor of the gymnasium. The sports staff were *not* pleased . . .

The Henry Compton school had a great tradition in sports, particularly athletics. I had a go at everything – 100, 200 and 400 metres as well as all three jumps; long, high and triple. The high jump was the worst. These days, you land in a bed. Then, they had sand, usually unraked, and if you landed badly all the wind went out of your lungs and you would be in serious trouble. Mind you, the long jump had its own particular problems because it was usually necessary to jump over any dog shit which the teacher had failed to remove before the start.

I had no particular preference, I just did every event I could. The first time they asked me to compete in the 400 metres, I had no idea how to tackle it. One lap of the track! That was a long way. My teacher said, 'What you do is run hard for 200 metres, and then pick up'. Of course, I ran flat out for 200 metres and then I realized – Man! there was no picking up . . .

I did reasonably well at school. I was one of the fastest kids for my year, and that gave me a sense of achievement. We had some guys at school who were quick and it seemed that every year someone else would come out and run pretty fast. But I was always in the top two or three. I was okay. I ran in house games at the Hurlingham track and then took part in school championships at the West London Stadium. I remember one particular occasion when I was actually a bit upset about being asked to run for the school.

There was a rule which said that anyone who was late more than twice would be caned. One day, I fell foul of that and, a couple of hours later, my name was called over the tannoy. I could not imagine what this was for because I had already received my punishment. In fact, the teacher wanted to ask me to run for the school. I have to admit that I was pretty pissed off. I thought, 'he's caned me and now he wants me to run for the school!' At first I refused but, eventually, I was persuaded.

The London Schools Championship was the major event, a really great occasion. The West London Stadium would be absolutely packed and it was common to find some of the locals laying bets! Nowadays, nobody turns up; the London Schools

Championship is nothing like it was. The problem is that nobody wants to do it. Sport no longer seems to play such a big part in school life. There are too many distractions and, in any case, I don't think the teachers are as keen to play their part. My teachers would think nothing about taking the kids to the track after school hours – extra sports would be common. But teachers don't bother now. Maybe they feel the kids do not show enough appreciation.

Perhaps it has more to do with the lack of subsidies. The government is trying to put something back into the schools on the sports side – but it's too late. We have lost too many potential competitors along the way, not just from athletics but from football and other sports. Because they play such an important role, I firmly believe that teachers should be as highly paid as business people. It seems that the government wants to keep standards low because if there are too many educated people then there is the danger that they might realize what the government is doing!

The Henry Compton school covered a large variety of sports, among them fencing, judo, boxing, cricket and rugby – which I hated because it was always so cold. Most of the time I played football. I made the school team on a couple of occasions and I thought I was a decent footballer. But my parents did not encourage it. They were not keen because it was felt that sports were only for people who had nothing to do. As far as they were concerned, the important thing was to get yourself an education and then a job. Football was not on the agenda.

Despite my appreciation of soccer, I have never been to a football match in my life. I have been a Manchester United supporter from around the time Rodney Marsh left QPR. I had always wanted to meet Alex Ferguson, the 'Big Man' at United, and the occasion arose not long ago at the Yardley/

Daily Express Awards in London. Martin Edwards, the Manchester United chairman, was also there. He had heard that I was a supporter and he offered the club's hospitality any time I wanted to bring along a few friends to see a match. I actually felt a bit stupid at the time because I must have been acting like a little kid!

As far as my parents were concerned, going to a football match was uncalled-for. But that was mild compared to their feelings about dog racing. A Mr Jones lived a couple of doors away from us. Not long after the White City Stadium had been turned into a dog track, Mr Jones asked my parents if he could take me along. My dad hit the roof! He was very polite to Mr Jones but, when I kicked up a fuss, dad went berserk. Dog racing was for gamblers; a sinful thing. There may not have been any betting at a football match but the attitude was, if I went there, I would either get beaten up or become a hooligan. There were things to be done in the house, which meant football matches were out of the question. You never miss what you don't have; I learned to accept that.

My father's views on gambling must have rubbed off. I don't gamble and I wouldn't recommend it to anyone else. I think I've done the National Lottery once since it started. I don't mind having a flutter in a casino when I'm away, and the occasional light-hearted bet, but I wouldn't go into a bookmaker's and bet on horses regularly.

When my elder sisters moved out, I was the oldest child at home, which meant I had to do various chores while my mum and dad went out to work. I must have been thirteen or fourteen when my dad said 'Right! Into the kitchen; you're going to learn to cook.' I didn't want to know because I thought cooking was a woman's thing. Why should I learn to cook when my friends were outside playing football? Why should I be in the kitchen, being a sissy? But, once again, I had no choice. Dad tried to teach all of us but I was the idiot because I did it right. My brother, Russell, didn't want to learn, so he would burn the food and do everything wrong until my dad reached the point where he could stand it no longer and threw Russell out of the kitchen. I, like a fool, got it right more often than not – which meant I had to cook all of the time.

I became pretty good in the kitchen; I could produce Sunday lunch although I never really enjoyed doing so because I just did not want to cook. But, when I left home to live on my own, I looked on things differently and realized that all those hours spent slaving over a hot stove were actually quite important. Now I really enjoy cooking.

I got on well at school – but not as well, perhaps, as I should have done considering I had been able to read and write at the age of four. Any child who does that now in England would be considered gifted! My parents felt originally that I might become a doctor or something like that, but I don't think they were living in the real world.

Even though I was really into sport, becoming a PE teacher was not the sort of thing to be considered when I left school. I didn't really see it as a job because I didn't realize that you went to college in order to become a sports teacher. The attitude was, 'Why do you need a degree to show someone how to kick a ball around?'

Believe it or not I wanted to be a chef! My careers teacher thought that was a good idea because my father's compulsory training had taught me to cook well. But nothing came of it. Looking back, I agree with the saying that school days are the best days of your life. If I could be at school now, I would be! No Income Tax, National Insurance, no responsibilities, nothing to worry about. Just go to school and do your work . . .

Eventually, my dad decided that I should be an electrician. When I left school, I was at a rebellious stage and chose electronics – anything but being an electrician. I went to work for VisionHire. Because I was an apprentice, they gave me nothing of interest to do. The attitude was, 'Sit down, watch TV; get out of the way.' I could tell you how many squares there were on the test card – but very little else. I was bored; my heart wasn't in it. After about four weeks, I left and found a job at the Co-op, doing accounts. It was easy then to get a job. I enjoyed accounts even though I thought the store manager was a right bastard. He was a young guy and in my view he treated people like scum.

The only other drawback was having to work on Saturdays; it interfered with my budding career as a runner! One of my school teachers, Mr Jones, had reckoned that I was pretty good at athletics. He was keen that I should not waste my talent and he took me to West London Stadium, where I joined London Irish. Athletics put enjoyment into my life and much of that came from being a member of London Irish. They were a breakaway club, very receptive and largely set up for Irish people. The Irish make great distance runners but, as sprinters, they don't have it! I had no problems joining in except that even though I was the fastest in the team, they made me run in the B string. The guy who ran in the A string was a lot slower – but he was Irish. Even so, I loved running for London Irish. We had a pretty good team and I remember one particular occasion when we entered a junior relay at Crystal Palace – and won it. When they called out 'London Irish', you can imagine the reaction from the crowd as four black guys got up on the rostrum . . .

I hardly bothered with training, but I enjoyed the races. The trouble was, they were usually on Saturdays and, of course, I had to work. Saturday is a busy day for a department store and the accounts had to be done.

Working as such didn't bother me; I needed to work to support myself and I think the fact that I had worked helped when I turned to athletics full time. A lot of the young athletes today have never had a job, so they don't know what it's like. When they finish with athletics, what are they going to do? They have no work experience. Having a job prepares you for athletics because training is working. It's discipline.

After a couple of years, I became chief cashier at the Co-op Wandsworth branch, in charge of all the accounts departments. I liked figure work, not that I had particularly enjoyed maths at school. I knew I had to work, so I just got on with it and found I was pretty good. I was earning £19 per week, which meant I brought home between £16 and £17, after tax. I thought I was made! My dad was working as a porter at the BBC in Shepherd's Bush and my mum was a nurse in the Royal Marsden. My mother had trained to be a nurse when she came to England but she was also a dressmaker, one of the best I have ever seen. You could show her a picture of what you wanted and she would make it. My sisters had more clothes than the shops! Mum had a room to herself, piled high with material and all sorts of bits and pieces. Being a girl in our family was good news.

My dad made me pay rent. He said I had to learn how to budget for myself. As a teenager, I was convinced he was being greedy; I thought that he hated me. Of course, I was going through a learning process which my parents were operating the best way they could. It worked because I think I handle my finances efficiently today.

The same could not be said for my athletics training at the time. Wandsworth must be one of the worst places in Britain for traffic. I had to catch the 220 bus and crawl across Putney

Bridge and all the way through Hammersmith to Shepherd's Bush. I would finish work at around 5:30 p.m. and not reach the West London Stadium and start training – such as it was – until 7:00. I was tired by then. Finally, when I reached home, my parents would start nagging me about the time I was spending at the track. To make matters worse, I would sometimes injure myself during training. My mum would hit the roof. 'This thing is killing you!' she would shout. 'You leave here fit and well and you come back, limping and crippled. Stop this thing! Stop this thing!' It was out of concern more than anything else, but it became pretty wearing at the end of a long day.

Eventually I left the Co-op and went to work in the tax office. We had this vision that wearing a suit and working for the government was a prestigious thing to do. I did it for my parents really, but I wasn't happy. At least it meant I could run for the Civil Service. I won everything there was to win; I was the bee's knees. But the office where I worked in the Elephant and Castle was a horrible place. I stuck it for two years, then I had to get out. I just couldn't stay there a minute longer.

I was still running for London Irish and at the time, I couldn't understand why I was not being invited to the various meetings. As I said earlier, Irish runners are not regarded as good sprinters and I hadn't realized the significance of the name Linford Christie being typically Irish. In fact, people used to think my name had to be Christy Linford. Even worse, a guy called Ade Mafe was also on the team and they thought his name must be Paddy Murphy!

I seemed to have a natural talent and found it quite easy to run respectable times for the 100 metres. I managed to beat guys who were training regularly. My attitude was, 'So why the hell do I need to train?' I eventually got to the stage where I could do anything I wanted to do; long jump, high jump, anything. It became easier to get races while I was running for London Irish. Thames Valley Harriers, on the other hand also trained at the same West London Stadium but they had the big names, which would have made it difficult for a little fish like me to find races. At London Irish, I was gathering experience. I was, in effect, serving my apprenticeship.

The races were usually inter-club affairs. There were six or seven teams in our division and we would race every Saturday, one of the high points being the Middlesex Championships. But that was a fairly local event compared to the England Schools Championship in Nottingham, which I was eligible to enter until I was 19. I went there for the first time in 1979. As far as I was concerned, it was like going to the Olympic Games.

It may be hard to believe, but that was the first time I travelled on an InterCity train – and I found it a frightening experience. I'll never forget that journey. I was out of my seat, standing by one of the doors, when a train suddenly went past in the opposite direction. It made that violent whoosh! and scared the life out of me; I had absolutely no idea what it was and I ran away. Then I had to pretend that I wasn't scared, while I was shaking like a leaf.

Athletes at the England Schools Championship were only allowed to take part in one event; that way, everyone had a chance to compete. I ran in the 200 metres against a guy called Phil Brown, a fully-fledged international. This was in the days of the 'Afro' hair-do and I had mine in plaits. I was tall but gangly, with my hair flowing, and they nicknamed me 'Horse' because of the way I appeared to gallop rather than run. I came off the bend with quite a lead but, being inexperienced, I thought, 'I shouldn't be here'. I began to slow down and, of course, Phil Brown steamed past and won the race.

I remember the sense of occasion. I was not overawed by the procedures or anything like that, but I was impressed by the number of people. Running against other schools in London was one thing but competing against the best in England was something else. There was an impressive feeling of team spirit; all the kids were screaming for their particular favourites. We stayed with local families – and all I can remember about the home I stayed in is that they had a big, shaggy dog!

Everyone was given a packed lunch, which provided ammunition rather than nourishment as tomato fights broke out all over the place. I was swept along by it all and really enjoyed the day. It was the biggest race I had ever been in. The whole event left a lasting impression.

We were each given a form, asking what could be done to help young athletes improve. I wrote 'more competition' without really believing that would happen. Next thing I knew, I was entered in races alongside the likes of Don Quarrie, Hasely Crawford and Allan Wells – big names at the time. But I wasn't really overawed by them which, I suppose, helped to make me what I am today.

I never had heroes. I never looked up to people and said 'I want to be like Don Quarrie', or whoever. The only athletics sportsperson who really impressed me was Sonia Lannaman. To me, she was one of our best ever, but so unlucky with her injuries. I remember I wrote 'SL – Speed Queen' on the side of my spikes – and told my friends it was her autograph.

Not having heroes made life a lot easier for me. If you have heroes you don't want to beat them. I just wanted to beat everybody. Some people go through life just being casual because they feel comfortable like that. Others have ambition. I must have got mine through my family. My grandmother was a very determined person. And my father went through a lot, coming from Jamaica with very little money to a country where he didn't know anybody. I must have picked that up although determination in itself is not enough; I still had a lot to learn about athletics in the early days.

Hasely Crawford was such a big guy. He intimidated me like nobody's business. On one occasion, we were lining up to race and there was water in his lane. My lane was dry. He walked over, picked up my blocks and dropped them in his lane. Then he looked straight at me and said, 'I'm smoking! I'm smoking!' I was the little skinny kid, he was the big guy. I couldn't do anything. We are really good friends now and I still remind him of it.

Intimidation was different then and not particularly subtle. Just as we were getting ready to race, someone would say 'Your mama's a whore' or 'Your wife's real ugly'. Try that today, with people being more temperamental, and you are asking for a fight. At the time you had to ride the waves because, if you became angry or upset, then you would be beaten. On one occasion, a guy called James Gilkes was racing against Allan Wells. On the bend, Gilkes was talking to Allan, calling him names and so on. As soon as they got to the straight – whoosh! – Gilkes was gone.

They did not play that game with me because I was not a factor at the time. But, even though I was green, the experience helped me a lot. When I reached the stage where I really had to start racing these guys, I wasn't scared.

I started running indoors at Cosford, a Royal Air Force station out in the wilds, somewhere in Shropshire. They used a huge hangar and I broke the British indoor record there for 200 metres. I remember thinking, 'Oh yeah! I'm The Man!'

I was running against a guy called Peter Little. He was

younger than me but he was good, really good. He held the British 200-metre record at 21.9 seconds for a heck of a long time. I came along and ran 21.8 seconds. I was as pleased as punch.

This was my first taste of standing on the rostrum and appreciating the reaction of the crowd. They really enjoyed their athletics at Cosford and I was a virtual unknown who had beaten Peter Little's long-standing record. It was quite an occasion for everyone; I was very much aware of that. I really celebrated because it was my first British record and yet it seemed to me that I hadn't really tried that hard. I began to realize what the possibilities might be if I trained a bit harder. But I soon slipped back to my old ways; training still did not seem that important.

The win led to my selection for the British team for an indoor event against Germany in Dortmund. A long-jumper called Trevor Wade became an international at the same time and he called for me on the way to the airport. I could tell immediately that he had been through the same drama with his parents that I had suffered. My mum would not let me out of the house without a collar and tie. Trevor was a few years older than me, but there he was dressed in his best suit. It was tradition among black people. If you had to dress up just to visit the doctor, then going to the airport was a major event. Trevor and I were on the train to Heathrow when we saw team members wearing ripped-up jeans and dirty trainers. I couldn't believe it. Nowadays, nobody really bothers although I still tend to dress smartly on these occasions. If you are representing your country then I believe you should look smart. As far as I was concerned, I was representing Britain in the best possible way because I went to Dortmund and won the 200 metres in 21.7 seconds, breaking the British record again!

Winning in Germany gave me my first taste of international

success, and that meant a lot to me. All I wanted to do after that was compete for Great Britain. There was a return match at Cosford, our only indoor arena at the time, but no 200-metre event had been planned because of its comparative unpopularity. But I really wanted to compete and that desire lead to the first of many clashes with Frank Dick, the man with the title 'Director of Coaching' even though, in my view and that of many others, he had very little to do with coaching most members of the British team.

When Frank told me there would only be a 60-metre race, I asked if I could guest in that event. He said there was no space. When I said I would like to do the long jump, the answer was also no. Lynn Davies, the Olympic long-jump champion, was team manager at the time. He was very easy to talk to and, on the plane home, I was telling him how much I had enjoyed my first international and how I thought it was a shame there was no 200-metre event at Cosford. He said I could guest in the 60 metres and, when I repeated what Frank had told me, Lynn said there would be no problem finding me a lane.

I was delighted. But that soon changed when we reached Heathrow. Frank Dick stormed over and said, 'Didn't I say you couldn't guest, that there's no lane?' I agreed that he had, but explained that Lynn Davis had said there would not be a problem. Frank Dick's response really shook me. 'If I say you can't run, then you can't run. Don't you ever go behind my back and ask anybody else.'

I felt about two inches tall. I thought we were all adults, part of the same team. I was about twenty and yet I felt that he spoke to me as if I was a kid. It took me a long time to get over it. I could not understand how anyone could speak like that. I never had any problems with the guy – it was the first time we had met! How could he treat me in this way?

There were a lot of black people on the team, so race did not come into it. But I was the youngster and this was Frank Dick's way of impressing what little authority he had. I had not been precocious or anything like that; I was a mouse, compared to what I am now! Thanks to help from Lynn Davies, I got my lane in the 60 metres – and I beat all the athletes trained by Frank Dick. That probably did not help a relationship which was set to go from bad to worse. He would pick on me for no obvious reason. I have had a personal dislike of Frank's attitude ever since.

Chapter 3

LEARNING THE HARD WAY

Despite what people may say, I was never a heavy drinker. In a previous book I referred to drinking rum and black, and I think the image grew from that. If you take one drink, then I suppose you are a drinker. But I was put off alcohol in a big way while still at school. I'll never forget it.

I was in the sixth form. We had our own common room and someone brought a bottle of vodka along to a party. I drank the vodka like it was water. They also had rum, and I drank some of that too. I was fine – for as long as I was inside the building. When I stepped outside and into the cool breeze, I couldn't understand what was going on. My head started to spin and I was thinking 'God – what's happening, what's happening?' I don't think I was drunk as such, but I was on my way. I was still aware of what was going on when they took me home; aware enough to start to panic because I knew my parents would kill me.

In our house, if my parents were at home when I got back

from school, I had to go in and say 'Good evening mum, good evening dad'. It was a compulsory thing. That day, I went straight downstairs to my room and fell into bed. I slept for ages. I was fine when I woke up but when I went upstairs my mum asked, 'What happened? You came in and went straight to bed.' I said I had been playing football and that I was tired. I was tired all right. But I was also panicking . . .

I've never been like that since; never wanted to. The press like to say that I was a serious drinker. Yes, I would go out and drink rum and black. But if I managed two, then I had done really well. Generally, I would have the same glass for the entire evening, preferring it that way because I did not want a repeat performance of the vodka incident.

We used to smoke. Most kids do, which is why I can tell them 'smoking is bad for you'. Part of the wall in our school playground used to stick out; we would stand behind it, in 'smokers' corner', and puff away. It was cool to buy a good brand of cigarette. One guy used to bring in Peter Stuyvesants and if you had the thin, brown ones called More, then you were 'The Man' because you had a long cigarette. We progressed to menthol cigarettes in the belief that our parents wouldn't be able to smell tobacco on our breath. It shows how stupid we were.

Inhaling was the thing. The cigarette would be passed around and if you simply sucked it and blew out the smoke straight-away, someone would say 'you bum-sucked it' because the end was wet and horrible. They used to say 'Take it in, take it in'. I didn't know what that meant, so they would tell me to swallow it. If you could make the smoke come through your nose, again, you were 'The Man'! Some of the guys knew how to smoke because their parents did. I would watch them suck . . . and get it down.

I still lived in Shepherd's Bush and my dad had a friend, a white guy called Johnny, who was a live-in tenant for a while. I'll never forget him. He used to smoke roll-ups and I stole some of his tobacco – it was either Golden Virginia or Old Holborn – took a Rizla and rolled it up. I thought 'Yeah! I'm going to practise because, when I go back to school, I'm going to be able to take it down!' I did it – and I have never, *ever* experienced anything like it in my life. My head started turning around; my hands, my lips – everything, started shaking. I tried to go upstairs and I got to the top step when something in my head starting saying 'Jump! Jump down the stairs!' I panicked because, again, I had never experienced anything like it before and I couldn't understand what was going on. Then I began to feel sick.

My younger brother started smoking and, as soon as he came into the house, my dad would interrogate him. He would say 'Let me smell your fingers', and Russell would try using washing-up liquid and various other methods which would make no difference. Obviously, smoking at home was out of the question and I began to think that if I could do without smoking at the weekends, then why did I need to smoke when I was at school during the week? In the end, I thought 'This isn't for me' and I stopped. That was it.

In any case, the guys at the track didn't smoke, which made the decision easier. And, by the time I had gained that first inter-national entry at Dortmund and established myself as a British indoor record holder, the thought of smoking never entered my head.

Indoor running seemed a lot easier to me than outdoor, even though some people found it quite difficult to run at places like Cosford. Indoor tracks are generally 200 metres round whereas each lap outdoors is 400 metres. Of course, you don't have to worry about the wind – or the cold – indoors, but the thing about Cosford is that the track itself was very steeply banked. I can remember seeing people running in the outside lane and literally falling off the top. On the other hand, if you had lanes one or two on the inside, then you couldn't run because it was far too tight – especially if you had long legs. People thought at first that I would be too tall to run indoors but, despite being 6 feet 2½ inches, I adapted really well. I found the track a lot easier and a lot shorter – so I just did it!

The surface at Cosford, a mixture of wood and concrete I think, was very hard. Cramp was common after an event. We would play cards and dominoes on the train going home from races and a guy called Randolph Charles always had cramp. We'd be sitting there and he seemed to get smaller and smaller because he was sliding under the table. Cramp would pull you down and hold you; it was a right bastard. We went through a stage where we ate little glucose sweets which were supposed to give energy and prevent cramp. All they did was make you pee; you would spend your time running to the toilet. It was almost better to take a chance on not having cramp.

I didn't suffer too badly – certainly not as much as Randolph. Training was not a part of my schedule because I still thought I was pretty good. We used to go to parties on Saturday nights, coming back at about ten o'clock the following morning. It would be a race to see who could go home, get changed and be first to the track. Training, if you could call it that, was literally running home to Shepherd's Bush and then to the West London Stadium. Having no car, I used to run it. That was the way I prepared for the races.

Part of the deal was wearing our tracksuits on the street. There was enough time to go home and change after racing, but we didn't do that. We wore our Great Britain tracksuits after races because we wanted everyone to know that we were part of the team. Sometimes we would get changed on the train and put on our kit so that we could walk down the road from the station! It was one of those things; being an international was the business. We would wear our tracksuits as often as we could. Now, nobody bothers. Do it today and you feel like a show-off.

You go in for that sort of thing when you are young but then, I suppose, you become complacent. Ten or twelve years on, it doesn't mean so much. Everybody knows what you do. These days, if you've got to tell people, then you haven't done anything. Even so, I think tracksuits should be worn. We should have a sense of belonging, of being proud to be British in the way that the Americans have pride in their country. They are taught that from a very early age and they have this feeling that they're great – which is something this country lacks.

When I was at school in Jamaica, we would sing the British national anthem. When I came to England, I found that nobody bothered. Kids should be made to feel that they belong and I believe that's one of the reasons why we have problems. A lot of black people don't feel part of Great Britain. If children are taught to be proud of their country, then they will grow up with a lot more self-confidence. I often feel that this country no longer has any morals. We should start straight away with the younger generation; the kids should stand up in school each morning and sing the national anthem, be proud to be British. If they had done that when I was at school I think we would have much more respect for the royal family, even though they do not always behave themselves properly. But we've missed out on my generation, and the one after that.

My family went to church every Sunday. Mum and dad were deeply religious people and I think, in a way, it was forced upon us as children. But it was something I got used to. I became really involved and enjoyed it at the time. It was a Pentecostal Church – one of those happy 'Make a Joyful Noise Unto the The Lord' kind of churches – which is very largely West Indian. It was the same kind of church we had attended while living in Jamaica and therefore promoted the sense of unity. You called everyone Brother and Sister. My parents were trying to bring us up in the ways of the church from that early age, a unified church where you were supposed to always be there for each other.

As a family, we have never been into Catholicism or the Church of England, which I believe was brought across to Jamaica in the colonial days. I think Jamaican people thought otherwise and did their own thing. I was one of the smart kids in the church. I knew the Bible very well. Everybody tries not to discuss religion with me – even now. Maybe I could have been a good preacher! Perhaps it's not too late . . .

My attendance lapsed once I started to travel and became caught up in the world. Every now and again I think maybe I should go back to it. I believe in God; I don't accept Darwin's Theory of Evolution or anything of that nature. I think it's very important to believe in something; there's got to be a greater being. Society shows that there are people who are higher and better and you therefore have to have somebody who is better than all of those people. That's where God comes in. I think my talent to run is a God-given gift and I give thanks to Him for that. I was brought up in a very religious home and that is something you never forget. I believe God guides and protects me. He has helped me, through athletics, to become strong.

People sometimes ask me about the problems my family had with the police when they came into our home more than twenty years ago and gave us a bad time for no reason. I was very angry at the time but you can't sit back and think about things like that for ever. Life has to go on. It's history and I think athletics has helped me to cope with that kind of situation. I have realized that just because someone has done you wrong, not everyone else is the same. Yes, we had a problem with the police but that was only a minority in the force and I don't believe the majority should suffer as a result. There are some great policemen. I've met some really nice guys and I think they would agree that there are one or two policemen hellbent on giving the rest a bad name.

You have to take people as they come. I don't hate those particular policemen with their racist attitudes, I just feel sorry for them. You can forgive and forget, or you can choose not to; it's up to you how you want to deal with it. I cannot sit back and dwell on those things because doing that will hamper my progress. I am better off than those people now. I am where I am today – and where are they?

The police in my youth were different from the police of today because, when I was young, if you did something wrong, the local policeman would tell you off or clip you round the ear and take you to your parents. Nowadays, the first thing they do is take you to court to make sure that you have a criminal record. Some of the things they do are totally unnecessary. Maybe that's because society has become such an evil thing. But I think the police have lost touch. The respect which we had for the police in my youth is gone now. Part of the problem seems to be that the police recruits are so young. They have had no experience of life, of dealing with people. All they know is the little bit they've learned from college, which is not enough to help them deal with the pressures of police work.

The problem with racism will always occur in any society where there are people of different creed and kind. It's up to each individual to work out how to deal with that kind of thing but, by doing what I am doing, by representing my country, I'm trying to show that there is really no need for the problems we have. More than sixty per cent of the British athletics team is black. A lot of football players are black, all doing their bit for the country and easing the racial problems. I think it's working because kids are not only saying they want to be Gary Lineker or Paul Gascoigne; they're saying they want to be Ian Wright or Colin Jackson as well. When I was young I wanted to be Georgie Best; that's how it used to be, but things have changed. In a sense, black sportsmen are uniting the country. We need to go out there and spread the message. When people see how harmonious the athletics team is, they will say, 'If they can get on, then why can't the rest of us?'

I have to admit, there was not a lot of harmony in 1982 when I told London Irish I would be leaving. During all the years I had been there, I had never been asked for a penny in subscriptions. But, as soon as I left, they started talking about back-dated subs. At the time, I had no money, so I knew it was going to be difficult for London Irish to get anything out of me. But that did not stop them from giving me a lot of hassle. Apart from that, I had no problem with the club. I was leaving because I wanted to progress. I wasn't getting anywhere racing and beating the same people every week. I needed something else.

At the time, Thames Valley Harriers was the best club. London Irish was in the Southern League while Thames Valley Harriers was in the British League. I respected an international runner called Les Hoyte, one of the fastest guys around at the time. He was beginning to help me and it was his suggestion that I should join Thames Valley. It was very serious competition there; I would be running against members of the British team. But it was still fun. Once I got into the way of life with

TVH and became accepted by the people in the club, we would relax and enjoy ourselves once training had finished.

I had started to think more seriously about training by paying more attention to a coach called Ron Roddan, someone who was destined to play a major part in my life. I had met Ron a few years before on my first visit to the West London Stadium. I didn't know who he was but he was in charge of training one of the biggest sprint groups at the stadium. It was not a question of going to Ron because he had been recommended or because he was someone I thought I would get on with; Ron was in charge of sprinters, he had a good reputation, so that's where I needed to be.

When I asked if I could join in, he said it was no problem and told me to warm up. I didn't have a tracksuit at the time – I didn't really know any better – so I jogged round in my jeans and trainers. Eventually, I got back to Ron and he told me to go round again. I went round and round and round and round. When I came back to him, Ron said 'go home'. That was it.

It didn't really bother me. I don't think I went back to Ron for quite a while and, even though I was at the track, it didn't seem to trouble Ron any more than it did me. If you force young kids to do things against their will, then you will get nowhere. Ron did the right thing by allowing me to do as little as I wanted without pushing me. That's what training is all about. You train because you know that if you don't bother you are going to get beaten. You do it, not because your coach says so, but because you want to do it. There is a lot more personal satisfaction that way.

I would train in the summer because, usually, it was warm and I would do short sprints. In the winter it was cold and I would do nothing at all. To be honest, even when it was warm, there were times when I didn't bother. Ron knew that was part of my learning process; I had to find out for myself. Now, of course, I don't even think about it but I can understand the dilemma youngsters face: 'I want to go to a party but I also want to train. What do I do?' A lot of young kids are lost to athletics at that point.

I think Ron might have thought I had reached that stage in 1982 because it must have seemed like I was not going to bother at all. I was running quite well although, looking back, I'll never know how I managed without proper training. I was never scared; I would race against anybody. A lot of guys were frightened to race, just in case they were beaten. That was never a problem as far as I was concerned. I would race and if I lost – then I lost. My attitude was: the time will eventually come when I will win.

I began to want success a little bit more and yet I wasn't really prepared to put the work in. The contradiction was still there because, in 1983, I won the Middlesex 100-metre title by beating the favourite, Buster Watson. This was at the West London Stadium and caught the mood of the rivalry between west London and north London. I don't recall it as being a big occasion as such but, certainly, it was light-hearted and fun. I set a personal best and a county record of 10.4 seconds – which still stands. They had clocked me electronically at 10.32 seconds but gave me a 10.4. Either way, that was moving. I was getting into the big boys' league.

That win did a lot for my confidence just as I was heading for Edinburgh and the United Kingdom Championships, an important event for the guys who were training and looking to the first World Championships later in the year.

The boost to my confidence obviously worked because I reached the 100-metres final. It was a miserable day and I took care over warming up. I was feeling really good and ready to run when it was announced that the race would be delayed because of a dispute. An athlete trained by Frank Dick had missed out on the final even though he had run the same time as the last man in. Frank's protest meant the race was delayed by more than an hour. We had to leave the track. I had never been in that sort of situation before. Warming up is not something that a coach will cover in great detail. You just learn as you go along; you watch people stretching and so you begin to stretch. As the years go on, you learn more and more.

Inexperience when it came to warming up again meant I went from being one of the favourites to finishing third behind Buster Watson and Drew McMaster. They were pretty hot internationals at the time but, even so, I was mad as hell because I felt I could have won that race.

There was some consolation from the fact that third place earned me my first outdoor international; I was selected to run against Finland at Lapinlahti, where I won the 100 metres in 10.46 seconds – beating Drew McMaster.

That was in June and I suppose my training, because of the weather, was as good as it was going to be. But I still preferred to spend my evenings in the nearby café playing dominoes. I would train one day and if the session was too hard then I would play dominoes the next. We played dominoes the way black people do; quite different from the more gentle method used by British players. Our domino games were exciting! We would talk, tease each other, make up catchphrases, play with a flourish, slam the dominoes down. And if the game was really tough and you knew you had the one domino which was going to win, you would get up, go to the door and then run across to the table and bang that domino on the table! Really good fun.

Sometimes I would be in the café from 6:30 p.m. until

midnight and wouldn't give a thought to training. I reckoned I had all the talent in the world. Guys who were training couldn't beat me. So why did I need to bother? Training was so tedious.

My life didn't have any real direction. I liked going to parties and, by this stage, I had become a father. I had been going out with one of my sister's friends and she had become pregnant. Her father threatened to kill me. My parents threatened to kill me. There was panic all round – not least from me! We all make mistakes and apart from the obvious reasons, mine was made worse because I was supposed to be taking exams and sorting out my future.

After leaving the Civil Service, I had gone back to college, mainly as a way of giving myself something to do. I was supposed to be studying sociology and English, but I didn't learn much, certainly not enough to pass exams. The most significant event at college was the day when I saw this girl walk across the common room. I took one look and thought, 'Damn! This is me!'

But she didn't like me. I did everything I could and got nowhere. I was completely smitten. To me, she was the prettiest girl in the whole college and I was not going to let her go. Her name was Mandy Miller but I used to call her Princess because she was so beautiful. I've got this knack; I seem to be able to do things and get away with it. I always mess around without being too serious; it's hard to get fed up with me. I wasn't coming on heavy with Mandy. On the contrary, I would make her laugh because she was so quiet. Eventually – I think it took a couple of months – she saw sense! We got together and I just couldn't keep away from her. Everything else went down the drain. But I have no regrets, none whatsoever, because we're still together to this day.

It was around that period when I decided to leave home. I was twenty-three and my dad told me it was time to do my own thing; I had to be a man, learn about my responsibilities and discover what life was really all about. At first, I thought my father didn't like me, but then I realized it was for my own good. When I see guys in their early twenties still living at home, I tell them to get out and accept their responsibilities. They always say they haven't got any money, but that's not the problem. When I left home, I had no money to speak of, but the whole experience did me the world of good.

I had been planning ahead. When living at home, I had saved up and bought pots and pans and various bits and pieces. I was partly prepared when I went to the Housing Association and rented a one-bedroom flat in a converted house in Scrubs Lane, just on the edge of west London. I bought myself a recondi-tioned gas cooker and someone let me have a little fridge. Mandy moved in with me and her grandmother gave us some money to buy carpets. I think it was about £150; I remember we had cash left over once we had carpeted the whole place! My mum and dad had given me their sofa, I already had a television in my room at home and I managed to put together a hi-fi from various bits I either had or bought or borrowed from friends.

Things weren't always good; I had ups and downs like everyone else. But I don't regret one bit of it. It was a really great experience and it helped me learn to cope. Of course, luxuries such as holidays were out of the question. My family had never been able to afford them and it was no different now. When at school, the kids would come back at the start of a new term and talk about where they had been. I used to make things up and say I had been to Cornwall when I had never set foot outside west London. Holidays had always been time spent quietly at home.

My athletics career had been going through a quiet period and, when I was not selected for the relay team in the 1984 Olympics, I was extremely disappointed even if I tried not to show it. At the time, I wasn't good enough to be an individual athlete but I had thought I was capable of making the relay team. When I watched the Olympics on television, it was not a case of desperately wanting to be in Los Angeles; I felt I should have been there. If I wanted to be on the team, then I would have to do something about it.

At a post-Olympic meeting at Crystal Palace, I won the 100 metres with a time of 10.44 seconds. I had beaten a top-class field and I began to think seriously about taking up athletics full time. I went to see my grandmother in Nottingham and talked it over. She said 'Do it because *you* want to do it. If that's what you really want to do, then do it. Don't go through your life saying, "if only . . ."' I had good chat with my dad and his attitude was the same: 'Do it and, even if it doesn't work, at least you've tried.'

I think they were right. The worst thing is to have the chance and not use it. I went to school with boys who were fast and, in later years, they would say, 'If only we had taken it up as seriously as you did, then maybe we could . . .' They've got to put up with that for the rest of their lives. Then you get the person who says 'Hey! I used to beat you.' And the answer is, 'Big deal. It's not what you used to do that matters, it's what you do now.' In the autumn of 1984, I made my big decision.

By coincidence, I received two letters which helped convince me I was doing the right thing. Ron Roddan wrote that I should either come back and take things seriously – or forget it. I must have gone missing for quite some time because he said something along the lines of 'Come back and get down to work like I know you can do. But don't waste my time any more.'

Ron was not the sort of person to come out with something like that, so I took note of what he said.

But there was an even bigger surprise when, not long afterwards, I had a letter from Andy Norman, the promotions officer for the British Athletic Federation. He said that if I changed my life style and my attitude, I could become the best in Britain. And, maybe, one of the best in the world.

Everybody was wary of Andy. But he was always fair even if his methods were sometimes very direct. He gave out invitations for meetings and there had been one occasion when I was due to run at Crystal Palace. I was just about to leave the house when the phone rang. It was Andy. He said, 'don't bother turning up'. When I asked why, he just replied, 'because I've given your lane away'. He had found a bigger name and that was that. I was gutted. It was part of my apprenticeship because, nine times out of ten, if he said you were going to run then you would get a race. But he would always ask for the favour back later on.

Andy did not suffer fools gladly and, when he sent that letter, its effect can be imagined. I wrote back, thanked him and promised that I would work hard. I said I wouldn't let him down. Mandy was working as a receptionist at an optician's; we would manage to get by. So long as there was food on the table, that's all that mattered. I began my first serious winter's training – at the age of twenty-four.

Chapter 4

BEYOND THE FIRST ROUND

When granny died, I was devastated. I remember, when I was young, saying my prayers at night and asking God to take years off my life and add them on granny's. I wanted her to live for ever. I don't think it's possible to love anyone in the way I felt about my granny; the next stage must be a kind of obsessive love. There was a very special bond between us; she was the person who shaped and moulded me into the person I am today.

Her mother was born into slavery and I suppose it was inevitable that granny should become a cook. But, as far as her family was concerned, she was everything; doctor, dentist, wise counsel, friend and story teller. She had cures for everything, she knew it all. I confided in granny, telling her things I would not have told anyone else because I knew that, with granny, it would go no further. My mum and dad always said they would never hide anything from each other. That's fine – but I wouldn't tell them everything as a result.

Like my dad, granny had a story for every occasion. Evenings in Jamaica were so interesting as we gathered round and listened to those wonderful tales. Granny said we were one, big happy family and she missed that badly when we moved to England and split between Nottingham and London. But she battled on, refusing to be beaten, doing everything for herself. She seemed indestructible because, at 5 feet 8 inches, she was an impressive figure. Right up to just before she died, she cooked, washed her own clothes and climbed the stairs on her own. And, always, she was immaculate.

She was over ninety and she died peacefully. When we heard that the end was very near, my dad, younger brother and I drove straight to Nottingham. She was dead by the time we got there, but she still had one eye open. A few seconds after we walked into the room – the eye closed. It was as if she had been waiting to see us, just making sure that we had arrived.

I still miss her. Certain things happen which I would like to discuss with granny because she would have known what to do or say. At the time, I recalled very clearly our last conversation about my future. That was yet another reason to work hard.

The effect was noticeable the minute I started to compete in 1985. Andy Norman was helping me quite a bit by finding races. He sent me back to Lapinlahti in Finland on the understanding that I was not to tell anyone, otherwise there might have been a few complaints. I travelled with the distance runner, Steve Harris, and ran the 100 metres in 10.20 seconds in windy conditions. That at least showed me that I would be capable of a really quick time in the right circumstances.

The morning after the race, Steve and I were kicked out of the hotel at around 7 a.m. What little expenses we had were used up by getting to the airport, where we had to wait for five hours. Our tickets were not transferable and there was no alternative but to sit there and watch the other athletes come by and get on their various flights. I was fuming.

As soon as I got off the plane, I went straight to Andy Norman. 'What's going on?' I demanded. 'How come there were flights every hour and we had to wait until two in the afternoon?'

Andy's reply was typically direct. 'Listen', he said. 'Don't you come in here making noises at me. You couldn't fill a phone box and, until you can, just be happy with whatever you get.'

It wasn't that I was ungrateful for the race. But we had been in the airport for a long time and I felt he could at least have given us decent tickets. I just wanted to get home sooner. Nevertheless, Andy had made his point.

I was still making the British indoor team but, apart from Ron and Andy, no one seemed to recognize my talent. At the time, Frank Dick was coaching Cameron Sharp and he said I would never beat the likes of Cameron or Mike McFarlane. According to Frank, I was wasting my time trying to be a sprinter. 'You should take up the long jump,' he said. I thought, 'Right! I'll show you.'

I had received another incentive when I went to the European Indoor Championships in Athens. This was my first major international meeting and I was impressed. The stadium was huge; I was overcome by the occasion. I was running in the 200 metres and for the first heat I was drawn with the Italian, Stefano Tilli, who had set a world indoor 200-metre record of 20.52 seconds earlier in the season. That was a heck of a time; more than a second quicker than my best outdoors. It made me pretty nervous, particularly in front of more people than I had ever seen before. I tried my best but it was not good enough. I promised myself that, the next time I was selected for a major championship, I would progress beyond the first round.

Before that, though, I was going to have to sort out a

recurrent injury problem. My running technique was such that I was putting unnecessary stress on my hamstring and this was causing a lot of trouble. By chance, I met Anna-Lise Hammer, a Norwegian freelance journalist who was also the press officer for the Bislet games in Oslo. She came to watch a meeting somewhere and they wouldn't let her travel with the athletes. I managed to get her on the coach. She sat next to me and we started talking. We discussed a number of things, including my hamstring problem, and she said she knew a really good physiotherapist who could help me out. That was all very well but I had no money. I had a job as a youth worker at a west London sports centre but Mandy was still helping me out financially. Anna-Lise and I became good friends and, when the hamstring trouble flared up again during the Amateur Athletics Association (AAA) Championships, she bought me a ticket to Norway and paid for the treatment.

It was Anna-Lise's way of investing in me. Andy Norman looked after my races but I did not have an agent from the commercial point of view. Anna-Lise obviously saw a way of fulfilling that role and helping me. But, if you are going to be an agent then your product has to be good. Anna-Lise was making sure that I was in good shape before she started to market me.

At around this time, I received a letter from the British Amateur Athletic Board (BAAB) saying that I was in with a chance of being selected for the European Cup, which was an important event at the time. I was ranked in the top three or four in the country and, as I went across to Norway to sort out my injury, I was pretty confident that I would make the team.

I made sure Frank Dick knew where I was and I had gone to a lot of trouble to sort out my passport at short notice. I still held a Jamaican passport but, in order to take part in a major meeting such as the European Cup, it was necessary to become a British subject. It had meant a lot of hanging around in the London passport office in Petty France but I was sure it would be worth it.

Frank called a relay practice at the training centre in Loughborough but he was told that I couldn't get back from Oslo in time because of a problem with the flights. I arrived in London the next day and went to Petty France to collect my British passport. As far as I was concerned, the injury problem had been cleared up; I felt good about my running and I was ready to compete.

As I left the passport office, I bought the *Evening Standard* – and read that I wasn't in the team. The BAAB didn't have the guts to tell me before announcing the team to the press. I was very pissed off.

I went straight to the BAAB offices, looking for Frank Dick. I felt prepared to punch him because he could have told me the bad news rather than let me read it in the newspaper.

When I eventually found Frank, I blew my top. Nigel Cooper, the General Secretary of the BAAB, was in the room at the time and he said, 'Well, Linford, it's good to see that you're angry. It shows you're keen.' I thought he must be joking. I told them some home truths and then I walked out in disgust.

The effect of all this was to make me realize that I would have to make sure I was much better than anyone else so they would have to pick me. It meant I would have to work bloody hard for 1986; but that incident really drove me on.

I suddenly realized what hard training was really all about. Sitting in the café during those cold winter nights had not given me the slightest appreciation of what Ron was up to on the track outside. I can't say I enjoyed training. In fact, I hated it. But the results were soon evident. I was selected for internationals –

and my career took off from there. I went on to win my first major title.

The European Indoor Championships were held in Madrid and I was up against two Soviets. One of them, Aleksandr Yevgenyev, had won the 200 metres at these championships for the past two years running. He was the bee's knees. Even when Ade Mafe was at his peak, Yevgenyev was unbeaten. The other Soviet was called Nikolay Razgonov and these two, along with Mafe, were favourites. I was second string because Mafe was rolling at the time – I was just the young kid. It's true that Ade was pretty strong; he had won the A A A indoor at the beginning of the season and Frank Dick had said that Mafe was the greatest up-and-coming athlete he had ever seen. Not long afterwards, I ran against Ade at Cosford – and beat him. So, where did that leave me in Frank Dick's estimation?

I was certainly very pretty confident when we went to Madrid for the European Championships, totally different from the way I had felt in Athens a year before when I went no further than the first round. I ran really well and made it to the final.

I was drawn in a good lane but pretty sure that everyone was thinking that I would finish third at best. Mafe had pulled his hamstring in one of the early rounds and that more or less led to his demise; he never really got over that injury. Meanwhile, it was left to me to do the business in Madrid.

It was a strange track. The length is normally 200 metres but this one was 164 metres, which meant you seemed to run that little bit extra. Yevgenyev was leading as we came off the bend and it looked like I was going to finish second. Then I found this extra gear from somewhere and I passed him on the home straight. That was it. I had won my first major title. My emotions went wild. This was the biggest achievement of my career and I had managed it after training seriously for just a few months. There was no question now that I could see the value of all that hard work.

There was a match with Russia not long after at Cosford and hundreds of tickets remained unsold. I wasn't going to run but Andy Norman persuaded me. When they announced my entry, the tickets sold out immediately. People wanted to see what this guy Linford Christie was all about. I won the 200 metres and the crowd went crazy; they had found a new star.

I was surprised too. Every time you achieve something important, even though you may have hoped to do well, when you do actually win it does come as a surprise. In the middle of all this excitement, I remembered the Finnish flights barely a year before and I went up to Andy, glanced round the packed arena, and said, 'Big phone box, innit?'

We still have a good laugh about that. I don't hold it as a grudge against Andy because he helped me a heck of a lot. His letter changed everything and, without his encouragement, I honestly don't think I would be here today. That European Championship title in Madrid was just the start of it.

I was on a high when I went to Oslo, where I ran two personal bests; 10.33 seconds in the 100 metres and 20.79 seconds in the 200. These were phenomenal jumps in performance yet, even though a lot of people began to take notice, they still didn't think I was going to be a major threat. I knew if I kept going at this rate, that would soon change.

Not long after, I was back in Madrid, this time for an important outdoor meeting on 4 June. I was there thanks to an agent by the name of John Bicourt who was taking a small team to Spain. This was the first time I had more or less been on my own at an event like this. I wasn't part of a British team, I just had to go out and run – for myself.

Before I left for Spain, I had been in the weight-training room at the West London Stadium with a few guys, including Clifford Mamba, who has since become an ambassador for Swaziland. We were discussing the entry for Madrid, particularly an American called Emmit King who was the man to beat at the time. They said I had no chance against Emmit King because, along with Carl Lewis, he was one of the fastest men in the world. I said, 'how can they be the fastest men in the world when they haven't raced against me?' That was my attitude. I genuinely did not see how anyone could call himself the fastest man in the world if he had not raced against all comers. That argument had no effect. They were sure I was going to be beaten and eventually Clifford said he would bet on it. When I asked him how much, after a bit of humming and hawing, he said, 'If you beat Emmit King, you can come back here and punch me in the mouth, that's how confident I am.' That was the deal, and we shook on it.

I didn't give it much thought once I got to Madrid. The weather was perfect from my point of view – very hot! In many ways, I was pretty green, particularly in such impressive company. Apart from Emmit King, the American contingent included Thomas Jefferson, the Olympic 200-metre bronze medallist. Roger Black and Seb Coe were representing Britain, Roger being as surprised as I was to be there. I did a couple of laps jogging with Seb; normally you would do two warm-up laps but I did about four. I was doing everything I could. This was the new Linford Christie!

Jefferson won the first heat and I lined up with King in the second. I won in 10.25 seconds, which was pretty good at the time and, I must admit, surprised me as well as everyone else. But, more importantly, Emmit King ran 10.84 seconds. I thought, 'Right! I must be in with a chance here.'

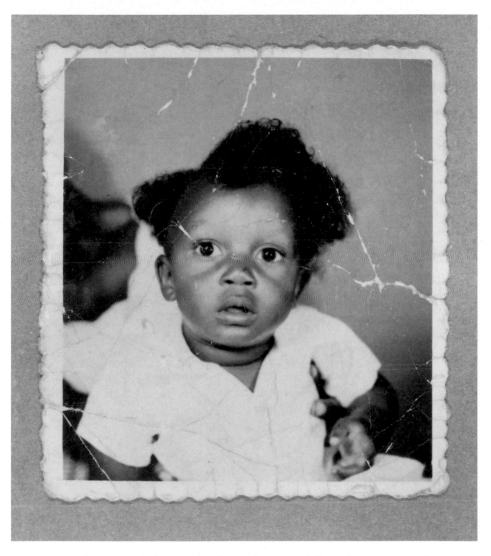

1 This is me aged two. That hairstyle was in fashion then, I promise!

2 (*facing page top*) With Colin Jackson's grandparents in Tampa, Florida.
3 (*facing page middle*) Heather Oakes and I become godparents to Les Hoyte's son, Justin.
4 (*facing page bottom*) With my oldest sister, Lucia, my oldest brother, Trevor, and my mum, Mabel, who is holding Lucia's son, Kevin. This photo was taken in Lucia's house in the States.
5 (*above*) Receiving my honorary degree at Portsmouth University, with Mandy.

6 Mandy and me with Colin's sister, Suzanne Packer, perhaps better known as Josie from Brookside.

7 Time for a hug with Mandy during training in Lanzarote.

8 Showing off in Gold's Gym, Florida.

9 Ron and Mandy in Lanzarote. The two people, outside my immediate family, who have done the most to help my career.

10 With Colin in Narrabeen, Australia, 1990. We had just come face to face with the most enormous iguana I've ever seen. I think I ran my fastest time that day to get away from it!

11 The British 4 × 100 relay team at the Commonwealth Games in Auckland, 1990. *Left to right:* me, Marcus Adams, John Regis, Clarence Callender.

12 Receiving the British Athlete of the Year Award from the
Duke of Edinburgh in Buckingham Palace.

I don't know what happened in the final, I just ran the race of my life. You never know how fast you are going, you just run and obviously you know you have been fast if the opposition has been beaten. But, as for the exact time, you have no idea.

The clock stopped at 10.01 seconds – which was world class. There weren't many people who had run faster than that – and it hadn't been a tight finish. I couldn't believe it, and neither could the officials because they deliberated over the time for ages. They obviously thought something must be wrong. A guy can't come from the middle of nowhere and run that kind of time; I could have won untold Olympic gold medals at that rate.

The Americans were saying 'Shit! Can you believe it? Some guy from Britain just ran 10.0! No way. Nobody from Britain can run 10.0.' The American view seemed to be that nobody could run fast, apart from them. That attitude still prevails today.

Eventually it was announced that I had run 10.04 seconds, which was a British record. I think I was ranked something like 150th in the world at the time and this put me fourth in the list. I was pleased as punch.

As a matter of routine, I rang Ron at his home. When he asked how I had got on, I told him I had run a 10.4. He said 'Not bad, not bad. So long as you won, that's the main thing.'

Then I told him the truth. '10.04', I said. 'I ran 10.04!'

Silence. Then he mumbled something – and the line went dead. It shocked him so much that he hung up. I had to ring back – it cost a fair bit of money in those days to ring from places like Spain – to check that he was all right. '10.04!' he said. 'You must be bloody joking! That's good!'

When Ron Roddan uses the word 'good', then you know you have done better than that because he's not someone who flings praise around. He's not the sort of person to make you big-headed. Mind you, there was no chance of that as the news began to sink in at the stadium. I remember one particular reporter who was covering the meeting for one of the athletics magazines. He asked 'Surely you're not going accept the time?' When I asked why not, he said I couldn't run that fast. 'You're going to be so embarrassed when you come up against guys who can really run that kind of time,' he said. 'They're going to beat you. What are you going to say then – that it's a fluke? You can't, can you?'

I replied that I had not given the time to myself; it came from the officials. But that sort of reception was to be typical of what was waiting when I returned home. To be honest, I was expecting headlines. After all, I had just broken the previous British record of 10.11 seconds set by Allan Wells. And yet I had about three lines in the newspapers – half of them missed it. But a very nervous Clifford Mamba was aware of the result. He looked pretty relieved when we just shook hands . . .

Some time later I was with Nigel Walker, a good friend of mine who went on to play rugby for Wales but used to be a hurdler. He said he had been talking to a few well-known athletes who shall remain nameless. One of them was the best ever in his event and Nigel had asked him what he thought about Linford Christie running 10.04. 'Be serious,' came the reply. 'Christie can't run 10.04. Maybe 10.4. But 10.04 . . . no way.' When Nigel put the same question to Frank Dick, the answer was predictably similar.

I don't think they had realized just how much my attitude had changed. A lot of the guys were saying 'Well, if Linford can do that sort of time and we can beat him, then . . .' One even went as far as to say that if I could run a 10.04, then he could do 9.04.

Adding to the hype would be selection for the Commonwealth

Games and the European Championships later in the year – which meant the AAA Championships at Crystal Palace assumed much greater importance than usual. Two Australians, John Dinan and Chris Perry, were the supposed stars of the show. Dinan had run 20.19 seconds in the 200 metres and Perry had done 10.3 seconds in the 100. Mike McFarlane, still one of the top sprinters, was also there; it was the best entry for the three As in a long time.

With everyone believing that they could beat me, I was obviously not expected to do much. In one of the semi-finals, it was taken for granted that Mike McFarlane and Donovan Reid would finish first and second. McFarlane did 10.22 seconds in the heats, which was a personal best for him. But I ran 10.21 seconds. People started to pay attention.

In the final, I just blitzed it. And yet my technique was not good; my starts were rubbish. I would end up giving the likes of McFarlane three or four metres at the start and then have to chase him. But now I could catch and pass him. I ran 10.22 seconds to win the final. Doubts about my performance in Madrid were fast disappearing.

I think, from that day, the opposition realized that Linford Christie was going to be the man to beat. They seemed to stop trying after that. It was as if they accepted the fact that they were not going to win – which was great for me because it made my job much easier. Man, I just loved that!

The knock-on effect was that I stopped looking to be the best British athlete. It seemed to me that so many runners were happy just to be British number one. Andy Norman had talked about that attitude among the British and I had never really understood what he was getting at. He had always said that I should aim at being European number one. Now I knew what he meant. I wanted to be the best European – and then the best in the world. Why worry about being the best in Britain? If I was number one in Europe then it should follow that I would be British number one. In any case, I had beaten just about everyone, with the exception of Allan Wells, who didn't run in the three As.

There was supposed to be a race between me and Allan Wells not long afterwards in Birmingham. The press were more or less saying that Wells simply had to turn up in order to win. Come the day of the race, Allan Wells didn't run – he was a little bit like that at the time. He had not done much since being sidelined by injury the year before and I was still aware of the fact that he had not bothered to offer congratulations after I had beaten his record. That was the usual form among athletes, regardless of any personal feelings. Allan and I would meet before the end of the season but, first, I was to receive confirmation that there was still work to be done on my technique.

Ben Johnson had become the man to beat and the press were trying to build up a rivalry between us. My confidence had never been higher. As far as I was concerned, I would beat Ben. I had run a 10.04 seconds, which was close to Ben's best. I had won more or less every time I raced. We were to meet for the first time at the Alexander Stadium in Birmingham, not long before going to Scotland for the Commonwealth Games. I thought, 'Yeah! I can beat Ben.'

He just got out of the blocks and moved. He blew me away. His time was 10.06 seconds. That's when I realized there was a lot more to be done.

Chapter 5

WEARING THE FLAG

Colin Jackson and I hit it off straight away. We were introduced by the hurdler Nigel Walker – like Colin, another Welshman – when Colin joined the British team in 1986. Nigel and I had roomed together and, when Nigel failed to make the team, Colin took his place as my roommate when we travelled abroad. We have the same sense of humour; we're just crazy when we're together. We seem to know exactly what the other is thinking without anything being said. After something has happened, we will look at each other and burst out laughing. Sometimes even Mandy does not understand our sense of humour.

It made a big difference having a friend like that because, until then, I would spend a large part of my time with just two or three other athletes when going to races. We got along all right but we were not close friends. Having Colin around made things seem so much better; he would encourage me and I would him. We were always there for each other.

Colin was born in Cardiff but his parents are from the same part of Jamaica as me. Colin and I are on the same wavelength in every respect and I suppose it was only natural that we should eventually team up to form our own business several years later.

The two friends who I see most at the races – Philip and Bernard Henry – actually started out having no interest in athletics. We met at college and they knew nothing about track and field events. They used to make me go training by saying they would come and meet me when I wanted to go somewhere other than the track. But they wouldn't turn up, knowing that I would then have to go training instead. Now, they are clued up; they know everything about athletics and yet they will not talk shop when we go out – which is the way I like it.

Ben Johnson and I got on well together. Maybe it was because we were both from Jamaica originally – he was brought up in a small place called Falmouth and he is now a naturalized Canadian – but, regardless of the controversy surrounding his athletics, I have always found him to be a very nice guy. We met again a few weeks after Birmingham at the Commonwealth Games in Edinburgh, where the competition was badly affected by a boycott. Only twenty-six nations competed after Caribbean and African countries withdrew in protest over New Zealand's sporting links with South Africa. The 100-metre heats were a bit of a farce as nineteen runners competed for the sixteen places in the semi-finals. I won my semi and Ben won his, assisted by a wind measured at 3.11 metres per second.

'Wind assisted' is officially anything above 2 metres per second. Any time recorded under those circumstances does not count as a record. Of course, you can have any amount of wind against you! Apparently, according to scientific research, wind assistance helps me a lot more than it would help a smaller athlete; conversely, 'wind against' is in their favour because I'm bigger and broader and therefore create more resistance. When running, you are aware of wind assistance although, if it's small, you can't tell by how much. But when it's against, it makes a big difference. You can run really hard into the wind and yet your time will still be slow.

The wind is measured by a machine. Don't ask me how it works but the officials reckon that they can measure .01 of a wind. I'd love to know how they do that. In a 200-metre race, they take the wind measurement on the straight and not on the bend. It is possible, for instance, to have a wind assistance of 4 metres per second through the bend, but only 1 metre per second on the straight. They should have one gauge on the bend and one on the straight, and work out the average.

The British Amateur Athletics Board promotion department once dreamt up an incentive that any official time which put an athlete in the top four in the world would be worth a bonus of £50,000. One night in Portsmouth, I ran a 10.04 seconds, which should have earned me £50,000. But, when they checked the wind reading, it came up 2.01 metres per second! I couldn't believe any machine could be that clever. I lost £50,000 thanks to .01 of a wind. The guy must have sneezed!

Ben won in Edinburgh and I just held on to the silver medal after feeling a twinge in my hamstring about five metres from the line. I was on the sidelines for the rest of the games, which was worrying because the European Championships were only a matter of weeks away. I stayed on in Edinburgh after the games, supposedly to make use of the physiotherapy facilities which were on hand. I found it strange that the physios said they couldn't work on me every day; they complained about my muscles being too hard. What did they expect when asked to massage an athlete?

The village itself was a boring place. It was very cold (this was in July!) and the highlight of my week was meeting the Princess of Wales. She was gorgeous; she laughed the whole time.

There were very few smiles on another royal occasion in the village. In one particular race, a British athlete, Heather Oakes, had beaten Angela Issajenko of Canada. Charlie Francis, the Canadian coach, had accused the British athletes of cheating. He was also claiming that, according to his calculations, Ben Johnson should have been given 9.99 seconds for the 100 metres. The Queen was due to come to the village for dinner and, while we waited for her arrival, I went over to Charlie to sort things out. All of this was going on just moments before the Queen was due to arrive. I have great respect for the Queen – I had never been in her presence before – but I was not going to have Charlie Francis saying stupid things about the British athletes. It was a heck of a way to start our relationship but, surprisingly perhaps, Charlie and I became quite good friends after that. By the time the royal party arrived, everything was sorted out and all the athletes were introduced to the Queen.

On my way home, I stopped off at Gateshead to watch an invitation match between Great Britain and the Common-wealth. Most of the medal winners from Edinburgh were there – joined by none other than Allan Wells. There had been a lot of controversy because Allan had not been selected for the Scottish team in the Commonwealth Games. I don't think he had taken part in the trials; he was expecting pre-selection. Quite rightly, the Scots didn't pick him; they preferred to choose people who had competed regularly in the various championships. There was a lot of hoo-ha, but the Scottish officials stuck to their guns.

Wells appeared for the 100 metres wearing a pair of cut-down black tights, like cyclist's shorts. We had never seen anything like it before and there were all sorts of comments. But Allan was to have the last laugh. Everyone was talking about Ben Johnson, of course. Wells smoked him! He beat everybody. Then he was allowed to guest in the 200 metres – and he beat Atlee Mahorn, the Commonwealth champion. It was another superb run. I have never seen anything like it. The crowd went wild.

Allan Wells started to say that they should pick him for the European Championships in Stuttgart. He was selected on the strength of those two races, which was a big mistake in my opinion. Allan had been fresh and focused whereas the competition was in a state of anticlimax; they had done the more important business in Edinburgh.

Of course, that did not stop the build-up in the newspapers. Now that I had recovered from my injury, the European Championships would be the first serious head-to-head between Allan and me. And, once again, it was almost a matter-of-fact thing; according to the media, Allan Wells was going to win the European Championship 100 metres. He was going to beat me.

I can't remember if I was favourite in Stuttgart but I know I was running really well. In the 100-metre heats, I had been faster than Allan Wells every time, but the media, particularly television, continued to give him a big build-up. I couldn't help but think that they were living in the past. Now I had to prove it in the final.

Allan made the best start and led for the first thirty metres.

But then things went according to plan and I smoked past him and won, quite easily, with a Championship record of 10.15 seconds. Allan finished fifth. Some of the newspapers were kind enough to suggest the next day that, if I took my running seriously, I could be quite good.

This was the first time that Britain had won the 100 metres in the European Championship for forty years. I felt a great sense of pride when I stood on the rostrum with a Union Jack, given to me by a British supporter on my lap of honour, draped around my shoulders. But even that would cause trouble.

I was later reprimanded by the European Athletic Association for wearing the flag on the podium and many people in the black community back home were upset that I did not appear to be showing solidarity with them; it was a typical reflection of the fact that a number of black people did not feel a part of this country. I was representing Great Britain; I couldn't somehow stand there and say, 'Yeah! I'm Jamaican.' But I knew my roots and, as far as I was concerned, this was kudos for Jamaica too. Wearing the flag was an impromptu thing but it said everything about how I felt. I have no regrets whatsoever.

In some ways, the sense of occasion was almost too much. I should have been resting and preparing for the 200 metres the following evening but, instead, I stayed too long at the stadium doing press conferences and interviews. I qualified comfortably for the 200 but, in the semi-final, I was sluggish. There was nothing there, no surge of adrenalin. I finished fifth and failed to make the final. Allan Wells took fifth place in the final.

We were to meet one more time in 1986. The McVitie Challenge at Crystal Palace on 12 September was the final event of the British season. I had run in Brussels the previous evening but, due to a mix-up with the flights, I did not arrive at our hotel in London until about 3 a.m. I hadn't eaten properly either. Meanwhile Allan Wells, not having competed in Brussels, was resting and getting ready for the race.

On the day, he made a blinding start and beat me in a photo-finish with a time of 10.31 seconds. It was close. Allan almost broke his neck as he dived for the line and then did a somersault! He was happy. That was Allan's last good race. He was thirty-six and I look forward to seeing if I can top that . . .

From my point of view, the race was significant because it would be the last time I would be beaten by a British athlete in the 100 metres. Nevertheless, I had earned my first British number one ranking. I've held it ever since.

At the time, though, I was still struggling financially. Despite my status in athletics, I had no sponsors and no money. Mandy helped me, but she couldn't support me. Since I wasn't working, I was receiving unemployment benefit. Mandy and I were still living together and, since she had a job, we could pay the bills. That helped me out a lot.

The most important thing in athletics is that if your home life is going really well, then that will be reflected in your running. It's like an electrical circuit. If one of the connections in that circuit is gone, then the power isn't going to surge through. Fortunately for me, the circuit was very strong and I have Mandy to thank for that. I can remember the times when I have had problems, Mandy was always there. I wouldn't go as far as to say I 'owe' Mandy because neither of us look upon it that way; we were no different from any other couple struggling to get started and I would hate to see the relationship being described as one 'owing' the other. But I would have no hesitation in saying Mandy has been wonderful; she has always been good to me.

Mandy is pretty smart; she has always managed to find good jobs. As I said earlier, she worked as a receptionist with an optician. Then she had a similar job with a marketing company before working for United Distillers. The last job Mandy had was with a pharmaceutical company. She does not work now because I prefer that she doesn't. Mandy is young and she should not need to go out and work if I am in a position to keep her. She takes care of the fan club and, as with everything else, she makes a very good job of it. But, so long as I can take care of her, then I can see no reason for Mandy having to go through the daily grind in an office. If the worst comes to the worst, she can find employment until she is sixty, so why rush into work? When I was working in the Co-op or wherever, my dad always used to say, 'Don't rush to do overtime. The money is good, but you've got until you are sixty-five to do overtime. Enjoy life while you can.' That's the way I look at it now but, of course, in 1986–7, we didn't have that luxury.

I went into the new season as number three in the world 100-metre rankings behind Ben Johnson and Chidi Imoh of Nigeria. In 1985 I had been about 150th! But all of that was put to the back of my mind when I literally began to see spots before my eyes not long after the season had started.

Having won the AAA indoor 200 metres, I went to Athens, confident that I was going to make up for my poor performance in Greece two years before. Off-season training had been going brilliantly thanks to avoiding the British winter and making the most of the warm weather in Lanzarote, but even the best laid plans can suffer an unexpected setback.

I was rooming with Nigel Walker – I think there were just three British athletes in Athens; myself, Nigel and another hurdler, Lesley-Ann Skeete – when I noticed a little spot on my arm. I brushed it off and thought no more about it. When spots started to appear on my nose, I put it down to the humid conditions. As I prepared to go home the next morning, the spots were getting worse. By the evening, they were appearing everywhere.

I didn't know what was wrong. I went to Charing Cross Hospital and sat for ages in casualty, only to find that they didn't know what the trouble was either. The doctor told me to go home and come back if it didn't get better.

The next morning, I was completely covered. I started to panic because I thought I had caught something contagious. I went to Hammersmith Hospital in Du Cane Road, which runs along the back of the training track. A nurse told me to take off my clothes, put on a gown and lie on the bed. She left the room and I did as I was told.

Then a doctor came in. He was wearing a mask, gloves – everything! I nearly had a heart attack. I thought, for the doctor to be dressed like that, I must have something really contagious. Mandy was with me and I blurted out 'Hold my hand! Hold my hand!' I thought I was going to die!

It was nerve-racking because AIDS was emerging at the time as a major concern and nobody really knew how the virus was passed on. It was not common knowledge that AIDS was mainly sexually transmitted; I thought that maybe I had got it because I had drunk from an infected cup or something. I was convinced I was in a very bad way. The doctor took one look at me and said, matter of factly, 'You've got chicken pox.'

Chicken pox! I hadn't thought of that. Not long before, I had been on *A Question of Sport*, in the same programme as Princess Anne – a brilliant woman with a great knowledge of sport. Unfortunately, she was on the opposite side with Emlyn Hughes, so Bill Beaumont's team lost! It was a great laugh and that particular programme drew the biggest audience *A Question of Sport* has ever had. As much as I admire the royal family –

and as much as I fancy Princess Diana! – I think the Princess Royal is the nicest; she's great. It so happened that one of her children had just had chicken pox and I think she was the carrier. That's my story, anyway. As far as I was concerned, I had caught the Royal Chicken Pox!

I was in bed for a week. I have never experienced anything so bad. When you catch chicken pox at the age of twenty-seven, you know all about it. I had spots where you wouldn't think you could get spots – on the soles of my feet, between my toes, in my mouth, up my nose, in my ears, in my hair – everywhere you can think of. Yep! There too.

My doctor said that I shouldn't have a bath for a couple of days; I was to dab on calamine lotion and leave it. I was in a terrible mess. I used to wear a T-shirt to bed and one night, when the spots started to pop, I could not get the T-shirt off. Mandy had taken time off work to look after me and, when we finally removed the shirt, there was no alternative but to throw it away. It was an unbelievable sight.

Eventually, I was allowed to have a bath. God, that was nice. After about four days I went out shopping with Mandy and found that I had to wear dark glasses because the light was affecting my eyes so badly. But, a change is as good as a rest and, when I started training again, I discovered that my times were better than ever. I was flying. When I was picked for the European Indoor Championships at Liévin in France, I had no hesitation in accepting.

Chapter 6

TROUBLE INSIDE

My family didn't come to many meetings in the early days. I think they saw athletics as a pastime rather than a serious business and, even now, they will only attend the more important events. The fact that they don't come that often doesn't affect me too much. In some ways it has probably been good for me; part of the process of allowing me to get on with my life. It has helped make me a more independent person.

I'm always happy to get them tickets if they want to come. My sisters have been to the races a few times but, to be honest, if my family is present when I'm competing, I can't help but wonder if they're all right. Even though it is a nice feeling when they cheer and scream, I prefer them to come every now and again rather than all the time.

Mandy usually comes to the major championships because a few of my friends will be there too. I know then that Mandy can sit and watch with them, have someone to talk to and hang around with because, if I am in the village, she is not allowed in. So, it relieves some of the pressure to know that Mandy is in good hands. Sometimes I hardly get to see her; she has to go back to her hotel and I have to return to the village, and that's it. It's not easy.

Sometimes my friends will arrange to come without telling me. They hide and say to Mandy, 'Don't even wave to him. Let him concentrate on what he has to do.' I think that's the best way. It leaves me free and, of course, Ron is always there. He is someone I can go to if I want to talk, he gives me reassurance if I need it.

The championships always seem to come too early. You always wish that you had one more week; you are never, ever ready. But Ron is always there to provide a confidence booster by saying I've trained well and I'm ready.

For Colin Jackson, it is completely different because his parents are real athletics buffs; they are sports-mad. Colin and I had become really good friends and, when we went to Liévin, his mum and dad were there. But it seemed that each time Colin's parents visited the track, I would get injured. It was a stupid thing but, when they came to France for the European Indoor Championships, I wanted them to see me run really well. Colin was rolling and I wanted to do the same, be a part of it.

I pulled a hamstring in a 200-metre heat. My body was still weak from the virus and that injury put me out of the World Indoor Championships, scheduled for Indianapolis in March.

I went to Norway for treatment. Proof that I was fully fit came in the 1987 European Cup in Prague, where I became the first British athlete to win gold in both the 100 and the 200 metres. Now I could claim to be the number one in Europe.

My standing in the world rankings was about to be measured in the World Championships in Rome at the end of August.

Before that, however, I was to set a new British record of 10.03 seconds in a 100-metre event in Budapest. I was obviously well prepared but my thoughts, which should have been focused on winning in Rome, were being occupied increasingly by the latest stage of what was turning out to be a battle of wills with Frank Dick.

Trouble had flared up in the relay team once more in Prague. Frank had changed the running order and our poor record in the sprint relay was upheld by a disqualification at the first baton changeover. I felt it was due to Frank altering tactics on the day, when he had me running second rather than my preferred anchor, or final, leg.

A young newcomer to the team, David Kirton, had been given the first leg, which was not a problem in itself, but Frank had insisted that David make a downsweep with the baton on the changeover. David is quite short compared to me and, what with my fairly upright style when in full flight, it seemed to me quite likely that things might not run smoothly. They didn't – and criticism flew in all directions.

The composition of the sprint relay team for Rome began to fill my mind much more than it should have done. Perhaps that explains why I eventually ran badly, finishing fourth (a poor 10.14 seconds) in the World Championships behind Ben Johnson, who stunned everybody with an incredible 9.83 seconds. As I dipped for the finishing line, I felt a twinge in my hamstring, and that kept me out of the 200 metres.

I was far from happy. One way or another, Rome was a disaster, the lowest point having been an almost inevitable bust-up with Frank Dick.

For a while I felt that although I would run in the relay team in the small events, when it came to the majors, Frank wouldn't pick me and I couldn't understand why. It seemed that I was doing the dirty work. I felt he was resting everyone else while I was running my backside off – and then he wouldn't pick me for the relay team when it mattered.

Now I was number one I was bound to be selected but, even then, Frank had wanted me to run first leg. I couldn't see a lot of sense in that because, at the time, I was having problems with my blocks. The reason I was losing races was that I was giving people three or four yards at the start and then trying to make up lost ground at the finish – which I couldn't do because I had been so slow out of the blocks. I didn't want to run first leg. I was the fastest guy on the team and I wanted to run either second or last – the anchor. That way I could use my long stride and my strength to best advantage.

I have always felt that if you run where you want to run, and everyone else is happy, then you are going to give 110 per cent. If you are not happy where you're placed, then you're only going to run eighty per cent. When I had arrived in Rome, I found that the guys on the team were far from happy. In general, they were fed up because Frank was killing us with relay practice. He would call an early practice at Crystal Palace and then he would arrive late, or not turn up at all. He would even demand a relay practice on the day before we were due to go out and run our individual events.

Now the team was arguing about the relay race itself and Frank's decision about where people should run. We sat down, had a talk about it and made up our own minds about the running order. 'Okay Linford,' they said, 'you're the top guy in the team – so you tell him.'

We went to see Frank and I told him what we had agreed. 'Isn't that so, guys?' I said. And everybody shut up; nobody backed me. I was left looking very stupid.

They were scared stiff. My place on the team was secure because I was the fastest. But, for some of the guys, being part of the relay team was their only chance to do anything. Frank knew that and he would use it. He was the sort of person who would deliberately pick an argument, knowing that most of the guys dared not respond.

Anyway, the same day when I had been made to look so stupid, Frank called a relay practice. There was a track very close to the village in Rome, but he wanted us to use a track which was half an hour away. We couldn't understand why.

Frank and I had an argument about the running order. 'You're running first leg. Like it or leave it,' he said. I replied that if we couldn't discuss it sensibly, then I would leave it. Tempers flared and suddenly I was aware of cameras clicking. I lost my cool completely. I swore at the cameramen and went into a rage. I made headlines everywhere. I was more famous for that than for my previous results.

I may have been number one in Britain and in Europe but this also proved that I didn't know how to handle the media. I was inexperienced and I was learning my lessons the hard way. I was upset because I felt I had gone out of my way to help the media in the past. Now they had turned on me. I felt very bitter about it.

The problem with athletics is that we have no training in how to cope with the media, which is ironic because athletics is one of the few sports where the competitors are allowed to deal directly with the press. By that I mean the media are permitted to stay in the hotels and training camps with the competitors; they become too familiar with the athletes as a result. That's one of the reasons why we get so much flak and it's something which the press office of the British Athletic Federation (BAF, the organization that took the place of the BAAB in 1991) should be doing their best to avoid. Instead, the media have access to athletes in situations where it should not be allowed and, to make matters worse, the officials – the people who should be dealing with the flack when things go wrong – are actually shielded from the press.

The incident in Rome made it obvious to everyone that Frank and I just couldn't get on. I told him my view was that we both had jobs to do and we shouldn't bother each other. I complained to the federation many times, but they took no notice. After the business in Italy, however, they decided to have an inquiry.

My idea of an inquiry is to hear every version of an incident because there are always three sides to every story; my side, his side, and the truth. They called me in, but Frank Dick was not there. I explained my version. I never heard another thing; I still have no idea what conclusion they reached, if any. I lost all confidence in the BAAB after that.

This was not a minor issue. There was obviously a problem between the head coach and the top athlete. The BAAB should have tried to resolve the situation, but they didn't. And, because of that, Frank Dick could carry on with his divisive tactics without fear of reprimand.

The problem was that the athletes were not sticking together. Frank would go to someone like Mike McFarlane and say that I didn't think Mike should be on the relay team. Then he would come to me and say McFarlane and the rest didn't think I should be on the team. This was our head coach playing silly buggers. As a result, the athletes were always at loggerheads and, for some reason, that's exactly what Frank wanted. There was no unity and the internal squabbles just went on and on and on, gradually affecting everyone.

For instance, there had always been rivalry between the west London team, coached by Ron Roddan, and north London team coached by John Issacs at Haringey. John Issacs was one of the top black coaches in the country and he wrote an article in a black newspaper about me and the relay team bust-up in Rome – and he hadn't even been there. I was gunning for John Issacs after that. I went to Haringey every day for about a week. I wanted to find John because I wanted to know just why he felt the need to do that. I never did succeed in getting a satisfactory answer.

But there is always retribution. If anyone was to set black people back in coaching, it was John Issacs. He kept crying out that he was being discriminated against because he was black. Eventually, everyone had had enough. Issacs was made National Sprint Coach but he left soon afterwards. What goes round comes round.

Meanwhile, Frank was still there and things reached the stage where I felt we could not go on arguing for much longer. I went to see Frank and I asked if he would help me with my starts. I thought that if we began working together, then maybe we could have a better relationship. We did work on my starting technique – but it didn't help our relationship.

One day Frank rang and suggested that we should have a talk. I was surprised that he wanted to meet me. We met in a little café in Wood Green to try to bury the hatchet. I thought that this was just to be between the two of us. A couple of days later, I read about it in a newspaper . . .

There were also difficulties surrounding Ron Roddan. Ron was my coach and yet he could never be on the team; it was always a problem to get him accredited. Eventually, the business of no accreditation got to Ron and I had to kick up a fuss. Frank brought in rules that personal coaches couldn't do any-thing unless he gave the go-ahead. When you've been with a coach all your life, he is all you know. It got to the stage where Frank asked for everyone's training programme. But Ron was smart. He never gave Frank his training programme because it is not written down. Ron keeps his programme in his head.

Frank was a great organizer; when it came to getting data and sorting out training camps, there was none better. But I felt he could not deal with people. Frank was not given accreditation by any of the home countries at the Commonwealth Games in 1990. It seemed to me that if I was running really well, Frank would be by my side, talking, talking, but if I ran badly, I wouldn't see him.

For me, relay has never been of any importance. It is some-thing which follows the individual events and it is good for unity on the team. The individual events are more important; once they are out of the way, then you can concentrate on the relay. I got the impression Frank wanted the relay team to succeed above all.

During the winter of 1987–8, I trained with Daley Thompson as we prepared for the Olympics in Seoul. We were working really hard, but having a good time along the way. Daley was a brilliant motivator, talking things through, discussing every level of performance and generally building up confidence.

He had a good effect on my performance as the 1988 season got under way. It had taken a while to recover from the injury in Rome the previous August. I had needed a break at the time and I went to New York, stayed with my sister, did the sightseeing bit and just relaxed.

But I did spend time thinking about events in Rome and I

could appreciate that it was dangerous to allow myself to be provoked. I had really blown my top and I was now aware that I would need to have some sort of inner protective barrier; a defence against people pushing too far.

I have always liked to keep myself to myself, and Mandy is more or less the same. We see ourselves as being very normal. Mandy likes to know all the neighbours. I'm not into all of that; I will say 'Hi' and obviously be polite but I wouldn't get into a conversation over the garden fence. I am not into gossip. I like to listen to it but I don't want to spread it. I don't want anyone to say 'Well, Linford says this and Linford says that.'

I can't be too careful because of the constant attention from the media, and that applies to things other than idle gossip. The night before Eric Cantona and Paul Ince were due to appear in court over an incident during a match at Crystal Palace when the Manchester United players became involved with some spectators, they were seen in a nightclub. On the day of the hearing, the newspapers carried pictures, showing the players allegedly 'living it up' on the night before a serious court case.

No sportsperson needs that kind of attention. Publicity is all very well in one respect because it satisfies sponsors, but I would prefer to stay at home. I don't like nightclubs; they're smoky and people end up standing on your feet, none of which is ideal for an athlete! I just don't seem to be able to enjoy myself and, of course, the problem is that people ask for your autograph all night long. I usually have no objection but there are times when I prefer to be off duty.

If we go out, it is to a restaurant or to the cinema, where we will arrive as close as possible to the start of the main attraction so that we can go straight in and sit down. I suppose you could say that Mandy and I are loners. Mandy is not one to go rushing about the place. She has one or two friends whom she sees regularly but she is not a party person, and she is not heavily into fashion, for example. But we do both like clothes; in fact, I think that presentation is very important. Saying you are the fastest man in the world is all very well but if you don't look good when outside athletics, then sponsors won't want to be associated with you. Mind you, details like that were the last thing on my mind at the time of my run-in with Frank Dick.

I had learned from Rome that I had been pretty naïve about the press. My attitude was not helped by the lead-in to Seoul.

Selection for the 1988 Olympics was based on results in the AAA Championships in Birmingham. You had to finish in the first two, or that was it. Some people didn't agree with the selection policy. The system did have its faults – an athlete who deserved to be picked might not make it on the day for various reasons; illness, injury, being generally off-form, whatever – but everyone knew what had to be done. I won the 100 and the 200 metres, which was the first time the sprint double had been won in these championships for something like thirty-five years.

I had run 10.15 seconds in the 100 metres and, when I went to Zurich for one of the last big meetings before Seoul, I did 10.07 seconds, my third-fastest time ever. But I finished fifth! Everyone – Carl Lewis, Ben Johnson, Calvin Smith – was there because, apart from being a pre-Olympic event, Zurich is one of the biggest meetings on the circuit. The city itself is slightly at altitude and the track is fast; that is the first attraction. The second is that Zurich is in Switzerland, which means it is adequately funded and very well organized. Andreas Brugger, the organizer, leaves nothing to chance. The food is the best. Everybody wants to be there; it is the meeting to win – but that does not come easy.

It is a very, very tough event. Even in a championship year, the Americans will train for Zurich because of its prestige and also the fact that it is usually just before a championship. It is the place to go to get the edge on your competitors. If you win in Zurich then, yeah! you are The Man.

The organizers can attract all the names because they have the biggest budget but, even if the money was no longer available, people would still go there because of the excellent treatment we receive. Some promoters are the exact reverse. They threaten you with statements such as, 'If you want to run in my meet, you had better not go to this person's meet.' And talk like that. Brugger never does anything like that. If you don't want to run, then that's not a problem. He's not going to say 'If you don't compete this year, then you won't be invited next year.' Some of the promotors are very quick to issue threats like that. They might also say 'If you don't do my meet, I've got certain friends in other places and I'll make sure you don't go there as well as not being able to come back here next year.'

I know of one promoter, whose name I will not mention, who once asked a foreign athlete if he had a camera. When the athlete asked why, he was told, 'Because you had better take a picture of this city as it is the last time you will see it.' The impression is that everything in athletics is so kosher. It's not. If the athlete has some clout, then the promoters will not dare to make threats. But that has never arisen at Zurich. My only problem was that I had finished fifth.

I was happy enough with my time (I had lowered the British 100-metres record to 10.03 seconds in Budapest the previous year) but none of this was good enough for the press. One newspaper headline proclaimed 'Fool's Gold'. They had an Olympic gold medal with my face in it and the same for Tom McKean and a few others. The article claimed British athletes were chasing fool's gold at the Olympic Games; we hadn't a hope in hell of winning medals. This was the send-off we were given to the biggest championship in any athlete's career.

Chapter 7

THE WORST DAY OF MY LIFE

The trip got off to a bad start. For some reason, the press had been booked on the same flight from London to Tokyo. Most journalists smoke and drink like nobody's business, and this was a long flight. So here you had athletes – all non-smokers – travelling to the Olympic Games and being killed by cigarette smoke.

On top of this, a story had broken concerning Tom McKean and a date he was alleged to have had with a prostitute at a nightclub. McKean had categorically denied this but it really had the press guys going, particularly the feature writers who are usually sent to the big sporting occasions. The timing could not have been worse because the story was in the papers on the day we left. It was embarrassing for Tom to see everyone coming on to the plane and reading about it. But the athletes just thought it was funny. Nobody believed the story because we knew what Tom was like – which was more than could be said for the journalists.

Apart from not knowing what they are talking about half the time, some of these guys would not have recognized Tom McKean if they had fallen over him – which was quite likely given the state of one particular journalist. Breathing alcohol fumes everywhere, he asked one of the swimmers if he was Tom McKean and we at least had a laugh at the writer's expense because the swimmer said he was Tom and he really strung the guy along.

The situation got no better once we arrived at the holding camp at Nihon, about sixty miles east of Tokyo. The facilities were the best I had ever seen and would have been the perfect place to prepare for the final move to the Olympic village in Seoul. But, to our disgust, we found that the media had also been booked into Nihon. We were there for a few weeks and, while the athletes may have had something to do, the press soon became bored. Perhaps as a result, Tessa Sanderson and I found ourselves in the middle of a controversy which took us completely off our guard.

At Heathrow airport, the photographers had asked if they could take a picture of me and Tessa Sanderson together, since we were the senior members of the team. Then they said 'Put your arm around her – you know, in comradeship.' I agreed quite happily, but perhaps I should have been more wary.

I think this had started during the trials in Birmingham when Tessa injured her Achilles tendon. I can remember the noise, even now; it was like someone cracking a whip. The injury was horrible and I really don't know how she managed to come back from that. But the point was, she had to take part in the trials otherwise she would not get picked. She couldn't even warm up and she was crying. I went over and gave her a hug and told her not to worry. That's where the story started.

Now they were saying that Tessa and I would disappear into

the bushes for several hours at a time. We couldn't have done that because there were snakes in the bushes and the place was cordoned off for security purposes. Threats had been made against athletes from some countries so there were guards everywhere, to make sure we were safe. There was no way Tessa and I could have been having an affair. We just laughed it off because it was such a stupid story. In the bushes for several hours! If I could have lasted for several hours, I wouldn't have been a runner. I would have set up in business! I could have made some money on the side.

But it was no joke when they went to see Mandy at home and asked what she thought of her boyfriend having an affair with Tessa. Mandy didn't know any better at the time and answered the questions without realizing what journalistic licence was all about. She didn't believe any of the things they were saying but, obviously, it doesn't help either of us to be thousands of miles apart when a story like that breaks. As I said before, the important thing in athletics is to have a home life which is going really well and if anything affects that, performance on the track is likely to suffer.

Mandy and I had been living together for a few years by this stage. We had moved from the place in Scrubs Lane to a semi-detached in Acton — and she knew me better than anyone. The business over my supposed affair with Tessa was an irritation more than anything else. At my end, the problem was that all of this was going on while Tessa and I were trying to prepare for the Olympic Games. We should have sued.

A tabloid journalist was chasing the Tom McKean story. One day, Tom must either have been playing badminton or he had gone for a run. When he went to take a shower, the journalist stripped off, got in the sauna — and tried to interview Tom!

I felt really sorry for Tom because he was trying to get ready for an Olympic Games. Regardless of who you are, you can't work under those conditions. Newspapers have an effect. I think that, mentally, I am one of the strongest guys on the track but even I am affected when I read some of the rubbish. In Tom's case, his preparation was messed up. If he had won a medal after that, it would have been a miracle.

If you are trying to prepare for an important event, you have got to have tunnel vision. You've got to concentrate totally. I accept that there have got to be times when the press can take a few pictures, but you can't have them there all the time. It was like stalking the royals. Everywhere we walked, there was a lens following. We weren't very happy with it; to be honest, I was totally pissed off.

Another story doing the rounds at home claimed that I was injured. Of course, that was not true. In fact, my training had gone well, except for the fact that Ron had had to return home after we left Nihon because, once again, he could not get accreditation. This was my first Olympic Games and my coach was not allowed in . . .

Just before I left for Seoul, I had a massage and fell asleep on the massage bed. The masseuse accidentally dug her elbow into my adductor. That panicked me because I was in pain. When I reached Seoul, I tried to do some strides with Colin Jackson and a few of my team-mates – but I couldn't run more than five metres. Now I was really worried.

Malcolm Arnold, one of the few coaches who Ron trusted to work with me, said I should rest, do nothing but rest. Malcolm's record is excellent and I took his advice even though it was very difficult just sitting around, thinking about the problem.

On the day of the 100-metre heats, we had to get up at an

unbelievable hour because the event was at about 10 a.m.
You have to be up and about, alert, have breakfast and get
yourself ready. It's so hard to eat breakfast on the day you
compete; nervous energy and everything else just kills you. I
felt completely knackered and I was knocking back the black
coffees to keep me awake – a crazy thing to do because you can
be found positive on too much coffee. It was naïveté on my
part because I thought I had nothing to fear; I had made a big
issue over the fact that I was not on drugs.

The previous December, *The Times* had run a series of stories
on drug abuse in athletics. One of the suggestions was that an
ex-sprinter had said there was no point in even thinking about
winning unless you were on steroids. I was the only athlete to
go on record afterwards by saying I was as clean as a whistle.
To show that I was a big supporter of the drug-free movement,
I wore T-shirts carrying messages such as 'Pure Talent. Body
by me. Training by Ron', and '100 per cent Natural'. I was
proud of the fact that I was doing everything through hard
work. I thought that was the ideal and I still believe it is the
way to do things.

But it does not alter the fact that I should not have been
drinking black coffee on the morning of the 100-metre heats in
Seoul. There were little makeshift shops in Nihon and I had
bought some ginseng. I had started taking that because it is
supposed to give you a feeling of wellbeing.

I began to do my warm-ups and found I was still limping.
These were my first Olympics, I was panicking like mad.
Malcolm Arnold took one look and said, 'Just get out there and
bloody run! If it falls off, then it falls off!' I ran – and didn't feel
a thing because the adrenalin took over.

Ben Johnson was not one of the favourites because he had
recently been beaten by Carl Lewis and Calvin Smith. Ben also

had an injury and, if that prevailed, he wouldn't win anything. I was down to finish fourth or fifth.

I ran really well through the rounds. Carl did his normal thing by trying to dominate from gun to tape; he always has to end up with the fastest times of the day. Psychologically, he tries to beat everyone else that way. I was confident I could pull it off in the final the next day although, deep in my heart of hearts, I knew I was just getting experience; I was still learning. But, being the kind of person I am, I really believed I could win! And yet I was so nervous that I couldn't stop shaking. I kept wanting to pee, I kept wanting to sleep – I was going through every emotion.

I was drawn in the middle lanes with Ben and Carl – and Ben just went. I don't think I'll ever forget that; he just went. We had been preparing with Ben in mind because he was known to be a sixty-metre man. He would go hard for sixty metres, and then just hang on.

So we had decided to train for the last forty. The plan was to work hard for sixty, stay as close as possible to Ben and, while he was dying, I would go past. It didn't happen . . .

Stride for stride, I was with Carl for about sixty or seventy metres. But Ben was already out of the picture; he had gone. Instead of dying, he picked up. I don't know what happened, to be honest with you. I don't know if it was ten or fifteen metres out, but he looked left and right – and just put his finger up.

He was looking for Carl. Ben hated Carl because he blamed him for spreading rumours that he was on drugs. They just couldn't get on. There had been a year when Ben had won everything; he was running really well and he lost one race to Carl. An athletics magazine which issues a ranking had made Carl number one. No one could work out how they reached that conclusion and Ben certainly wasn't happy with the ranking.

But, from pictures of the 100-metre final in Seoul, you can see from the look on Carl's face that he is the one who isn't happy. He also ran in my lane. The rules said that if you step on the line, then you should be disqualified. Carl actually ran a couple of strides in my lane. He just couldn't believe how far in front Ben was. And then Ben put his finger up. He ran 9.79 seconds. With his finger in the air! Damn!

I ran the race of my life in 9.97 seconds to cross the line in third place. I was the first European to get below 10 seconds. I was tested afterwards.

I was due to run in the 200-metre heats two days later. But, before that, we were all to be diverted by something totally unexpected.

I was woken up to be told that Ben had tested positive. Our press officer, Tony Ward, then arranged for me to do an early morning live television interview, which I think was a bit naïve of him considering I was due to run later that day. In my view, the team management should never have allowed that to happen but I went along and did the interview, and everything else besides.

I cried that day. I really cried because I have always felt that people who get caught for drugs should be banned for life. I had wanted the officials to catch these people. But I never expected it to happen to Ben. Believe me, I had been in Ben's company and I never thought he was on drugs – never, ever. He was such a nice guy. There are stories that people on drugs tear up the room and go loopy-loo. But Ben was so cool; he was really funny.

On the day he won the gold, we were on the rostrum and he

was admiring the girls carrying the medals. Ben had a stutter and he was saying 'You s-s-s-see that girl over there. T-t-t-tell her, Ben Johnson wants her.' He was a laugh. I knew he would be missed. The Canadian team got on with everybody and, I suppose, because of our West Indian background, Ben and I just clicked; we were great friends. I felt so sorry because it was a sad day for athletics. But I cried because I was just sorry for Ben.

By now, the rumours were out of control and a witch hunt began. The British papers said that there were more athletes in the 100 metres who had tested positive.

I recovered, took what little of the ginseng remained, and ran the 200 metres. I finished fourth in the final and set a new British record. It was strange because I didn't really know what I was doing. I found myself asking Lesley-Ann Skeete, a hurdler, how I should run the 200. I was supposed to be an experienced athlete but I had really only been on the international scene for a short time. And this was a big occasion.

Some of the guys had run the 200 metres in under 20 seconds; people like Carl Lewis, the greatest of them all. He had practised the 200; he really knew what he was doing. My personal best had been a 20.37 seconds – and that was wind assisted! To me, the 200 at this level was something completely new.

Don Quarrie, the former Olympic 200-metre champion, was part of the Jamaican team management and Lesley-Ann said she would ask Don how the 200 should be run. Apparently, he said 'Run the bend hard, save a little bit, and then go on the straight.' That's what I tried to do but, for some reason, I just seemed to be floating on air. It was a very strange feeling.

Despite the furore over Ben Johnson and the problems with the press, we had a good time in Seoul. I remember we shopped and shopped. You could buy made-to-measure clothes for next to nothing. I came away with a cashmere double-breasted blazer, a suit and a coat which I've still got – a long one with a big split in the back. It was so cheap! And you haggled with everyone; that was the way business was done. I even remember Colin haggling with a taxi driver because the fare was something like 40p instead of 35p! It was normal to do that.

Talking of taxis, there was one occasion when Sally Gunnell and I were in a cab driven by a woman. In Seoul, everyone spat with great gusto, it was horrible. But this taxi driver snuffed one up from her toes, opened the window and let fly. We were travelling at speed and it shot past our window and hit the back of the cab. Sally and I were close to being sick . . .

If you weren't in a cab in the city, then you were usually walking in the village. It was quite a way from our accommodation to the dining hall and the problem was, the dining hall was at the bottom of a steep hill. One morning, Colin and I took a short-cut across a field on our way to breakfast. This 'thing' – I know it wasn't a bird, but it was as big as a bird – started to follow us. It really got our attention. We ran! We jumped fences, cleared barbed wire – everything that was in the way until we reached the dining hall. Nobody would believe us when we explained why we were in such a state!

The road to the hall wound all over the place and then there were very steep steps once you got there. It was like climbing a mountain and, once inside, the air conditioning was bliss. Eventually, we discovered that there were bicycles available but the trouble was that everyone left them at the dining hall; nobody was prepared to ride them back up the hill! I remember, too, that the various suppliers – Puma, ASICS and so on – had kit on display. Bit by bit, the items would mysteriously disappear.

By the time we were due to leave, the athletes had even gone as far as stripping the dummies of their clothes!

It was all part of the fun. We had a good laugh and I remember, after the 200 metres, a group of us were relaxing in the village and generally messing around. Our team manager, Mike Turner, was a university don who caused a lot of jokes among the athletes because he would wear a GB tracksuit – with brown socks and shoes. But I didn't find anything funny about what he had to say when he came across and pulled me to one side.

He told me he had received a letter from the International Olympic Committee (IOC), informing him that I had been tested positive. Mike was a nice guy and I thought this was some kind of hoax. Me being tested positive? There was no such thing. I looked in his face and I could see that he was really serious. I just broke down.

I tried to hide it. I didn't want everyone around me to start thinking, 'God! Linford's done something' and panic. I had just got the silver in the 100 metres and finished fourth in the 200 metres. That had been a big boost for the whole team. The last thing I wanted to do was go out there and crack up in front of everyone, particularly some of the younger members who had even less experience.

We were all so inexperienced at the time that when the word 'drugs' was used, it was automatically assumed that the reference was to steroids. I said, 'If they want their medal, they can take their medal. I don't want it because I don't take steroids. Don't tell me that I'm on drugs, because I'm not.'

I went into a room at the athletes' apartment block with members of the British team management. They didn't know the name of the substance concerned, but they started a serious cross-examination. I suppose they thought they had to but I knew I hadn't done anything. They made me begin to believe that I had.

To this day, I don't know if I've forgiven them. It's not good to keep things like that inside you and it has taken me a long, long time to begin to feel better about it. But, each time there is a similar incident, it makes me mad because I remember the way I felt.

I almost started to question myself. They came into my room and took away all of my vitamins. I had to tell them everything – what I had eaten for breakfast, and so on. And I started to think, 'Yeah, maybe you did it. Maybe you did inject yourself with steroids.' It went on and on and on and I started to cry. I thought 'Damn. I've always believed in being fair in athletics; natural, with no drug abuse. And now they are asking me this. Making me believe I took drugs.'

An international coach had once said that it would be impossible for anyone to win an Olympic gold medal naturally. My ambition had been to prove that you could do it without drugs. Everything I had worked hard for had just gone down the drain. I was Ron Roddan's athlete and everybody would ask where I got the drugs from. They would assume that the drugs had come from Ron.

There was the embarrassment that came from thinking about my family and friends and the people who had supported me and believed in me. It would affect them too. If you take drugs and get caught, everyone associated with you is labelled as well. I could hear my friends saying 'Yeah, Linford's done really great.' Bang! That would be the end of it.

I just wanted to die. At one point I almost wanted to kill myself. Things like that went through my mind because they were really grilling me.

I realized very quickly that not everyone on the team could

be trusted. The rumour was out that two British athletes had been found positive and somebody on the team leaked my name to the press. My name should never have been made public. But it was. Obviously, there was going to be an inquiry. But, before that, I had to visit the British Olympic Association (BOA) headquarters and try to explain to them that I had not taken drugs. They told me to keep it quiet; it was supposed to be hush–hush.

How could I keep something like that a secret? If I kept quiet, then it would be a sign of guilt. I said I needed to talk to the team, I needed to tell my team-mates, because if I didn't do that and they heard through another channel, then it would be even worse for me. People would begin to talk behind my back.

I was sharing a room with Colin Jackson and he was one of the first people I spoke to. When I asked if he ever felt I took drugs, he thought I was joking. I told him I had been tested positive; he couldn't believe it. 'If you're on drugs,' he said, 'then I'm on drugs.'

Colin and I talked about it and I've never cried so much. I felt those people took away a lot of my humanity, they took away a lot of my self-respect; everything I had. I was confused, upset and angry. Shit! I should never have been put through a situation like that. After speaking to Colin, I told Malcolm Arnold. I told everyone because I wanted people to know that I didn't do it. I told them first-hand so that it wouldn't be such a shock when the story came out.

Malcolm Read, the British athletics medical representative, had been to the IOC medical laboratory. He discovered that the substance concerned was pseudoephedrine; the kind of stuff you find in cough mixture. I could have killed myself thinking it was steroids when, all along, it was bloody cough mixture. And the amount they found – they said they found it and I had no alternative but to go along with that – was so small, something like eight parts in a million. It was a joke. It seemed to me that this was a witch hunt; the IOC had caught Ben, made world headlines, and now they wanted to be seen to be catching everyone in their fight against drugs.

I had spent twenty-four hours believing they had found steroids before discovering that they were talking about pseudoephedrine. During that time I hadn't been able to sleep. It was as if my life was at stake. The doctor had had to give me sleeping tablets.

Colin and Malcolm tried to help me through it. And I must say that Frank Dick was very supportive. He was with Daley when I told him. I was crying again – I just couldn't stop crying – as I repeated that I had never taken anything in my life. Both of them were really good about the whole thing and that made me feel a lot better. I asked them if they thought I would take drugs; they said no, they didn't.

When I went to see Robert Watson, the Queen's Counsel appointed by the British Olympic Committee (BOC) to defend my case, he started by saying that I would have to go to the inquiry the following day and explain my case to the committee.

The QC suggested that I should say I had been taking cough mixture because I had a cold. They would probably accept that, give me a slap on the wrist and a three-month ban. I said 'No. There's no way I'm going to lie because I didn't do anything.'

Robert Watson said he was glad I had said that because now he believed that I hadn't taken drugs. 'I was just testing you,' he said. 'If you had accepted my suggestion, then I wouldn't have represented you. I would have thought you were guilty. But now I believe you haven't knowingly taken anything.'

During this time, the qualifying rounds for the relay were being held. I didn't run in the first heat because, if I was banned by the IOC later in the day, then the whole relay team would be disqualified. Of course, the rumours were going strong and the press were watching our every move. Frank suggested that I warm up as usual and then he would say that I had been withdrawn from my heat because of concern about a slight injury resulting from the 200 metres.

I watched from the sidelines. The American team won their race although they ran outside their box at a changeover. The white flag was raised but at first the Americans were not disqualified, even though the video proved the case. In the end, the Americans were thrown out after other countries protested.

By now, the news had broken in Britain. Linford Christie and Kerrith Brown, a member of the British judo team, had been found positive. Neither of our names should have been released. The hearing was still to come that evening. Having watched the chaotic scenes on television as Ben Johnson and his coach tried to leave Seoul airport, I thought I knew what was in store. But nothing could prepare me for the disgusting scene outside the hearing.

The inquiry was supposed to be a confidential meeting in a private place. The only British representatives present were supposed to be the management, Kerrith and people from his sport, the QC and me.

There must have been more press in the lobby of that hotel than when Camillagate broke. Everyone was there. I couldn't believe it. I was pushed and shoved, swept along by the throng with microphones and cameras shoved in my face. I said nothing. Nobody was supposed to know about this meeting apart from the team management and the IOC. So who was leaking information this time? It was a disgrace.

The inquiry followed the usual procedure. I had given two samples, an 'A' and a 'B'. I don't know why they bother because the samples are always going to be identical. It's the same urine, they just split it between two bottles. People become confused when they hear that the officials are waiting for tests on the 'B' sample. It gives the impression that the athlete has given another sample. That's not the case. If they say it's in your 'A', then it's going to be your 'B' as well.

I felt like I was in the United Nations. There were tables in a horseshoe and I was in the middle with people all around me. I was not allowed to speak unless a little light came on. Every country seemed to have a representative and the translations took time. Robert Watson presented a very impressive case. He showed samples of ginseng, which we now believed to be the prime suspect. The committee asked me questions but there was nothing I could really say. I told them I had always believed in drug-free athletics, just as it said on my T-shirts. After a few more questions, they said they would come to a decision.

The committee eventually accepted that I had not done anything wrong. In the press conference which followed, they said I had been given 'the benefit of the doubt'. The spokesman's English wasn't very good which is why, I think, he used a phrase like that. But the press picked up on it, which meant my name wasn't cleared properly. One British paper even went as far as to send a reporter to Jamaica to find out if I had known Ben Johnson when we were kids! I don't know when Ben left Jamaica, but I came to England when I was seven so, even if we had met, it wouldn't have made any difference. I should add, however, that one or two of the athletics writers had been very supportive; they didn't believe that I was guilty any more than I did.

Before we left Seoul, I tried to find out how my name had been released. The sample bottles carry numbers, not names. Names and numbers are kept by the top officials and it seemed that someone was being paid to divulge the information.

I knew the media would be waiting at London airport and I thought the answer would be to issue a press release. No one connected with either the BOA or our team was willing to put out a release saying that I had been exonerated. Nobody wanted to get involved. Tessa sat down with me at the back of the plane and, between us, we worked out questions which had to be asked. But I wasn't satisfied with that because I wanted to clear my name. I even thought about suing the IOC but decided against it.

I was to discover that there had been tremendous support at home. The welcome I received at Heathrow – people waving Union Jacks and cheering – was wonderful; just what I needed at the end of what had been a very long and trying five weeks.

Despite all that happened, some people still believe I was on drugs, even though the amount of pseudoephedrine concerned wouldn't have stimulated a child. I would have needed bottles of the stuff to get any effect. I have put it down to experience and I can say to people 'Don't take drugs, it's not worth it.' I only have to remember Seoul. I felt like a little kid who had taken a penny bubble gum from a shop and ended up in the Old Bailey.

I had discovered so many things. The IOC blamed the BOA, and vice versa, each side saying the other had released my name. The BOA denied it and I never did find out who was responsible. I've had very little to do with the BOA ever since. I go to the games, get my massage, run my race, collect my medal; just do my own thing. I have never felt comfortable with the BOA and I do as little as possible with them because I still haven't got over Seoul. I don't think I ever will. To me, it was the worst day of my life.

Chapter 8

DEALING WITH DRUGS

I don't think officials really understand how embarrassing it is for the athletes when they have to perform in the dope room, although I appreciate that close observation is necessary because I know some people will go to great lengths to cheat. It has been said, for example, that women have been caught concealing condoms of urine inside them; others have used catheters direct into their kidneys and so on. The worst, almost unbelievable scenario, concerned the athlete who was caught with someone else's urine in his mouth. That gives an indication of how far some people will go to cheat and the officials obviously have to cope with that.

But that does not take away from the fact that the athlete has to go in and pee in front of someone. It's difficult enough for men but twice as bad for women, as officials have to stoop to all sorts of levels to make sure there is no foul play. It is all a part of being an athlete, something which you have to learn to put up with – but can't.

I found that I was able to put my experiences in Seoul to good advantage. Each time there has been a drug problem since, the team usually contacts me because nobody really knows how to deal with it. The management called me, for example, after it was announced in Barcelona in 1992 that Jason Livingston had tested positive.

Jason and I had been together at training camp and he had been running really well. We had been talking about drugs and all sorts of things and, as always, I had said it wasn't worth doing drugs.

I was in bed early as I was due to compete the next morning when an official came to my room and told me Jason had tested positive. There wasn't much we could do at that point. Jason had been tested at an earlier meeting and yet he had come all the way to the Olympic village before the Sports Council informed him.

When you go to training camp, you have to let everyone know where you are so that you can be contacted if necessary. Yet it seems they waited until the day we went into the village before letting the BOA know that Jason had tested positive. They should have sent him home straight away. Once inside the village, it became an Olympic problem – which in my opinion it should never have been.

I had a chat with Jason and used the experience I had gained from being in the same position. But my case wasn't as serious because Jason had got himself involved with steroids – in this case methandianone.

I told the team doctor to give Jason sleeping tablets and to let him sleep in my room; I was supposed to be sharing with Colin, but he had not arrived at that point. Once again, the BOA wanted to keep everything quiet. But you can't. The press soon gets to know – and then the word is out. My advice was to tell the team as soon as possible. Then there would be no panic and no wild rumours inside the team. If nothing was said, then it would affect everyone's performance. I broke the news at a team meeting and it eased the situation.

Jason's case was straightforward – if you can ever call it that – compared to Solomon Wariso's case in 1994. That, to me, was a low issue.

Solomon was due to compete in the European Championships in 1994 and, according to him, the BAF knew about his positive test before we left for Finland. When Solomon failed to hear anything about his travel plans, he rang the BOA to find out what was happening. It was then that he was told about a letter they had received saying he had tested positive for ephedrine. It seems the letter had been with the BAF for a couple of days. They said they would fax him a copy.

The following day, when nothing had arrived, he phoned back to find out what was going on. It was a serious situation and he needed to know. He was told that, due to the confidentiality of the letter, it had not been faxed to him. Of course! Who would be stupid enough to think about faxing something like that in the first place? Instead, it should have been delivered in person or sent to him by courier. But the BAF just sat on it for another day.

Then, worse still, they said he should go to the games and compete – 'but if you're winning, you should hold back'! What sort of intellect does a person have who would tell an athlete something like that?

I heard about what had happened during the flight to Helsinki. One of the team members had been told and he passed it on to me as team captain. I went down to the back of the plane, sat with Solomon and talked about it. Earlier, Solomon had been asking me if I knew what 'Mah Wang' was. I thought that perhaps it was short for 'marijuana' but he said it wasn't that; it meant something else, but he didn't know what. He then explained that he had taken something called 'Up Your Gas'. I knew about 'Up Your Gas' because I had seen full-page advertisements for the stuff in the United States. The ads said there was nothing illegal in 'Up Your Gas' and claimed that athletes could take it. I had read the package; they were more or less saying 'The name sounds stupid – but this really is the business.' I can remember being in a health shop in the States when the assistant confirmed this to an athlete, saying 'It's all legal.'

Ninety-nine point nine per cent of athletes will take anything which is not illegal if they believe it will help. Solomon used 'Up Your Gas' and the test found that he had taken a banned substance – Mah Wang – which turned out to be the Chinese name for pseudoephedrine. It is actually Chinese slang; how are athletes supposed to know that? But ignorance was no excuse.

The immediate problem was that they had sent Solomon to the games. More athletes were finding out about the story but I discovered that Malcolm Arnold, our chief coach, didn't know. The BAF should have told the team management, regardless of the background. It is the management who have to deal with the situation – or at least try to.

They didn't really know what to do and, again, I was called in. It was the day before I was due to compete, but I didn't mind because I was team captain. I don't suppose, when they made me captain, that anyone thought my role would work out like this. Dealing with drugs had not really been necessary in the past but, since they were now an unfortunate part of the scene, I made sure that I accepted the responsibility and worked for the team.

We decided to put out a press statement. Athletes can't hold themselves back to avoid winning a medal. If the three guys in front fall over, you can't say 'oops', stop, turn around and run the other way! It is harder to run slowly in a race than it is to run fast. We produced a draft statement which had to be faxed to BAF officials for approval. Word came back that they didn't like it. They must have known that the most important move at this stage would have been to come to the village and brief the management on the situation. But they didn't. It was late in the evening, they were in their hotels, and they didn't seem to care.

While Malcolm and others were deliberating on this, the phone started ringing. The press were on to the story – which was exactly what we had feared. And, once again, there appeared to be a leak. Somewhere between the testing and the message reaching the BAF, somebody had told the press. The powers that be finally came down to the village to talk to Solomon.

Previously, Solomon and I hadn't got on. He used to train in our group, after joining us from John Issacs. He was talented, but he was strange in some ways. I remember once he had a foot problem. Ron and I came down to the track one evening and found him bounding around on the foot. Ron said, 'You're injured – so what are you doing that for?' But you couldn't tell him anything.

When he left our group, he started to say that Ron was rubbish. That annoyed me because Ron didn't have to take him in the first place. You can say what you like to me but I will not tolerate people insulting Ron. He has done too much for me; he's too much of a nice guy to have to take that sort of abuse.

When Solomon ran his first good race, he said I was old and he would be the man to beat. So when I saw him in the warm-up area at the next meeting, I went over to him, 'Solomon,' I said. 'You are telling people that I'm too old and that you're going to beat me. Well, you're talented. But you are also stupid, too stupid even to think that you can beat me.' He should have finished in the top three or four in that race and he actually ran slower than the women did. It proved that he was an upstart who thought that one good race makes a champion. It doesn't.

But I felt sorry for him in Finland. Having gone through the Jason story and my own case in Seoul, it seemed common sense to suggest that I help him out. Everyone agreed.

It was around midnight when I was called from my bed to talk to the management. I was competing the next morning but, since I was more or less Solomon's representative, I needed to hear what was being said and to ask questions relevant to his case. They finally asked Solomon 'What do you want to do?' Then they said, 'We don't think you should run. But we want you to pull out.'

I said to Solomon 'Don't pull out! If they don't want you to run, then let them pull you out. They should never have let you come here in the first place.'

The fact was that if Solomon had wanted to run, and the BAF were against it, then that would have been it; he could not have run. So why did they wake me up to listen to such crap? They kept asking Solomon why he wouldn't pull out.

Now I was getting cheesed off. 'If you don't want him to run,' I said, 'then pull him out. You are the team management; he has to do what he's told. He's only the athlete, we are only the minnows after all.'

They deliberated and deliberated. I started to ask questions and I was told that I shouldn't be putting questions like that, it was up to Solomon to ask them. I said I was there as Solomon's representative and my job was to ask questions relevant to his case. I asked another question which they couldn't answer; and another. I was told that I could not bring up the subjects in question because they were not to be discussed in front of some of the people present.

I lost my cool. I said, 'We're all here to try and solve this puzzle. We all know it is confidential; that's why we are here at this meeting, trying to talk and sort it out. There shouldn't be anything which we can't discuss but I seem to be doing nothing but standing here just listening to you lot. I haven't got time for this; I've got a race tomorrow. You're all a bunch of wankers. You can't even make a proper decision.'

To be honest, even now, I can't see what was so difficult. They could have said 'Okay, Solomon. Because of the serious-ness of your case, we think it best that you don't run. You are withdrawn.' But they were trying to get Solomon to make the decision. It was a let-out in case, in the unlikely event that the 'A' sample had not been correctly tested and the 'B' sample showed a different result, the case was dropped and Solomon tried to sue them. Then they could say, 'We didn't pull you out; you did.'

That is no way to operate. I was so hurt because it just brought back all the memories of what I had been through in Seoul. I had to hold myself back; there were tears in my eyes. I was so mad. I just walked out. After I had gone, Malcolm explained to them that I was very sensitive about the situation because of having been through the business in Seoul. Anyway, Solomon didn't run.

The following day I discovered that a press conference for Solomon had been arranged between my heats for the 100 metres, the hope being that I would miss the conference. I found out about it and went over to the press centre.

Solomon is an intelligent guy, but sometimes he seems to lack a little bit in the common sense department. Inexperience plays a part, too, but once he finds himself in a situation like that, he doesn't seem to know what's going on. They left Solomon to the mercy of the press. The more questions they asked him, the more he dropped himself in it. It was like feeding a baby lamb to the wolves and expecting the lamb to fend for itself. They just cut him to pieces.

As soon as the formal part of any press conference finishes, the person concerned is then swamped as he or she tries to leave. I could see that was going to happen to Solomon and he didn't need that. He had got himself into enough trouble. I grabbed him and said 'Solomon! Get up! Get out!'

Someone said, 'But we need Solomon to do *Grandstand*.'

I said, 'Solomon, don't do *Grandstand*. Shut your mouth, don't do anything else; just leave.'

The next day, I discovered that Solomon had appeared on *Grandstand*! I told him that the drugs situation should not be glorified in that way. It was something he ought to be ashamed of, something which should be allowed to die down.

The inquiry came in due course and Solomon was found guilty. That brought the whole business of drug abuse back up the agenda as we went to Canada for the 1994 Commonwealth Games.

There were rumours floating around the village in Victoria that a few other people had been tested. But Colin and I were not really involved in that initially because, in order to avoid jet lag, we had decided to travel as late as possible. In my case, I was going to do the 100 metres and then return home. Originally, I had said I would like to run the 200 metres because John Regis was injured. In the event Toby Box, a young, up-and-coming guy, was picked for the 200 even though my times had been far superior to his. Fair enough; it was the management's choice. I finalized my programme, told everyone concerned, flew to Victoria and won the 100 metres. That's when I caught up with the rumours that one of our field eventers had tested positive.

I asked Alan Lindop, the team manager, about the story but he didn't want to discuss it. He said it had nothing to do with anyone else; there was nothing to be said; there would be no press release or anything like that until the appropriate time. I thought he was really good about it because that was exactly the kind of confidentiality we had been looking for.

I was talking about the drugs business with a few of our female athletes, including Diane Modahl. She was asking questions which were so naïve it was quite clear she didn't know anything about the subject. We were exchanging rumours. I was telling them the stories I had heard about me, that I was big and old in athletics terms and there was no way I could be running so fast unless I was on drugs! You shouldn't joke about these things but we were having a laugh, just to lighten the mood. At no point would I have believed that the people in the conversation were involved in any drug problem.

I left Victoria soon afterwards. When I got home I learned that two athletes, Paul Edwards and Diane Modahl, had tested positive. In Diane's case, I couldn't believe it. If Diane had been using drugs, she would not have been asking the stupid questions I had heard in Victoria. If she had actually taken the doses she was accused of, it was surprising she was still alive. Certainly, she would have been shaving! Five o'clock shadow would have been an understatement because we were talking about a male hormone. And yet there had been none of the characteristics you would expect. She hadn't been running the times; there was no drastic improvement in her performance to say Diane was taking drugs. This confirmed my serious doubts about the entire testing procedure.

At a meeting just after the World Championships in 1993, all of the top athletes competing had been selected – supposedly at random. Of course, I was one of them. Since there were rumours flying around, I decided I was not going to take any risks with my urine. I was going to be the one who handled it and made sure the bottles were sealed. I took Maurie Plant, an Australian official, in with me to act as a witness. I met the doctor, signed the forms and then peed in a plastic beaker similar to the kind used at parties. When the doctor went to pour it into the bottles, I stopped him. 'I'll do it,' I said. 'I don't trust anyone. I'm not taking any chances. You lot say I'm on drugs. I'm going to make sure you find out that I'm not!'

I poured the first sample into the 'A' bottle and sealed it. Then I began to pour the 'B' sample. I thought that if I squeezed the beaker I would make a better lip for pouring. I squeezed – and the beaker snapped! Pee went everywhere. All over the doctor.

It has got to be the most embarrassing thing I have ever done. The doctor was coughing and spluttering. I was laughing, not because I thought it was funny, but through total embarrassment. I was saying 'Sorry! Sorry!' The contents of the beaker had gone everywhere. He began to get angry and, because I was embarrassed, I reacted. 'I said I'm sorry. What more do you want me to do?'

Maurie was going red. The doctor's shirt was soaked. I didn't know what to do next. Mandy had bought me a really nice T-shirt from the World Championships and I had it in my bag. I gave it to the doctor so that he could change. They made me go again.

I had to wait until I could produce another sample; I was there for ages. As it turned out, everything was fine. But if I saw that doctor today, I would still be apologizing.

There can be dangerous side effects to the business of having to give a sample. For instance, it takes an hour and twenty minutes to warm up and, during that time, I have to hold my urine just in case I am tested after the race. They will ask for a sample and you have to stay in that room for as long as it takes. So I would hold my urine to the point where I was bursting. Apart from the obvious problems of discomfort while trying to run, I began to have bladder problems and my doctor told me I was developing a form of cystitis. He said I shouldn't hold my urine, otherwise I would pay for it later in life. I stopped and that has since cost me a lot of time spent waiting in the dope room.

I ran in Sheffield at the end of 1994, but I had to go to the toilet before the test because I was not prepared to hold on any longer. It meant I was in the dope room for three or four hours. Everyone else had gone home but my friends had to wait for me to produce a sample.

Eventually I got to the stage where, if I was ready to give a sample, then I thought the official should be in a position to deal with it. I was tested after winning the 100 metres in the 1994 World Cup. It always seemed to be me and, when I asked why I was being tested yet again, they said it was random. I said if that was the case, then I was prepared to bet any money I would be back again once the relay had been run the next day.

We ran the relay and one person from the team had to be tested. Who was it? Linford Christie. I was prepared this time and, against the advice of my doctor, held my urine for ages. Once in the room, the combination of nerves and adrenalin makes you want to give your sample straight away. They said I couldn't go because there was a queue.

'Are you crazy?' I said. 'You call me in here and I am ready to give a sample. My doctor told me not to hold my urine, I'm getting cystitis because of this and you are telling me that I've got to sit down and wait. I am not waiting. Either you take it now, or I'm gone.'

I asked the athletes waiting if they minded if I pushed in, and no one objected. The officials went off and had a quick conference, came back and said it was okay. They found a little room and I gave my sample. But I had made a fuss because I felt that it was relevant. These people don't have to go through the testing procedures, they don't appreciate the problems. If the facilities are inadequate, they should not call in so many athletes.

But I was also annoyed because the tests had gone from being random to the point where I was starting to feel victimized. Somebody actually said to me that if I didn't want to be tested I shouldn't run so fast! My answer was that they should test everybody rather than the same few athletes all the time. Then there can be no argument. I have been to events where another name and number were originally on the list of athletes to be tested and they had been scratched out and replaced by my number and name. And the testing is supposed to be random. I was always complaining to the team doctor. When he once asked why the name and number had been changed, the officials said they had made a mistake and my name should have been there in the first place.

The system should protect the innocent, but it doesn't. I thought that the more I competed and the more I was tested, the better chance I would have of proving that I am clean. But it has reached the stage where I feel like the more I compete and take part in tests, the better chance there is of being set up.

Everybody who gets caught on drugs will say they haven't taken anything. You can catch them with a needle in their arm and they will tell you somebody threw the needle! If they get caught, then they should say so: 'I got caught. Fair cop.' They know the score.

When told the test is positive, what can you do? Nothing. Nothing at all. You can't be tested positive and get off, since the federation is never wrong. They're infallible and they have never ever made a mistake – except for a Norwegian javelin thrower who sued her federation. Now they are bringing in clauses which prevent you from suing federations if they say you have tested positive and that turns out not to be the case. You have to go through arbitration within the system itself. Everyone makes mistakes, but nobody has been through the system and got off.

Medicines such as Nightnurse are banned. Half the population, when ill, will take Nightnurse or something similar. We are not allowed to do that yet the people who criticize and judge athletes can. As soon as athletes catch a cold, they are supposed to steam it. But athletes can't afford the time out and they can't train with a cold. They need to get rid of it as quickly as possible. You would think, with the sophisticated testing available these days, that officials could tell the difference between someone taking medicine to help a cold and someone taking an abundance of ephedrine to enhance performance. With the equipment available in Seoul, they reckoned it was possible to find a grain of salt in a swimming pool, and yet it is somehow impossible to recognize a common cough medicine.

There has been talk about regular blood tests – which is fine. But, with blood tests, if it is possible to go back two years and tell what an athlete has been taking, then why not? If they can go so far as determining who has fathered a child or who your ancestors were, then why not use blood tests in athletics on a random basis? It would cost money but if the sport is to be kept clean, then drastic steps need to be taken.

In major championships, for example, it should be compulsory to have all eight finalists take a blood and urine test. As an alternative, test the first four finishers in the final and random test a couple of others. In my opinion, that's the only way to have a fair system. There is no need to test the person who finishes last because if an athlete finishes last and he or she is on drugs, then they're in trouble anyway. They are going to take more drugs in order to finish at the front and they are going to kill themselves as a result. To be honest, who really cares if the guy who finishes last is on drugs? It ain't working. Save money by not testing them.

Things have reached the stage where, as a guard against over-ambitious parents, school children are being tested. That's ridiculous. If a child catches a cold, what is the first thing the parents are going to do? Pour Nightnurse down their throats to make them better. They go to school the next day, run in the school sports – and test positive. Little kids testing positive. What next?

The whole system needs overhauling. We need expert opinion to say whether or not, for example, five parts per million of ephedrine really would enhance an athlete's performance. Does it need, say, fifty parts? Who knows? The problem is that the athletes are losing faith. We have no confidence at all in the system; my experiences have proved that. It is bad enough to have to go through the embarrassing procedure of producing a sample but at least at the end of it, athletes deserve a consistent and fair system. I am all for having drug tests. But not the shambles we have at present.

Chapter 9

DIET FREE

I became captain of the British team for the first time in 1989. It was a great, great honour, made even better by the fact that it happened in Gateshead, one of the best venues in the country in my opinion. And we won the European Cup – brilliantly, as it turned out. To be honest, it was the best thing to happen in what was otherwise a terrible year.

Britain had never finished better than third in the European Cup. This time the meeting was on home soil and, for me, it would turn out to be one of the greatest I can remember. The mighty Soviets, the Germans, the French – everyone was there and Britain was up against it.

Les Jones, a great man and one of the best team managers we ever had, was a terrific motivator. He was from Northern Ireland and, along with Mary Peters, he did a lot of athletics over there. Les was a likeable guy; he was fun, he was fair and I don't think anyone had a bad word to say about him. It was a great shock to everyone in athletics when he died suddenly of a heart attack at one of the indoor meetings. I went to his funeral in Northern Ireland and that was a *big* event. It was a measure of how popular he was, just as the fact that athletics in Northern Ireland has perhaps not been on such a grand scale since his passing.

Les provided the encouragement we needed. Kriss Akabusi won the 400 metres hurdles; I won the 100 metres; John Regis won the 200; Colin Jackson won his event. Nobody wanted to be outdone by anybody else at home. We competed out of our skins and, against all odds, Britain's men's team won the European Cup for the first time.

They needed someone to collect the cup. When Les Jones came over to speak to me, I thought I had done something wrong! Having a team captain was not a regular thing – it was not a matter of routine. In fact, I can't remember the last time there had been a captain before I was appointed. I never did find out exactly why I had been chosen but it was a very great privilege. We had made history. And we had done it in Gateshead.

It may not be the fastest track, but Gateshead has some of the most knowledgeable and enthusiastic supporters. The Geordies are the nicest people; down-to-earth, warm and friendly. When I compete there, it's electrifying. There is something about my relationship with the crowd at Gateshead. I remember going to one meeting when I couldn't compete because of injury. The atmosphere never came alive. It just seems to be my place. Winning the European Cup in Gateshead is one of the highlights of my career. As I said, it was one of the few good points in a bad year.

1989 had started off reasonably well – very well, in fact. I won an unprecedented 60- and 200-metre double in the AAA Championships, which was a useful warm-up for the European Indoor Championships. But I never got that far.

The day before the start of the event, I was warming up on the track when I dropped the metatarsal joint in a toe on my left foot. I bandaged it, had injections and tried to do some running – but couldn't. I was in too much pain. That was it. Rehabilitation took ages; the foot was so swollen and my toes were unrecognizable. I just couldn't believe it, a little thing like that and I ended up on crutches. A few people who saw me on the street said I was finished, history. That made me even more determined to get back.

I was able to do weight training, just to keep my muscles in trim, but because I couldn't run, my weight went from thirteen to about fifteen-and-a-half stone. I was out for four or five months. It seemed to last for ever.

When you are injured while running for your country, nobody gives a damn. There are no phone calls to see how you are getting on; nobody cares. An athlete's body is like a car. There was a time when, if parts on the car went wrong, they would be repaired. Now as soon as a part gives trouble, they throw the whole part away and replace it. That seems to be how athletes are treated. People are only interested in the races. If you have a good one, everyone is happy. Have a bad one and it's 'cheerio'. At least if they say 'cheerio' you've got a reaction . . .

I knew there was nothing for it but to persevere. Once I was able to run again, I jumped straight in at the deep end. It was the only way I knew.

One of my first meetings was at Pescara, on the Italian Adriatic coast. I went to Italy with John Regis, Sally Gunnell and Colin Jackson, among others. And we all ran *badly*. It was expected that I was not going to go particularly well but this was the reverse of what was to happen in Gateshead later in the season when we lifted each other to new levels. In Pescara, one poor performance was reflected throughout the team.

When Colin and I train together, if he runs well, then I'm confident too. It works both ways. In Italy, we all ran badly and a headline in the paper said we should have brought our buckets and spades. Group morale is important but it can't be the only reason for athletes not performing well. Sometimes your car runs well, sometimes it doesn't. There is no deep meaning to it – we are human beings and that's how the body chooses to perform from time to time.

My foot gradually improved but there was always the threat that the toe might become dislocated once more. I was told that if the toe had actually broken then I would have been better off. But it just popped out and my left foot has never been the same since. I still have a lot of trouble with it. Certainly, it cost me a place in the Commonwealth Games trials later in the year. I won the 100 metres but I was doing enough to qualify in the 200 when, coming out of the bend, the toe just went. I was on the inside, in lane one, which didn't help. Lanes are sometimes chosen according to seeding, sometimes not. You never know what the officials are going to do. Lane one is not good because it is so tight. As for the rest, it depends on what sort of runner you are but the middle lanes – three, four and five – are generally considered to be the best.

Of course, lane choice doesn't matter for the 100 metres and I beat Carl Lewis for the first time in the Grand Prix Final in Monte Carlo. Even though I didn't win the race (victory going to Ray Stewart), it was an encouraging result near the end of a poor year. The best thing to do was focus on the Commonwealth Games, due to be run in Auckland the following January.

Usually, I try not to fly straight to a major event, which is why we use holding camps to complete our final training away from all of the hype and the hassle. In any case, you can't do much speed work in the British winter, so a holding camp in the warmth of the Australian summer was the answer. Or, at least, it should have been.

This was my first visit to Australia and it was nearly my last. The holding camp was at Narrabeen, about half-an-hour north-east of Sydney. Someone was supposed to have checked it out beforehand on behalf of the British team, but they must have looked at the wrong place. I can't understand how anyone could have passed Narrabeen as suitable for athletes making final preparations for an important meeting.

The accommodation was not suitable for adult athletes. We were crammed into rooms with bunk beds more suitable for five-year-olds. The plastic cups we were given to drink out of had been chewed by the kids. And as for the food . . . on one occasion, we had cake and jelly and the leftovers appeared in a trifle the next day. Anyone arriving five or ten minutes late for a meal got nothing. Not that they missed much. The toast at breakfast was pitch black but nobody said anything. After a couple of meals I couldn't take it any more. I went into the kitchen and complained. A woman started shouting at me, so I told her the truth about her cooking.

'You lot can't cook,' I said. 'Look at this toast – it's black. If you even presented the food properly, we might be tempted to eat it. But you can't give athletes rubbish like this. It's inedible.'

It shouldn't have been for me to complain but no one else wanted to know. It was worth it because, the following day, the food improved quite a bit. I ate there occasionally but I just could not get used to drinking out of plastic cups with chewed edges. Colin and I, Malcolm Arnold and a few others ended up going to a nearby McDonald's for breakfast – which may surprise people who believe athletes stick religiously to special diets. I don't bother with that; I eat everything. If you train, then you shouldn't need to diet.

I eat fruit, but I will have a fry-up if I feel like it. So long as everything is in moderation. People have problems because they go too far. I will eat a chocolate bar if my blood-sugar level runs low, say, at the end of a training session when I haven't eaten anything. Chocolate is the easiest way of replacing energy in the short term, but I don't do it that often. Everyone can eat chocolate even though the belief is that sweets give you spots and make you put on weight. That's rubbish as far as I am concerned. Colin Jackson eats more chocolate than anybody I know! He will eat a big bar of chocolate the day before he runs and there is not an ounce of fat on him. It is a matter of being sensible. Anyway, I think you should treat yourself now and again. Cutting things off only increases the desire.

Fortunately, I haven't got a sweet tooth. Ice cream doesn't appeal to me. I will not eat cakes – unless I bake them myself – and I avoid anything with cream. I eat red meat only occasionally, perhaps when I go to a Chinese and buy beef in oyster sauce, or something similar. Most of the time I will have chicken and fish. Pasta, I find, increases the feeling of hunger. It is supposed to be good from the carbohydrate point of view but my body doesn't need that much because I don't need to run that far. I will eat pasta occasionally but, to be honest, I'm not keen.

I defy the rules but I don't snack between meals. I can go all day without having anything to eat, particularly when I am training. It doesn't bother me. My liquid intake while training is not that large either. They say you are supposed to sip water, but I don't bother with that. I train during the hottest part of the day and find that I can't drink at the same time. If I have a drink beforehand, I am in trouble. If I am thirsty when I finish,

I will have water. But I can go nearly all day without having a drink. My liquid intake comes instead from the oranges, grape-fruits and other fruit which I eat during the day. They provide all I need. There are times when I sweat like a pig during training, but I've never had a problem. I can look after myself. The only trouble seems to come when I am in the hands of someone else.

The accommodation at Narrabeen was a complete contrast to the village which was waiting for us in Auckland.

When we got there I found I was running much better than before. In fact, I was faster than some of the guys who had been selected to run in the 200 metres but, of course, it was too late for me to be included in that race. I ran 9.93 (wind assisted) to win the 100 metres and anchored the relay team for another gold medal. All of that added to my enjoyment of Auckland; it was a lot of fun.

The minister of sport at that time was Colin Moynihan. When he visited the village, I didn't want to meet him and I think a lot of my fellow athletes felt the same. But I believe he eventually spoke to the swimmers. I am generally wary of politicians; I think they are always concerned about what's going to be good for them.

My competitive form continued indoors at home and then into the outdoor season. Maybe it was too easy. When Andy Norman claimed I was easing up before the line, I told him I needed an incentive. He gave me one by saying I would receive a bonus if I ran the 100 metres in under 10 seconds. I went to Portsmouth and ran 9.95 seconds.

'You sod!' he said. 'You knew you were going to run well. You've turned me over! I've never seen your legs move so fast.' He took it well. It was his way of encouraging me and we both had a good laugh about it. I really appreciated his support –

13 & **14** A rare moment or two of relaxation with Mandy at our home in Tampa. Life can be tough being the world's number one sprinter!

15 (*left*) Discussing plans in Australia with Sue Barrett, agent extraordinaire.

16 (*below*) With Ron in Tampa. I don't look knackered so this must be before training.

17 (*above left*) Being massaged by Chris Gringham in Australia.
18 (*above right*) What it's all about – getting down to training in the gym at Narrabeen.
19 (*below*) Lending a helping hand to Frankie Fredericks, with Adrian Patrick.

20 (*above*) Training on the track in Tampa. Colin is in the foreground with Paul Grey behind him. Sally-Anne Short sits in the outside lane and Mark McKoy, the 1992 Olympic hurdles champion, stands next to her.
21 (*left*) Talking training with Colin and Mark.
22 (*facing page top*) In full flight during training.
23 (*facing page bottom*) Coming up on the outside of Frankie Fredericks in a training run at Narrabeen.

24 (*facing page top*) Stretching out with (*from left to right*) Frankie Fredericks, Marcia Richardson and Adrian Patrick in Australia.

25 (*facing page bottom*) No pain, no gain.

26 (*above*) Running on lava in Lanzarote sure beats the track in London, particularly in winter!

27 (*below*) What a feeling! Winning the gold in Barcelona, 1992. *From left to right:* Davidson Ezinwa (Nigeria), Leroy Burrell (USA, now the world record holder - incredible thighs!), me, Dennis Mitchell (USA), Frankie Fredericks (Namibia).

28 I must have just run a 400 metres – I only ever look like this
when I've just run a 400 metres!

both moral and, on this occasion, financial! I think the sport did itself an injustice by getting rid of Andy in 1994.

Such good form seemed to turn on me later in the season. I'm not sure if it was the fact that I was running so well so early, but I was to go through a terrible phase when I raced against Leroy Burrell and he just blew me away – three times in ten days.

It's one thing to be beaten when you are not on best form but, because I thought I was in really good shape, I lost my confidence completely. Every time we raced, I had no answer to Leroy. My motivation started to go. I had begun the year by setting my sights on the Commonwealth Games. That had gone well but now this series of defeats felt like one big anti-climax.

My rhythm had gone. Running is all about timing, every-thing working together. It's as if there is a metronome inside you. In my case, the metronome was working but my legs weren't keeping in tune. I lost my coordination and, of course, that made me try harder. And the harder I tried, the worse I got. I was thinking about it too much.

I took some time out and didn't race, concentrating instead on intensive training. People tend to think that training is simply a matter of getting fit. That is only a part of it. Many people have the same amount of natural talent, and training enhances that – but only the right kind of training.

Sprinters have what is known as a 'fast twitch' whereas a distance runner's twitch fibres are slower. I have always felt that it is harder to be a sprinter than a distance runner. Distance runners would obviously disagree with me but I believe that you have to be born to sprint. No matter how much training you do, if you do not have those fast-twitch fibres, then you ain't going nowhere as a sprinter! On the other hand, if you put in the miles and do the right kind of work, then you can become a world-class distance runner.

Training can vary quite a bit, particularly during the winter. I do a lot of so-called overdistance work – in other words, I actually concentrate on running further than 100 metres. Not all sprinters feel the need to do that; they concentrate on 60 metres, 80 metres, 100 metres and maybe 120 metres. I will run anything up to 800 metres. That gives me strength and a little bit of endurance. I want to be able to run fast and hold that speed longer. I need to know that if I am running a race and I am down (slightly behind) for whatever reason, then I can pick up and have the strength to keep going.

That is why weights complement the track training because weights make you stronger. With the right kind of weight training I can become explosive, which is also what I need. But, if you are not careful there can be a downside to weights because, if incorrectly applied, they can slow you down. It is necessary to maintain mobility for elasticity, even though weights will increase muscle mass, and therefore body weight. You need to strike the right balance.

Some people step on the scales and think that they can decide whether or not they are in shape judging by their weight. When in training, you are going to be heavier – end of story. According to the statistics for an average man of my height and age, I am overweight. So long as I can carry that weight in the races then it's not a problem. If I am strong enough, then I should be able to cope.

Arms, stomach, back, glutes, quads, hamstrings, calves, ankles; every muscle is used. A sprinter will put between eight and ten times his body weight through his ankles and toes. During training I will carry up to 300 kilograms – more than three times my body weight – on my shoulders when doing squats. I need to call in all the muscles, which is why I prefer to use free weights rather than the machine weights you see in every gym. Free weights make it easier to work the individual muscles.

We alternate the training; weights one day, track work the next. They say it's not the training that makes you strong but how you recover between the work-outs. Muscle tissues are shed and little muscle fibres are torn during each session but, as they regenerate, they become stronger. Rest is a vital ingredient and I will try and take one day off each week.

Work in the gym will also be complemented by things such as resistance training on the track. That will involve pulling a heavy lorry tyre by means of a harness which will force me to lean forward and drive out. We can also use an elastic rope, attached to a runner in front, which will make me go quicker and increase my leg cadence (leg speed). I'm not worried about the length of my stride, 1 concentrate purely on moving my legs as fast as I can. The elastic strength of the muscles can be increased by bounding, which means leaping two-footed from a standing start over high hurdles.

Unless I use the right kind of weights and more or less teach the body about what is going on, work-outs in the gym will be of no use. One of my greatest assets is that I know my body and I can train for as long as I want until my body tells me I can't do any more. Then I have a rest. When I go out and run I am able to tell if my body is saying 'I can't do it today'. In which case I will stop. Some people are not so familiar with their bodies and they continue training when, in fact, they would do more good if they stopped.

Everyone works to the same basic rules when training but we each have our own variations. It's like reading the Bible; everyone reads it but there are different interpretations. The secret is finding the variation which suits you, it's trial and error. We've all got to run, it's just that some people get off on running 60 metres and 150 metres; others prefer 300 and 400 metres. We're all different and the fine details of training have to suit you.

Athletes are like racing cars. If you drove one on the public road and went over a bump, something would go wrong and you would probably need to stop the car. But you could take an old jalopy down the same road, you could even take it up on the pavement or off the road completely and it would still keep going. The more highly tuned you are, the more prone to injury you are likely to be. If I tripped and fell on the pavement I would most probably be injured, whereas the average person would not. Athletes feel every ache and pain but, because they know their bodies so well, they can take steps to prevent injury. However, as I got down to serious training after that run of defeats by Leroy Burrell, fitness was not the problem.

I worked with Ron, Colin and Malcolm on relaxation and technique. Gradually, the coordination came back and I was competing strongly again by the time we went to the European Championships in Split.

The heats for the 100 metres were run at a very early hour. It's sometimes difficult to rouse yourself and I did just about enough to qualify. My main rival was a Frenchman, Daniel Sangouma, and I saw him the following day reading a newspaper and having a laugh with some of his team-mates. They called me over and pointed out the headline. It read: 'Christie Faces French Kiss-off'.

This was the kind of encouragement I was getting before a major competition. And people wonder why I don't like the media. Of course, it made the French feel good because it increased their confidence while, at the same time, it knocked mine. Athletes know their rivals very well; I can read people like a book. The Frenchmen knew I would be down if I saw a headline like that. I tried not to show it, but I was upset.

I got through the next round and into the final. Sangouma really got out of the blocks and I had to dig in. I ran 10 seconds dead – and won. I had turned thirty the previous April and now everyone was making a big deal out of me being the oldest man ever to win the title.

Age has no relevance as far as I am concerned. I can only assume that the media chooses to comment because they think I must feel like they do once they pass thirty, or whatever age is in question. Their assumptions are so out of touch with reality. Because I am six feet two-and-a-half inches and weigh between fourteen and fifteen stone, then I must be an aggressive person because that's how reporters assume they would be. It seems that a lot of what the journalists write about me is how they actually see themselves.

At least they had something positive to say when the men's relay team set a UK record in the final. It was significant from our point of view because this was the first time the team had actually rebelled in their own quiet way against Frank Dick. We had run to his order in the heats and if we had stuck with that in the final, in my view we would have finished last. There were a lot of disgruntled people, so we decided to forget Frank and run to our formula. We didn't win, but it took a world record to beat us. It gave the team confidence; things were a lot better after that.

All in all, Split had been quite traumatic but perhaps the funniest moment – well, not for me exactly – came after my 100-metre victory. I was *so* thirsty and there was very little to drink. The late Maria Hartmann, chairman of the women's AAA, with the very best of intentions gave me a bottle of champagne to quench my thirst. Without thinking, I drank about half of it – and I was gone! They put me to bed for half an hour or so to allow me, as Colin put it, 'to gather my thoughts' . . .

The 1990 season ended at the new Don Valley Stadium in Sheffield, where I won the 100 metres in 10.32 seconds. The time was unsensational – but the same could not be said for my leopardskin body suit.

Athletes used to wear little shorts known as 'batty riders' because they would ride up your backside, or 'batty'. Allan Wells introduced the cut-down shorts in Britain in 1986 and I liked the idea. Apart from giving warmth and protection to the athlete's hamstrings, they were distinctive. It seemed to me that all runners looked the same. So I decided to take it a stage further by going for multicoloured body suits. I'll never forget the first time I appeared dressed that way. The other guys said: 'Yuk! How can you possibly wear those things?'

But the suits stood out. The crowd could recognize me. They no longer saw eight black guys who looked the same. Now they knew which one was Linford Christie. I became more and more outrageous. I would wear cutouts – suits with big holes in the side – penguin suits, anything. It was entertaining. Apart from watching the events, people came to see what Linford Christie was wearing. And Sheffield seemed to become a focal point. Every time I appeared there, I tried to wear something different. I had the suits made by Denise Vaughan of Deni Vee. Between us, we would come up with designs which I really liked. But some were pretty outrageous. On one occasion I wore a skeleton outfit. We got schoolchildren to think up various ideas and the winner drew a skeleton suit. I was racing against the Frenchman, Bruno Marie-Rose, and he couldn't stop laughing. He said he couldn't concentrate because he thought I looked so funny.

The crowd became a part of it. I used to wear the body suits all the time and the crowd would complain if the outfits were not outlandish. It was entertainment, a means of giving something back to the public.

From a practical point of view, the tights are much more comfortable than shorts. There is nothing flapping around and, as I said before, they keep my hamstrings in place. I wear my tights down to my knees to give the muscles extra support. There can be a lot of movement in the hamstring and sometimes it can twist and pull. Also, it pays to keep muscles as warm as possible.

If temperatures in Britain reach sixty degrees, we think summer has arrived. The Australians laugh at us. If we go to somewhere like Nice where we sweat in the heat, everyone else says it's cold. For the British, that is a good day. But warmth, and humidity especially, are good for sprinters because that keeps heat in the muscles. The warmer the muscles, the more elasticity you get out of them and the better the performance. Muscles become stiff in the cold and that leads to injury. So tights are the answer. That's the main reason I wear them; the second reason is for the benefit of the crowd.

Reactions to my outfits were varied. Maria Hartmann complained that wearing tights was too sexy. I said she should be watching my performance and my technique rather than how I looked. We had a laugh about it and she did agree that it brought a lot of publicity to the sport; it made men's athletics more recognizable and acceptable. Now everyone wears tights, of course, and my biggest regret is that I didn't patent them!

There is no doubt that the tights make the sport more colourful for television but, early in 1991, the TV people were trying to make their own spectacle and Leroy Burrell and I were stupid enough to get sucked in.

They were trying to build up a race between us at Cosford as a big grudge match. Leroy, a former long-jumper, had turned to sprinting in his native America. He had more or less appeared from nowhere and started to run the fastest times in the world. There had never been a problem between Leroy and me but the television people niggled and niggled. They had shots of the two of us facing each other; the whole thing was hyped like a boxing match. Athletics can't be marketed like boxing, it's a totally different type of contest. But those TV people weren't about to let go once they had established a theme.

Questions would be put to us individually and then the answers would be edited in such a way that it seemed as though we hated each other. They got Leroy to say things that he shouldn't have said, and they did exactly the same thing with me. Leroy had beaten me over 60 metres in Germany and, by the time we got to Cosford for this so-called 'grudge match', there was a lot of unnecessary antagonism in the air.

Leroy had broken the world record for 60 metres, so he was in good shape. He beat me at Cosford. There was so much animosity and aggression. He won in a time I was quite capable of doing, but I was so uptight about the whole thing that I just went tense. It didn't help anyone when he turned around and stuck his tongue out.

I didn't say anything but, when we left the arena, I went over to Leroy. 'Look,' I said. 'I don't mind you beating me, but if you ever do that again . . . Disrespect in front of my home crowd is something I just won't tolerate.'

We exchanged words; we were sizing each other up because I felt like punching him right there and then. It was nothing more than frustration on both sides. It was heated and yet we were arguing fairly quietly. Suddenly, we were aware of a television camera, so I sat down. That should have been the end of the matter but the television guys felt they had the sensation they had been looking for. This justified all the pre-race rubbish and they made the exchange seem bigger than it actually was.

ITV then compounded the problem by showing the tapes to the journalists. That was all some of them had come for and, instead of writing about the race, they developed this story for all it was worth – which wasn't much, in my opinion. The whole thing should never have happened in the first place.

Of course, it didn't stop there. The next day, before I knew what was going on, the newspapers were carrying headlines such as 'Burrell Says: "Christie Threatened to Kill Me!"'

A lot of people were getting angry now. They were annoyed about the way Leroy was carrying on. Complete strangers were coming to me and saying they were going to beat up Burrell. The whole thing was out of control – all thanks to television wanting to promote a grudge match.

I was upset more by the way the media had reacted. We are all working in the same sport but, it seems to me, if you want to be a champion then you have got to have a certain type of temperament to cope. The British media do not understand how to treat champions. America has many great sportspeople because the media builds them up. When they do well, the competitors are made to feel good and they go out and do even better.

They don't do that in Britain. All they want is to see you fall. We have some terrific sportspeople but, once all the initial euphoria of the new star has been dealt with, it is rare to read anything positive. This country could have a good boxer, for example, but the journalists will say he's not brilliant because they have not seen if he can take a punch. Why does the boxer need to prove that he can take a punch when he knocks opponents out in the first round?

The problem is that a lot of the writers do not truly understand competition. They should speak more often to sportspeople to find out what makes them tick. And if the writers did compete, they either failed to make a good job of it, or they made very little money. Either way, they feel bitter and that negative attitude comes out in print.

Over a period of time, a stance like that can wear you down. Certainly, it must have played a part in leading me to think during 1991 that I would retire at the end of the year.

Chapter 10

DOWN AND ALMOST OUT

I discovered early on that if you let people take liberties once, then they always will. I like a joke as much as anyone and I would describe myself as being a gentle person. But, if you annoy me, then you will know about it.

I have this reputation for being aggressive. As I said, I can only put that down to people believing that they would be ready to go out and fight everyone if they were big and muscular. That's not the way it works. If you are good at karate, you don't go around kicking everybody. There are other ways of doing things rather than being a bully. If I was as arrogant and horrible as one or two reports have suggested, then I wouldn't last long with the friends I've got. Colin Jackson, Mark McKoy and Frankie Fredericks would never train with me for a start. We make sure we have a good laugh when working together. But there is a time for everything – a time for jokes and a time to be serious. We can be practising starts and, once we get onto the blocks, the playing is over.

I'm not going to win races if I'm always grinning. If I'm smiling, then everyone will think Linford is a push-over. Of course, it can be quite useful at times to have people believe that I am always angry and aggressive because then they will be more cautious. But, even then, there is always someone who will push to the limit. There was a recent example when I was doing some work for the National Lottery and the press were present. The photographer from the *Sun* had come along with something which was wrapped up. It turned out to be a lunch box and he was about to try and have it in the picture to help perpetuate their pet theme. Fortunately for him my agent, Sue Barrett, intercepted before he got that far.

When it comes to stupidity such as that, my tolerance level is very low. The *Sun* may see it as a joke but, as my father says, 'What is a joke to you is death to me.' I think it is derogatory – but then what do you expect from the *Sun*? They don't talk about Sally Gunnell's breasts; if they did, there would be uproar – sexual harassment and everything else – and they know it. So, why do I have to put up with this?

There are times when I feel I've got to put my foot down. If people ask 'Why is he being like that?' it's because they don't think. They fail to understand that I work hard at my athletics. I don't play silly games and I fail to see the funny side, just as a newspaper editor would not be amused if someone constantly belittled his efforts or made very personal remarks. He has a job to do and I have nothing against that. But do unto others as you would like them to do unto you.

The joking was definitely over when I was beaten by Andre Cason in the 60 metres at the 1991 World Indoor Championships in Seville. He had improved his personal best to 6.54 seconds. I ran quickly enough in 6.55 seconds. It was close. In the 200 metres I should have run better than I did. I lost that too. It's true that I had not trained specifically for indoors, and I put the defeats down to that.

The indoor season is short and it's necessary to do a lot more speed work for events such as the 60 metres. You need to be sharp, get out of the blocks quickly and explode. Indoor work is supposed to suit shorter athletes and I would often be asked how I managed to compete so successfully in the 60 and 200 metres. I think it has a lot to do with strength and technique and I'm pretty strong in both areas.

It was the first time I had managed to do the World Indoor Championships. In the past I always seemed to be injured. Although I had been beaten, I felt I had run reasonably well considering that I was going through one or two personal problems. Physically I was in very good shape, but mentally I wasn't all there.

The main outdoor event of the year was the World Championships in Tokyo. I was running really competitive times in the 100 metres, but the final was unforgettable from the point of view of fast times.

I was drawn next to Carl Lewis. Alongside were Leroy Burrell – who had just broken the world record – and Dennis Mitchell. At the start, Mitchell got a flier but there was nothing anyone could do about it. The starter is supposed to wear a headset in which he hears a telltale sound if someone leaves the blocks early. The starter was not wearing his earphones and, when Mitchell moved prematurely, the starter had no way of knowing. They didn't call Mitchell back. That was it. Once the race has been run, you can't do it again. Certainly not this particular race.

I got out of the blocks ahead of Lewis but, as soon as he came past me, I went tight. You are supposed to relax and not panic but I went tight. Carl won the race in a world record time of 9.86 seconds. Burrell finished second, also inside the old record with 9.88, Mitchell got the bronze with 9.91 seconds and I ran 9.92 seconds to finish fourth. There were six people under 10 seconds; an amazing race. But, because of the emotional turmoil I was going through, I felt I had run as fast as I was ever going to run.

I was thirty-one. I had reached the point where the media were saying I was too old – and I started to believe it. They said I was past it, so maybe I was.

Someone wrote that I was beaten by stronger, younger, faster men. If that was the case, I didn't know where these younger, faster men were. I took the writer up on the point in public by asking if it was not about time that he was replaced by a younger and better journalist! He took offence and said we should talk privately if I had something to say. I said, 'No, let's talk about it here. You write about me and thousands of people read it. So why can't I talk about you in front of your colleagues?'

I decided, 'to hell with it'. I thought I had run as fast as I was ever going to run. Never in my wildest dreams had I thought I would run 9.92 seconds. It was a British, European and Commonwealth record. For the first time in my life I felt satisfied. I thought this is as good as it's going to get. It's time to get out and get away from all the crap the media were giving me. I didn't feel I was being appreciated. After all, I had just set the fourth-fastest time ever for the 100 metres and it took a world record to beat me. The trouble is, fourth is the worst place you can be; so close and yet so far. You can touch, you can smell – but you can't have. In any case, unless you win gold, there's nothing worth having anyway.

I decided I was going to retire, forget about athletics and step out of the limelight. I told the media immediately.

I hadn't bargained for an amazing response from the public. I received letters from all over the world, but from the British fans in particular. They all asked me to change my mind and many said they had already bought tickets especially to see me run in the Olympics in Barcelona the following summer. 'Please give it one more year', that sort of thing. It was really touching.

I had a long talk with Ron and he said I should give it one more try. The last thing I wanted to do was go out as a loser. Fourth place could not have been worse; I didn't want to be remembered for that. After further discussions with Mandy and some of my friends, I decided to do one more year. If it hadn't been for the response from the public, I would have stopped. And, of course, I valued Ron's opinions more than any other.

Having been an athlete, Ron understood the situation. More than that, we understood each other and had done so more or less from the moment we had met more than ten years before. I find that there are times when a stranger does not need to say anything to me and, as the expression goes, my spirit doesn't take to them. I realize we are not going to get on. I think I am a pretty good judge of character and I hit it off with Ron from the start, even though we did not exactly do a great deal initially in terms of training. The fact that he did not push me probably had a lot to do with it.

When I walk into a shop, if the salesperson gives me time to look around, then I am more likely to buy. If they jump on me – or if they reckon whatever I happen to look at is 'very nice, it really suits you', then I am not likely to respond. When Mandy and I were setting up our house in Florida at the beginning of 1995, we went shopping for curtains in Tampa. Each time Mandy asked the assistant, 'do you think this will match?' the lady said 'yes'. No matter what it was, she would say 'yes'. She didn't get the sale.

When I went to see Ron for the first time, I just wanted to take my time and build up slowly. Ron recognized that. He had the ability to eventually apply what he needed to apply without causing offence. Not many people can do that. It is like a boss driving his work force unnecessarily; they will end up hating him.

If you have been in that position then it pays to remember, when you take charge, what it was like to be pushed around. I don't know if Ron had been through that sort of experience but that's the way he worked. He understood perfectly.

If I say something is hurting, I am not making excuses. It's actual pain. So if I tell Ron I don't want to do the next bit of training, he won't question it. If you have been working in one job for ten years and you take a day off, there has to be a reason for it. It should not be a sackable offence. A coach has to understand that principle.

Ron knows how I feel when I run. I don't throw tantrums but Ron can look at my face and tell immediately how bad it was. Ron knows that sometimes I don't want to talk straight away. Best to leave me alone, let me relax and get over it. In a couple minutes, I will be fine. I might say 'Ron, that was shit!', and he will say, 'That's what I thought. Never mind, we can do this . . .'

On the other hand he doesn't gush with praise, and that suits me too. It's back to the sales assistant who constantly agrees with you; in the end, you don't believe anything they say. Sometimes I will run well but, even then, Ron will say nothing. Then, when I really do something, he might say 'yes, that was pretty good', in which case I really feel I've made progress. Ron knows exactly when to say 'You've done well.'

We are completely different and yet we know just when to

give each other space. It's automatic; nothing needs to be said. Sometimes I might not want to talk but Ron knows that, under the circumstances, it would be better if I did. We will go that way too. Invariably, he is right.

We are a fifty-fifty partnership. I know about one aspect of training – the weights – and Ron is still learning about that. But on the track, he knows a heck of a lot. We complement each other. Ron works out my running sessions – he tells me what to do, and I run. I do the weight session and he does the track session; it all comes together.

Ron has a good eye. He can tell whether or not I have run well because he can see things that I may not have noticed. When he looks back on a race, he can say, 'this is where you went wrong'. That's the point. Being slagged off is no good. I want constructive criticism, something I can learn from and incorporate into the next training session.

Ron can see my technique start to fall away and he can implement steps to put that right. It is possible to do too much racing and not enough training. You can more or less forget how to run. Ron can tell me when it is necessary to start training in a certain direction – and he can do it in a way which is not damaging to the morale.

One of the reasons we get on is that we can discuss things without falling out. There must be a compromise. It works every time and I trust him completely. In fact, it goes beyond a coach–athlete relationship. There are athletes half my age who are still chopping and changing coaches because they can't get on with each other. Ron knows everything about me but, unlike some people in the public eye, I don't have to worry. I can trust Ron not to pass things on.

If you haven't got trust in your coach, then you are not going to run well. Apart from one brief period with someone else, Ron has been the only coach I have ever had. Colin Jackson is the only other person I know who has a similar relationship; he has been with Malcolm Arnold since he was a schoolboy and Malcolm was the Welsh national coach. Sally Gunnell has been with Bruce Longdon for a long time. That sort of thing makes an important difference. It is all about mutual trust and understanding.

All I want from the people I work with is loyalty – I don't ask for anything else. The day I find that I can't trust someone I train with, then I have no further time for them. There is no way we can work closely any more.

There must be give and take and the important thing, in my view, is to have a laugh when training. All work and no play makes Jack a dull boy. Ron has begun to develop the coloured sense of humour and that makes training great fun. Our group will make the most noise, laugh the loudest – but train the hardest. Having a laugh while walking around takes your mind off the run that is to come. Then focus on the job again, do the run, really get into it, and relax once more.

There is a great danger in becoming too serious. I never think about training until I reach the track or the gym. I don't think about racing until the day, or maybe the night, before. Some people think about it weeks ahead and get nervous. If you get nervous six days before the race, what's the point? You can save that energy and use it on the day. If it's going to happen, it's going to happen. Some people think, 'Oh God, I am going to lose.' I never let that sort of thing cross my mind. If I'm going to lose, it has to be someone damn good to beat me. That's the way I approach it. Ron was instrumental in building up that inner confidence after I decided not to retire and made the commitment to run in 1992.

★

I opted to forgo the indoor season and spend time in Australia doing warm-weather training. The usual routine would have been to train in Lanzarote but the trouble with that was that I would be pressured into returning to Europe for the indoor races.

I trained really hard in Melbourne for the first part of the winter. I enjoyed being in Australia as such, although the business side of it was not so good. Some of the local athletes and coaches acted in a very strange way. If I was a sprinter, keen to improve, and one of the world's top athletes came to train locally, I would be interested in finding out exactly what he was doing. I would want to see what tips I could pick up. But the Australians just kept themselves to themselves. Apart from Cathy Freeman (the Australian and Commonwealth 200- and 400-metre champion) and her coach, none of the other sprinters wanted to train with me.

I ended up doing starts with long-jumpers and 100-metre sessions with 400-metre runners and hurdlers. It was really strange. Most of the time I trained on my own. It was not uncommon for me to turn up only to be told without warning that I had to train on the dog track around the back.

On one occasion, when we were hoping to practise starts, some people at the stadium were bringing the blocks out in preparation for a meeting. Ron asked if he could borrow a set, saying that we would be finished before the start of the meeting. The guy said no, we couldn't. When I went over and asked, he got really stroppy. I said, 'There's no need to be like that. What we want to do is borrow the blocks, do some starts and go.' And he said something about going back to the park with the elephants where I belonged.

Ron was more upset than I was and he let him have it. That was the first time I had seen Ron annoyed like that; he really told the guy what he thought. Mind you, this man was so old that, if he lasted out the year, he would have done well. But, even so, it wasn't pleasant. We had to phone England and have my blocks shipped out so that I could practise my starts.

I was to discover that a lot of the coaches in Australia think there is a secret to training. They seem to believe that because I am a rival and they train with me, I am going to get better and beat their athletes – which I was doing anyway. There's no secret to it. The answer is that of course I'm going to see what they do, but the reverse is also true and I would like to think they would learn more from me. Some coaches believe there is a secret, and they are the only people who have it.

I ran a couple of races in Australia and, in general, the people were fine. But the flies really bothered me. I was accustomed to seeing the pictures on television of people starving in various parts of the world and, always it seemed, there would be flies crawling all over their faces and into their mouths. I was a bit shocked to find the flies doing exactly the same thing in Melbourne. And nobody seemed to bother. Of course, I spent my time doing what they call the 'Pommy Salute' by constantly waving my hands back and forth across my face. It made no difference at all.

The plus side of training on my own was that it made me a lot sharper mentally; you have to concentrate that bit harder. We met Michelle Baumgartner, one of the greatest unrealized talents in Australia. She took Ron and I around quite a bit and introduced us to her gym. She was a workaholic and that rubbed off because I got through a lot of serious gym work. I was in very good shape by the end of it.

While I was in Australia, I heard that Jason Livingston had equalled my 60-metre indoor record of 6.51 seconds. Jason used to train at Crystal Palace and his coach retired unexpectedly. Jason was looking for somewhere to go and he joined our group. He was a nice guy, I got on well with him. He wasn't tall but he was well built; very similar in many ways to Ben Johnson. In fact, he was very quick out of the blocks – just like Johnson – which was why I called him 'Baby Ben'. He clearly had a lot of potential.

The day after I returned to Europe, I ran 6.55 seconds at Sindelfingen in Germany, so I was pleased with that. But, as far as the media were concerned, it was the same old story; another so-called grudge match was on the cards. It so happened that Jason and I were due to meet the following weekend in a GB v USA match. Straight away, this was billed as 'The Challenge'!

It was becoming so boring. Each time I was away, somebody would do a good time and immediately the headlines would ask if this was the next challenge for Linford Christie. Jason Livingston, Michael Rosswess, Darren Braithwaite, Toby Box; they would run times that I could knock out pretty easily. And yet, on each occasion, this would be 'The Challenge'.

It is all very well to run a time when I'm not around. But a race between us is a different thing. It becomes very hard for them to run as relaxed as they would like – they think, 'Damn! Linford's here.' The pressure is on because they want to beat me. But I know I can beat them. That's where the difference is – wanting and knowing.

They have to hope that if they are one hundred per cent, then I need to be no more than eighty per cent. They know that if I am ninety per cent, they are going to get beaten. And if I'm one hundred per cent, they are in serious trouble.

Jason had won the European Indoors and, to do that, you have to be pretty quick. He had a really good start but then I got my usual surge and that was it. End of 'The Challenge'. But it was a good race regardless of the hype.

★

The outdoor season was busy – Sheffield, Rome, Edinburgh, Oslo, Lausanne and Gateshead – with some encouraging results in the 100 metres and the 200. It was the perfect build-up to Barcelona.

My feeling was that having run 9.92 seconds at the end of the previous year at a time when I was not in the best frame of mind, then judging by the times from 1992, if I ran 9.92 seconds in the Olympics I would win the gold. An athlete must always believe he or she is going to win, otherwise there is no point in running. You go into every race thinking you are the best and you are going to win. If you feel the other guy is better, then what's the point in doing it? You can't afford a negative attitude.

People ask if I watch videos of races and examine my rivals. If I'm at a meet then I'll watch other people race, but I don't go to the length of getting videos of other events. It's not like boxing where, say, a fighter might change his style from Southpaw to conventional and you can watch that on video to see how it's done.

In athletics, a sprinter might get out of the blocks really well and run a good race. You watch that and, when you meet, you decide he's good out of the blocks so therefore you will follow him out and then pass him. So, you are watching this guy and he has a bad start. Meanwhile, someone you are not watching makes a really good start and you are left behind because of gauging your performance by the first guy. You don't really learn much by watching videos unless you are trying to pick up a little bit of technique here and there. But there's not much you can take into consideration. You have to do it your own way.

I hadn't actually run against Carl Lewis that summer. In fact, Dennis Mitchell had won the American Championship and

Carl hadn't made the Olympic 100-metre team – which was a surprise. Deep down I thought I was good enough to beat Dennis and that gave me an indication of how well the rest of the Americans were running. I felt I was in better shape than they were; I didn't really have to worry about them. My main rivals, I felt, would be Oladape Adeniken from Nigeria and Frankie Fredericks from Namibia.

Final training took place in Monte Carlo. It was very productive because I did a lot of work with Colin Jackson and Mark McKoy, two of the fastest people in the world over 30 and 60 metres. I didn't always expect to beat them over 30 but I could judge my progress by seeing how close I could get. I was running faster than ever over that distance; the rivalry was really good, we worked hard but had a lot of fun. I was ready for Barcelona.

Chapter 11

THE FASTER YOU RUN,
THE EASIER IT IS

I arrived in Barcelona three days before I was due to compete. The most I did was a little jogging but, otherwise, it was a case of having a massage, stretching, having a massage, stretching and, in between, finding my way around. There was not much to see.

The village was terrible and the accommodation was even worse. We had beds that were so tiny it was unbelievable. Colin and I shared a box room which was so cramped we had to leave our suitcases in the corridor. There were eight or nine people sharing two bathrooms. We had a big metal shutter on our bedroom window but it broke not long after we had arrived and we couldn't use it. It was an awful place, certainly nothing like the image people have of athletes travelling the world and visiting all these exotic locations.

It is the responsibility of the organisers of the major championships to provide accommodation. The athletes are in their hands and, as a general rule, the more important the championship, the lower the standards. Be it the Olympics or whatever, it is as if the organisers do not need to try that hard to please.

It is generally assumed that we stay in four- or five-star hotels but the village in Barcelona was just about as far removed from that as you could get. So why not move out and check into a hotel? There would be nothing to stop me but it would hardly set an example to the rest of the team if the captain went elsewhere and left them to it. I couldn't turn round and say to the kids 'yeah, I know how you feel' if I were staying up the road in comparative luxury.

I don't like the idea of finding accommodation outside the village because we go to the games as a team. We might as well shack up together. If I'm having chicken, everyone's having chicken! I can't be having an à la carte meal somewhere and thinking these are my team-mates when it appears I'm trying to say that I am better than they are. The top American athletes stay in the big hotels. But that's not me.

Along with everyone else, I had to put up with what we were given in Barcelona. I had to sleep with the pillow underneath my stomach because I had a lot of problems with the bed. It was just awful; my feet came off the end of it. Philip Henry and his brother Bernie came to watch me run and, when they paid a quick visit to the village, they couldn't believe we were living in accommodation like that.

On the plus side, however, the food was fine – they provided a 24-hour service. The main benefit was making new friends. That's one of the nicest things about being in the sport; you can meet people and you can have a really good time.

The day before I was due to run, I was told that Jason Livingston had tested positive. He was crying and pretty distressed about the whole thing and, as I described earlier, I was asked if I could help.

There's not much you can do. Jason was luckier than I had been in the sense that he had been told the substance was methandianone. In my case, nobody knew what it was. Mine turned out to be ephedrine and I had been thinking it was steroids, whereas Jason's case was more clear-cut – not that it helped him much.

Once again, there was this secret CIA-type behaviour from the officials. They sent him home the next morning and then came the headlines and uproar. As I said before, in my opinion it should never have been an Olympic problem.

Jason had great potential. I felt that when I retired Jason would become The Man because of the promise he showed at that time. He was very young and he was training with our group; he couldn't have had it better. We trained in Lanzarote together and he was beginning to get quite a bit of publicity. Sponsors were showing interest because he was a new face. When I then said that I thought he had the potential to be the next number one, his chances of being sponsored increased even further.

I found the whole business in Barcelona very disappointing, but that was nothing to how I felt when rumours started to suggest that I had given Jason drugs because I was afraid he was going to beat me. Sometimes you wonder about the mentality of these people. They wanted to find out where Jason had got the drugs from and, when he refused to say anything, the suggestions began that it must be in our training group because Ron and I had to be dealing in drugs.

It was embarrassing more than anything else. Ron had been helping Jason although, by that time, Jason had left the group. We had been doing start sessions with another sprinter, Lennie Paul, and we had a great time baiting each other. But Jason said that he couldn't train with us any more because we had intimidated him and we were trying to psyche him — which was certainly not my intention. Even so, Jason and I were still friends. His being found positive did not change anything. I felt sorry for him because he was a youngster. He was twenty-one and he had thrown his entire life away. He had everything in front of him and everything to gain, and yet he had lost it all in one incident.

I had to get on with my own race but, as usual, they had allowed the press into the village. My motto is: 'keep a low profile'. When it comes to major championships, I have got work to do. I am not talking. I don't want to be lured into the sort of question where I say 'of course this runner is not as good as me', or whatever, because that will play into his hands. 'Christie doesn't think I'm as good as him; I'm going to show him!' It makes the guy go out there and try that much harder. I just wasn't interested in playing games like that and I had no intention of posing for photographs at this stage.

The Spanish officials had placed computers in the village, a very good system which enabled you to do anything from discovering lane draws to sending messages. I was standing with Colin at a screen when I felt a tap on my shoulder. As I turned round, a photographer put his camera in my face and the flash went off. It made me mad and I grabbed him. He got hold of me but I decided it wasn't worth punching him. I was going to give him a slap because he was out of order but Malcolm Arnold persuaded me to let the photographer go.

There was also a journalist who kept bugging me. I told him to leave me alone, I had come to run and I wasn't in Barcelona to help him out with stories. He persisted, so I took his notebook. He said he would go away if I gave the notebook back. I said that if he had gone away when I had asked, this would not have happened. I left the notebook in the BOA office.

The next day some of the newspapers claimed that I had been rude to a member of the public, that I had been effing and blinding. It was so far from the truth. The people concerned were not members of the public. They had come to the village in search of stories and they had got out of hand. That did nothing to improve my relationship with the media. If I had punched the photographer, things would have been much worse even though I would have felt a lot better . . .

I certainly felt good during the 100-metre heats. I was cruising, running 10.07 seconds in the second round. Leroy Burrell ran 10.08 seconds and, in the semi-finals, he ran 9.97. I ran 10 seconds dead. I was in control the whole way, whereas Leroy was running really hard.

There were arguments over just who was the favourite. Dennis Mitchell was saying he was the best; Leroy Burrell claimed he was going to win. They asked me who was favourite and I said Dennis and Leroy both were. I wasn't getting into that kind of discussion because I didn't give a damn who the favourite was. Certainly, I didn't want it to be me; I wanted to sneak in around the back.

I knew that Leroy had one good race in him so I felt sure he was going to be in the reckoning. In the semi-final, I sat behind him all the way, feeling that I could run past him at any time. I just left it at that and let everyone continue the debate over who was favourite.

Meanwhile, the British team was in disarray. As I prepared to compete, I had found there was no physio present. It was a very important race and that's what the physios were supposed to be there for. They were elsewhere in the village and it reminded me of the time when I pulled my hamstring, went to the room, knocked on the door and the physio came out and said she couldn't deal with me because she was just about to wash her hair! That's one of the reasons why Colin and I prefer, if we can, to bring our own people with us, although it is very hard to get them accredited at the major championships. Malcolm Arnold had to give me my massage on this occasion. Now I was ready.

It was an impressive line-up for the 100-metre final: Frankie Fredericks, Oladape Adeniken, Leroy Burrell, Dennis Mitchell, Ray Stewart, Bruny Surin, Davidson Ezinwa and myself. Each athlete has their own way of preparing for the start. Dennis Mitchell has his kung-fu kicks, everyone has their individual routine and I made a change to mine in Barcelona.

After losing at the World Championships in 1991, when I panicked as Carl Lewis came next to me, I decided I had to find some way of concentrating even more intensely so that I could block out everyone else. If someone came up to my shoulder, then I wouldn't become tense and seize up. Ron summed it up by saying that there was nothing anyone in the other lanes could do to help me win. Just forget about them and concentrate on my particular lane.

I had read an article on Carl Lewis in which he had said he didn't go on to the track to race other athletes. He went out to run the best he possibly could and, if he did that, then it should be good enough to win. Barcelona was the first time I went to the blocks imagining my lane was a tunnel, with everything else on either side a blur.

In the 100 metres, people think you let rip from gun to tape. It's not that at all; technique and concentration play a big part. When you are in the blocks, you should be waiting for the 'B' of the 'Bang!' and reacting like a missile once the gun goes. Obviously, you have to go forward in a crouching position.

Some people come out of the blocks, stand straight up and then go forward – but that's too late.

The idea is to stay low initially and then the body will bring you up. And once you are upright, you raise your hips, pick up your knees, your arms start pumping – and away you go. If only it was as easy as that.

The foot on the front block is the one with which you push off. Some people prefer to lead with the left, others with the right but, whichever one, it is the ball of the foot that gives the push, with the back leg coming through.

Obviously, the start is important but it is not necessarily the fastest man out of the blocks who wins the race. It is the guy with the best pick-up and the one who can maintain top speed longest and stay relaxed who wins. Of course, it's great if you get a good start; it makes your job a lot easier. People talk about reaction time but it's not how quickly you move out of the blocks that's important, it's how fast you put your foot down while running that makes the difference. It's not how fast you start. It's how fast you finish.

You can come out of the blocks and start doing long strides straight away. Unfortunately, the longer your stride, the slower you are going to be. You don't need full strides until you are up to speed. When you leave the blocks, the strides should be short and fast. You have to run as quickly as possible and the only way you can do that is to have little tiny strides until your body is upright. Then the long strides come in.

The more you strike the ground, the more fatigued you are going to become, and then your knees start dropping. It is like a boxer. The more you punch him in the ribs, the less protection he is going to have for his face because he is going to automatically start dropping his arms. It is the same principle with sprinting. When your knees are coming up, you have a chance to stretch your stride. If you don't, then the strides will be short, and you can only do so many of those.

You can see fatigue starting when a sprinter's shoulders start coming up; the idea is to keep the shoulders down and stay relaxed. You won't win simply by being fast, the trick is to run fast and stay relaxed for longer than anyone else. The faster you run, the sooner your muscles will begin to tie up. If you get the technique right, you can stay relaxed and keep the speed going. You can only maintain top speed for so long before your performance starts to fall off. And once you start to fight, that's when you begin to slow down. Staying relaxed is the thing.

I run with my palms open. A clenched fist is a sign of aggression and, when you are pushing too hard, you become very tight. You have to be aggressive but it has to be internal anger. Your face is very important because, whatever your facial expression, your body will follow. If your face is relaxed, your body will stay relaxed. If your face expresses anger then your body is going to do everything that way. Once again, the idea is to stay relaxed. Don't clench your fists.

Your arms have to pump backwards and forwards, using the ball and socket joints to the full without moving your shoulders. The stronger you drive your arms back, the better. The faster you move your arms, the faster your legs will go. It is similar to freewheeling on a bicycle. Swing your legs forwards and nothing happens. But if you swing them backwards, the bike will do a little jerk forwards. It is exactly the same with your arms and legs. The drive is at the back, so you push off from the back. That is what propels the body forwards.

Your back has to be straight and your hips have to be high. But if you lean back too far, apart from running the risk of injury, you are not getting full power through your body. If you stay too far forward, that also leads to problems. It is essential to find the right angle and remain upright.

You have to ride your hip over the lower half of your body. As soon as you strike the ground with one foot, the other leg starts to come through. The idea is to strike and keep that foot on the ground for as long as possible. Keep your knees up and don't put the other foot down until you have got maximum stride. A lot of people don't do that. They recover too quickly, which means that they will have better leg cadence but, because I am getting maximum stride throughout, I can pull away. Taking shorter strides may be faster, but I am gaining distance all the time.

It is wrong to believe that I am at an advantage because of my long legs. It is the reverse, in fact. It takes more time to get going because of my long limbs. It's like a sports car that gets away quickly but eventually uses more petrol and runs out just as a larger car sweeps past.

When viewed from in front or behind, it looks as though I'm throwing my legs out as I run. In fact, it only seems that way because, if you look at my thighs, the big muscles are on the outside and that helps create the impression of the legs being thrown to the side. I have to call on the big muscles – glutes (in the cheeks of the backside), thighs, hamstrings – and I have to push sideways, particularly when leaving the blocks, in order to get those big muscles to work. It's actually very difficult to run in a perfect straight line.

People sometimes imagine my legs to be bigger than they actually are. Size is not a sign of strength. The biggest man in a gym is not necessarily the strongest. Because my legs are not that big, it does not mean that they are lacking in strength. In comparison to my body they are in proportion even if, as I said before, their length goes against me initially.

My advantage comes in the second half of the race. Because I am stronger, I lose speed more slowly than most runners. It looks as if I am accelerating but, in fact, the others are slowing down more quickly. It is impossible to maintain top speed right to the end and I believe I reach my maximum somewhere between sixty and seventy metres. I can hold it for ten, maybe fifteen metres and then I start to tail off. The stronger you are, the longer you can hold off the slowing process.

The shorter guys reach their top speed much sooner and they can only hold it for ten metres. So, say they reach their maximum at forty and they can only hold it to fifty metres, then it's all over after that. If I am close behind and still accelerating, I am going to come through. This is where the training for speed endurance comes in; I can run fast and hold on to that speed for a greater distance.

It is perhaps difficult for an outsider to understand that all of this can be going on in such a short space of time. It may be just ten seconds to the onlooker but it feels like a lifetime to me. When I am actually running, it seems a lot longer than ten seconds. I have trained myself to do things which, normally, you would not be able to do in a ten-second period.

I have to be able to drive forward, pick up, pump my arms and increase my leg speed if I need to overtake. I need to be aware of the tightening up which comes if my shoulders start to rise; I have to try and drop them and stay relaxed. If everything goes well and I am running fast, it does not feel that way at all. It is actually easier to run the 100 metres in 10 seconds or under than it is to do it in 11 seconds. The faster we run, the easier it is. If I went jogging, I would end up being more tired than if I had run flat out. Running flat out means using all the muscles while your body is relaxed. It sounds a contradiction but, if it is taking 11 seconds, then there isn't time to do all that because you are not doing it right, you are still working on your technique.

In the 100 metres, I don't breathe at all. People say you should breathe, but I don't – it's not a big problem to hold your breath for 10 seconds. When I train with weights it is the same thing; I don't breathe while I am lifting. I find that when I hold my breath I am stronger. Again, that goes against the popular consensus, but who cares? If it works, it works. You do what you feel comfortable with. But I am always willing to learn. That's why I was ready to try thinking only of my lane and nothing else as we went to the blocks for the 100-metre final in Barcelona.

I was going to give it everything, right from the 'B' of the 'Bang!'. I made a good start and, when I got to 60 metres, I knew I had won. There were still 40 metres to go, but I just knew I was heading for the gold medal. Everything had gone according to plan. I had been the only guy to go quicker in each round. Ron had always encouraged me to try and build up gradually during the heats, saving the best for the last. And here I was, doing just that.

I can't tell you anything about the reaction of the crowd. You don't hear the noise when you're running. It's like being in a trance. If you hear anything, you are not concentrating. You can see through the side of your eyes when people are getting close. I didn't see anybody and when I don't see anybody, I know I'm winning.

About three or four metres from the line, I started thinking to myself, 'what have you done, what are you doing?' I knew from that moment on my life was going to change. No longer would I only be back page sports news; I would be inside as well, the subject of features. I actually had time to think about the repercussions because the final few metres seemed to last for ever. But I soon forgot about that as I crossed the line. I had time to put my hand up and that split second felt great. Olympic 100-Metre Champion. *Yeah!*

Then came a huge anticlimax. There was supposed to be a cloud nine feeling, a sense of walking on air. I was waiting – but nothing was happening. Of course, I was very, very happy. I was happy for Ron, for all my friends and sponsors, all the people who had been supporting me. This was what they had been dreaming of. To be honest, it was more Ron's dream than mine. The pinnacle of every athlete's career is to be Olympic champion, for every coach it is working with the athlete towards that ambition.

The lap of honour was great. I was looking out for my two friends, Philip and Bernie. They were the only two people in the crowd wearing Linford Christie T-shirts. I saw a few others I knew, including Jackie Jackson, a girl I hadn't seen for years. It is a wonderful feeling having people who you know personally in the crowd.

There were loads of interviews and there was a lot to talk about. I had covered the 60 metres in 6.48 seconds, which was faster than I had ever done before. My overall time was 9.96 seconds; no one else had got under 10 seconds. At thirty-two, I was the oldest Olympic champion.

Receiving the medal on the rostrum was the best part of the whole thing. When I heard the national anthem, it came home to me that I was the reason they were playing it. The stadium was packed to capacity and millions of people all over the world would be listening to this. The British national anthem. I had beaten everyone. There was definitely a lump in my throat but I had to fight it; there was no way I was going to cry. I always remember that Michael Johnson cried once and that picture was used over and over again. I was not going to give them the chance to do that to me.

People become reflective on occasions like that but my first concern is to find out if I have run the perfect race. That's my only fear because the day Ron says 'yes, that was perfect', then I will know that I can't run any more. I will have to stop there and then. But you always find fault somewhere along the line; there is always room for improvement. The only problem in Barcelona was that I couldn't find Ron. Unknown to me, he had sprained his ankle getting onto the bus taking us to the stadium that morning and he had been receiving treatment on the physio's couch.

I found him eventually when I got back to the village. It was a great scene, everyone leaping around. And there was Ron, tears in his eyes. I've never seen him like that before, because Ron is the kind of person who shows little emotion. He's a hard guy. It was such a picture to see his face. I was thinking, 'stop it or you are going to make me cry'. He was so happy.

When I began to wind down, I felt mentally exhausted. It may be ten seconds but that had been ten years to me. Mentally, physically and spiritually, it's tough because of the need to dig in, concentrate, avoid mistakes and get everything right. For those ten seconds you are putting everything you've got in your body into running 100 metres. People say 100 metres is not that far. They should try running it. It's a long, long way. Sometimes I wonder how we cover it in under ten seconds.

I was drained and yet I still had the 200 metres to run. I was trying to pace myself but it is hard to come back to reality. You have to forget about the 100 metres, get back into the game and concentrate on the next race. But the trouble is you're in a buzz and, as much as you try to put your feet back on the ground, all the things which you have to do after winning a race –

interviews, presentations, more interviews – take too much out of you. I tried to pace myself through the 200-metre rounds but I got knocked out in the quarter-finals. But that would not detract from my feelings on the night of winning the 100 metres.

When I went back to my room I thought about it quietly for a while. When they had given me the medal, I had dropped it. There was a dent in it, but that didn't matter. It was a great moment because it is the pinnacle of every athlete's career. I began to think back to the times when I used to say that one day I would be British champion. People laughed at me because I preferred an easy life rather than going training. I remembered when Frank Dick told me I would never beat the likes of Cameron Sharp.

Everything came flooding back. I remembered the people who had helped me, particularly Ron Roddan and Andy Norman. Andy always had faith in me. He knew when I was going to run well; he chose my races. It always worked.

You think back on all of those things. You wonder what you can do in return. All you can do is say 'thank you'. And the best way to do that is to go out there and prove them right, prove all the doubters wrong.

I didn't have any thoughts on the fact that I had said I would retire the previous year. As far as I was concerned, that was history. I had changed my mind and I had been looking forward ever since. You don't go to the blocks thinking, 'I wouldn't be here if I had followed through with my earlier decision to retire!'

You wonder just what effect a win like that will have on the outside world. Then the stories start to filter through. There was supposed to have been a Michael Jackson concert at Wembley on the same night as the 100-metre final. Jackson cancelled at the last minute and the crowd was really cheesed off. To help make up for it, the organisers said they were pleased to announce that Linford Christie had just won the 100 metres in Barcelona. Apparently, the place went crazy and the mood was a lot better after that.

A man told me he had been camping with friends and they had been saving up what little battery power they had left just to watch the TV. They went out all day because they wanted to have enough current to watch the race that night. I don't think I have ever won another race which has given people such pleasure.

I think the fact that the 100 metres had always been considered the property of the Americans had a lot to do with it. How jealous I used to be when I saw them waving the Stars and Stripes. I remembered saying to Colin that one day I would go out there and win for Great Britain. Now I had done it. It was a brilliant feeling.

Chapter 12

BIGGEST, BADDEST, BEST

It didn't take long for the rumours to start. The newspapers began to ask 'Would Christie have beaten Carl Lewis?' I was not really surprised, particularly after I had heard that some members of the British press in Barcelona had been genuinely happy, whereas others had made no attempt to hide their disappointment after I had won.

There are bound to be ups and downs. I appreciate that the journalists have a job to do; it works both ways. But I am only human and, if they upset me, then of course I am going to say something. Claiming that Carl Lewis would have beaten me was guaranteed to set me off.

Carl himself decided to jump on the bandwagon by agreeing with the view that he would have won. As far as I was concerned, he was talking rubbish but the annoying thing was that our papers were giving him space. I really don't believe it would have been the same in the American newspapers had I gone over there and started to criticize Lewis.

Carl hadn't been good enough to make the American sprint team. I can only beat the people I race against and I can only race against the runners in the line-up for any given meeting. He was never going to beat me in any case. In 1992, Carl Lewis had no hope against me – or any other decent sprinter. He was getting his ass kicked left, right and centre by those who had finished behind me in Barcelona. But still the stories continued.

It went on and on and Carl started to say I was avoiding him. I ignored him because he was insignificant in 1992. I was racing the American number one, Dennis Mitchell. Carl wasn't even number three, so why should I bother about him? However, at this rate, it was clear there would have to be a showdown at some point.

I hadn't trained much after Barcelona and I was beaten by Adeniken in Cologne. I beat Burrell and Mitchell with a 9.99 seconds in Berlin and, for the rest of the season, I decided to run only when I wanted to. I was becoming my own man in every respect because it was around this time that I decided to set up in business with Colin Jackson in order to look after our interests in a more productive and efficient manner.

My first agent had been Anna-Lise Hammer. Andy Norman had been looking after my track activities but Anna-Lise realized I needed to have someone working on sponsorship deals and she showed me how to go about it. I worked on my own for a while and then came into contact with Laura Lisbon, who worked for Ralph Halpern, the boss of Burton's. Laura worked with me for three or four years before Colin and I sat down one day and decided that we should have a company where we would have the say. Not only would that capitalize on our success, the company would also provide us with something to focus on when we had finished with competition. The question was, who would help us run it?

At one stage I had been sponsored by the National Dairy Council and, during that time, I had worked with Sue Barrett, who represented Alan Pasco Associates. We got on well and I have to admit I was impressed by the way she stood up to my sometimes blunt methods! Not long after Barcelona, I called Sue and offered her the job. Naturally, she was reluctant to give up a good position but the challenge of virtually being her own boss while working for Colin and I must have been appealing. She was venturing into the unknown in certain respects and I know I was pretty happy when she accepted. Now we had to choose a name for the company.

We went through the usual list of names with a running connection – 'Striders', 'Sprinters' and so on – but it was Sue who came up with the final solution. She had noticed that black people had a habit of coming up and saying 'Yo! 'Nuff' respect!', meaning, 'Yes! Enough respect. You've earned it, respect is due.' That sort of thing. Sue said she had been running through the various names with friends when they suddenly hit on the idea of simply calling the company 'Nuff' Respect. It seemed very appropriate, a part of the black vocabulary which had spread into the street talk of white society too. It is a name which has a ring to it as well as being one which people could identify. More than that, it was part of our roots. 'Nuff' Respect it would be.

We do personal management for Colin and me, John Regis and Tony Jarrett, among others. Sue and her assistant, Alison Morgan, help us sell the various packages to sponsors as well as organizing our schedules and arranging interviews, track activities, appearances and so on. The girls do a brilliant job.

Once we had the company up and running, the immediate benefit from my point of view was that I could concentrate on my running. I would not be able to go training for as long as I do if the phone was ringing and I was losing potential sponsors. I speak to Sue on the phone and receive faxed details of important news clippings every day. Sue knows to give me as much space as possible but I am always kept informed, no matter where I am in the world.

The great thing about the company is that there are no workers or bosses as such; we work as a unit and make joint decisions. It has been a very successful operation and, against the predictions of one or two doubters who thought we would fail completely because we didn't know what we were doing, 'Nuff Respect is flat out all the time. It is true that we are sometimes quite gullible because of being keen to help other athletes. I am inclined to take the problems of others on my shoulders and I have this urge to go out and see that justice is done. Unfortunately, that does not work very often in the real world.

During the winter of 1992–3, I returned to Australia again for warm-weather training. The decision was helped by the fact that Keith Connor, the former British triple-jump champion, had become a coach in Sydney. It's always nice to see friends when you're away from home. Anyway, training in Australia had worked the previous year, so why change?

While I was there I ran a few races and then returned to do more work in the gym. I was warming up by doing cleans and, as I picked up a weight, it slipped. I felt a twinge in my back. I thought it was just one of those things; as they say, 'no pain, no gain'. Certainly, if I wake up in the morning and I'm not in pain, then I don't think I am in shape. I am more or less in pain twenty-four hours a day.

I tried to lift the same weight again. My back was really sore, so I decided to leave it. Then I went to squat – there must have been 200 kilograms on the bar when I picked it up. I did the squat and returned the bar to the rack. I tried to walk away, and couldn't move. The pain was excruciating but I couldn't scream out because there were people in the gym. It was one of those things; even when you are tired, you can't allow others to see it. I stood still for a while and eventually the pain eased a little. I went outside with Ron, tried to straighten up, and couldn't. I was in a bad way.

We left the gym and decided to go back to England. I was taking painkillers but travelling on the plane was a nightmare. When I got home, I started seeing physios and chiropractors and that gave me some relief. I carried on training but, one day in the gym, I heard a click in my back – and the trouble started all over again.

I was supposed to be going to Portugal but I knew I would not be able to do anything if I went. So, while everyone else headed for the airport, I stayed behind for a couple of days' rest. When I got to Portugal later in the week, everyone said they were glad I had arrived because Ron had been so grumpy; he was lost without me. He really is like my second father.

I was still suffering. You can buy Ibuprofen, a really strong painkiller, over the counter in Portugal. The normal dose in England is 200 ml. In Portugal you can buy 600 ml. I was taking about 1,200 ml of this stuff, four times a day, to enable me to keep training. Then I would take more at night so that I could sleep. It was awful. When I finished training the painkiller would wear off and I wouldn't be able to walk more than ten metres without being in pain. I was in such agony that I started increasing the dosage to 1,800 ml.

My body was numb but I was still training. I felt I couldn't afford to take the time off. On the other hand, we didn't know what was wrong with my back and it seemed stupid to carry on. I was about to call a halt when I got into conversation with some German athletes. They gave me the name of Dr Muller-Wohlfhart, a really good back specialist in Munich.

Then, a few days before I left Portugal, I was doing some block starts with Colin when I pulled a tendon in the back of my knee. That was it. I told Ron I was going home to sort myself out. I returned to London, asked about Dr Muller-Wohlfhart and was told he was really good. I got in touch and, luckily, he was able to see me the next weekend.

The worst part about it was that I had arrived home on the Tuesday and I wasn't able to go to Germany until the Friday. I now had a throat infection as well, so there I was, on my own, with all these ailments. I could hardly eat, I hadn't trained properly for a couple of weeks and I was still on the Ibuprofen. Talk about feeling sorry for yourself . . .

When I finally went to see Dr Muller-Wohlfhart he asked me about my throat. I opened my mouth and showed him and he left the room, coming back with a huge swab. Then he put antiseptic on it and shoved it down my throat. I nearly hit the roof. The nurse looked at him as if he was mad and, when I finally recovered, he did it again.

Then he started sorting out my back. He did some tests – making me raise my legs and so on – and then gave me sixteen injections in my back before sending me for a massage. I went to him three times and I had sixteen injections each day. On the third day, the pain had gone. I went home and started training again with no problem at all. I couldn't believe it.

I didn't take part in the indoor season and I began to play myself back with relays in Portsmouth and Rome. Thanks to having missed so many weeks of training, my times over the 200 metres were poor but I returned to win the 100 metres in 10.26 seconds at one of the British meetings.

There had been a bit of a fuss because Toby Box had beaten me in one of the semi-finals. There are no medals for winning semi-finals. Toby Box finished fifth in the final but, for some reason, the fact that he had beaten me in the semi made the headlines. If Toby Box had pipped me in the final, okay, then we could talk. So the next Trivial Pursuit question was, 'Who was the first British athlete since Allan Wells to beat Linford Christie?' The fact that it was a semi-final did not seem to matter when it came to creating a story.

But the sports pages really went to town when the subject of footballers and their fitness came up. At the time, it was being said that Paul Gascoigne was not fit. I was asked for my opinion. I said I thought 'Gazza' was unfit but, if he asked for help, I would gladly give it. In my opinion, a number of the footballers were unfit.

The subsequent headlines claimed: 'Christie Accuses Gazza of Being Unfit'. I suppose I should have expected that. But it became really stupid when someone produced a study to show that footballers were fitter than I was. This was in *Athletics Weekly*! Our magazine! They reckoned footballers had the strength capacity of Roger Black over the 400 metres, the stamina of Eamonn Martin throughout a marathon, and irrelevant rubbish such as that. Then it was reckoned that Rory Underwood, the England winger, was faster than Ben Johnson at his best over 30 metres. It really got out of hand.

Not surprisingly, Gazza took offence – as I would. He was in Italy and someone must have called him and said something along the lines of 'Linford Christie says you are fat and unfit – what do you think?' Then they came to me with 'Gazza says this and Gazza says that – what's your reaction?' I told them to forget it. I wasn't going to play that kind of game. It went on for a long time and the point was, the press had been saying for some time that Gazza was unfit. But suddenly, they were blaming me. None of the soccer players said anything; I don't think they could, in all honesty. Eventually Gazza realized what was happening and he stopped rising to the bait. We left it at that.

I later met Gazza at the BBC Sports Personality of the Year awards. I have always found him to be okay, despite the impression given in the newspapers. Deep down, I think sports-people understand each other and we got on really well. We sat next to each other and talked the whole night. The subject of fitness was never raised.

Meanwhile, I was back on form, winning the 100 metres in the European Cup meeting in Rome and then equalling the all-comers' record of 10.06 seconds in Edinburgh at the beginning of July. Around this time another American runner, Andre Cason, decided to jump on the Christie bandwagon. He claimed that if he and Carl Lewis had been in Barcelona, I would never have won. Cason hadn't made the team and said he had been watching the race on television with his father. When we reached 60 metres, they looked at each other and he walked out of the room because he knew that he would have won if he had been there. So I thought, 'Okay, that's cool. We're both running in Oslo, so I'll give him the opportunity to prove it then.'

In fact, he never got the chance. I won my heat, he won his heat but then he pulled out of the final, owing to sickness.

Carl Lewis was continuing to say that I was avoiding him, that I was chicken. Even before I became Olympic champion I always raced when I was ready to race, and not before. I have my pride on the line and I was not prepared to run on a whim. When I go to a race, nine times out of ten I am in shape; Ron always sees to that. Finally, a proposal was put to me and I agreed to race Carl Lewis.

Now the hype really started. Once I had accepted the race I gave no interviews, none at all. That was the only way to avoid getting into a false confrontation with Lewis but, from the journalists' point of view, it meant they were not getting a story and, therefore, not making money. Someone resorted to a transatlantic interview with Carl. Predictably, he said he was going to whip my ass. The media wanted to know my reaction to that. I simply said it was one ass-whipping I was obviously going to have to take.

Gateshead had been chosen as the venue. I had no part in the decision but it suited me very well. I look upon Gateshead as my track. I am number one there and I feel the same way about the people. Carl came to Gateshead by Concorde, private jet and Rolls-Royce. I arrived by scheduled flight and taxi, but I continued to avoid answering questions. If I lost and the media wanted to talk to me, I would talk. If I won and they wanted to talk to me, I would talk. But my motto beforehand was to say nothing and avoid trouble.

Meanwhile, Carl was on television and radio. The race was being built up like Godzilla and King Kong, the clash of the Titans. Carl was saying that all his fans should come to Gateshead and wear bandanas. He claimed I had never beaten him in twelve outings, he was in good shape, he was ready. I thought, 'well, Carl, we'll see'.

Many of my friends came to Gateshead. I received lots of letters and people were stopping me in the street. The message was, 'You had better beat him.' I knew I was fit and I knew that Carl was not going to beat me. But talk about putting on the pressure! This race day was going to be one of the longest of my life.

I don't have a rigid routine on race day, in fact I don't have much of a routine at all because it is pretty straightforward.

Breakfast depends on how I feel. Usually I can't eat much on race day, but I try to have something because I am going to be at the track all day. I may have a couple of slices of toast with jam and a cup of tea – but it's difficult because the nerves are building up.

The races can be at any time during the day, sometimes there can be one in the morning and one in the afternoon. Once at the stadium, I work backwards from the start time. I usually have to report either thirty minutes or an hour beforehand so that my number can be checked and I am issued with a leg number which is used in the event of a photo finish. But I bear in mind that I need an hour and twenty minutes to warm up before doing all that.

The purpose of a warm-up is simply to warm up the muscles. A jog starts the process and then I begin stretching. It is a case of stretch and hold rather than jerking the muscles, because that can tear the tissues. Sprinting puts muscles through a lot of stress and warming them beforehand allows you to stretch them further. If you take a piece of chewing gum out of the packet and try to stretch it straightaway, it will snap. But once you start to chew, you can stretch it for as long as you want. It's the same with muscles but on the understanding that if they become too flexible, injury will also result. If you are not flexible enough, you will be hurt. You have to find a happy medium.

It is necessary to keep a little bit of resistance in the muscle so that it goes bang. Taking the chewing gum analogy once more, if you stretch the gum and let it go, it will not go back to its original length. On the other hand, an elastic band will. You want to be aiming to have your muscles like elastic rather than chewing gum.

If you simply stretched and then ran, problems would result. You also need to prepare the muscles for what is to come while getting the rest of the joints working. The drills – stepping and running – which follow get you in the mood. Start off slowly and the movement gets faster and faster. It is like starting a car. Turn on the engine, start revving it hard and that's a recipe for a broken crankshaft. Better to start revving slowly before driving away.

The warm-up track is at, or very close to, the main stadium. Some athletes may decide to do a little bit of warming up in the hotel room before coming along to the track but, usually, everyone makes use of the warm-up area. The press are not supposed to be there but sometimes cameras are allowed in – which I think is absolutely disgusting. There are times when you want to be alone and this is supposed to be an area restricted to athletes and their coaches, a place where you can either collect your thoughts before a race or reflect on it afterwards.

There is a period of waiting after reporting to the officials. Apart from running the race through your mind it is necessary to keep moving. If you wait around too long, the muscles will begin to seize up again and that will definitely lead to injury when you start running flat out. Provided the temperatures are not too high, I will keep my tracksuit on for as long as possible. But, no matter how hot it may be, I will always wear thermals – sometimes top and bottoms; Marks and Spencer do really good ones – and tights, right up to the last minute, just to keep the muscles warm. The only time I wear shorts during training is when I am lifting and doing gym work. Otherwise I prefer to wear long tights.

Further drills ensure the muscles are kept in shape; having started the engine, it is kept revving while sitting at the kerbside. The elastic band has been stretched and is being held, ready to fire. You have warmed up, done your drills. Now you are ready to race. That's when athletes become irritated when officials, who don't know any better, call them on to the track long before the race is due to run. Tempers flare because they are stripped off and all that aggression is bottled up, waiting to be released.

People have their ways of building up mental aggression. I am not focusing on one particular athlete, I want to beat *everybody*. My idea is to go out there and win. I concentrate solely on that.

The way I feel at that stage is as if I am going to do something dangerous, rather like the buzz people must get before bungee jumping. The adrenalin is flowing throughout the period when I am getting ready to run. Sometimes I feel as if I am going to have a coronary, my heart is pumping so furiously. I really believe it is going to pack in.

And yet, despite that, I can be sitting, waiting for the call to the blocks and I will start to nod off. The adrenalin flow is such that it brings on a feeling of tiredness. I go past the stage of being over-anxious and, when I feel sleepy, I know I am ready.

People have wanted to monitor my pulse and so on but I'm not into all of that. Too much knowledge is a dangerous thing. It doesn't mean I am going to be a better athlete. I am not open to experiment and neither am I in a particularly sociable frame of mind. Colin and I are great friends, but when we line up next to each other for a race, that goes out of the window. For ten seconds, I can do without friends.

Television dictates the time spent immediately before the start. Having the camera focus on each competitor is good for the viewer and good for the athlete from a commercial point of view. The event sponsors need their exposure too, but I block all of that out of my mind. The only time it affects me is when it is a cold day and they make us strip off so that the sponsor's name can be seen, and then have us stand around for fifteen minutes before the off. That's when problems can arise. Ideally, competitors should be kept in their tracksuits or tights until the last minute. Introductions to the crowd should be taken care of first. I am aware of having my name announced, but it is on the fringe of consciousness.

I am looking where I am going. I am concentrating on my own lane and nobody else's. There is nothing in particular in focus. Just 101 metres, and that's it. I am getting my mind together, trying to block out everyone and everything around me. It is like taking a picture where the subject is pin-sharp but everything around it is a blur. That is how I am – everything around me is a haze but I can see my lane with perfect clarity.

It takes me a while to get into my blocks. Quite often I am the last to do so. It is not intentional, it is not a tactic designed to unsettle everyone else. I am just trying to get ready the best way I know, and that's it.

I have to make sure, when I am crouching and trying to feel right by getting my shoulders in the correct position, that I move around a lot just to make sure the starter knows I am not settled. It is like looking in the rear-view mirror while taking a driving test; the actions have to be exaggerated otherwise, if you simply move your eyes, you will fail because the examiner may not be aware that you have actually checked the mirror. If I don't make my movements obvious, the starter will say 'set'.

Sometimes, my back leg shakes like mad no matter how hard I try to keep it still. I just think of that as my twitch fibres being ready to go. It's all to do with nerves. The answer is just to let the leg shake.

If I have had the chance, I will have watched earlier races to get an idea of how soon after the 'set' the starter fires the gun.

Normally, it is a couple of seconds. Some starters do one after the other without a pause.

By now, the thinking has stopped. The concentration is totally on moving with the 'B' of the 'Bang!'.

Once away, whatever was left on your mind has gone completely. The adrenalin has prepared you for what you are doing; running like that is not an everyday thing and the body has to get ready.

In Gateshead, before the race with Carl, I was aware that this was hardly a normal day – even in terms of the races I had done in the past. My body was telling me from an early hour that this was going to be something pretty special.

Chapter 13

GO WITH THE FLOW

The race against Carl Lewis in Gateshead was the longest day of my life. We were warming up when Carl's agent, Joe Douglas, came over to talk to me. During all of the time we had been in the hotel the previous day, Joe had not spoken a word to me. Now he wanted to talk just as I was warming up and concentrating on a very big race. I went over and spoke to a well-known ex-athlete who had passed a message to me that he wanted to speak to me. He explained that Joe didn't want me at all, but he could see that my concentration might be disturbed and this was just an excuse to get me away. It was a nice gesture.

There was a capacity crowd. You would have been forgiven for thinking that this was the Olympic Games. My heart was thumping more than ever, I was as nervous as hell. To me, this was more nerve-racking than being in Barcelona because Carl was one of the greatest athletes of our time. I couldn't really understand why he felt he had to stoop so low as to try to belittle my achievements. He must have known what it was like when he was Olympic champion.

Ron and I had been working on my starts all winter because we knew that was where my improvement was going to come from. After watching videos of my races, we realized that I was losing out during the first thirty or forty metres. We concentrated on that.

Then we realized that Carl's starts were not that good either. He would finish really well, but he didn't get out of the blocks that quickly. There was little to choose between us in the final sixty metres. If I could get ahead of him in the first forty metres, then I was going to win. And I knew there was every chance I could do that as we prepared for the start. The atmosphere was electrifying.

As we left the blocks, it was one of the very few times when I was actually aware of the crowd. Jon Drummond was also in the race and my plan was to try and stay with him because I knew he would make a very fast start. Sure enough, Jon was out! He was away. But Carl was nowhere. Eighty, ninety metres, Jon Drummond was there. Ninety-five metres, I surged through. The place went wild. If it had been a boxing match, Carl would have been on the canvas; he would have been hammered.

It gave me so much pleasure. People like to talk about what you used to do. The important thing to me is what you are doing now. I had beaten Carl only once in thirteen outings – it did not mean he would win again this time. Circumstances change.

As soon as I crossed the line, a man came out of the crowd, ran straight to me – and gave me a smack on the lips. I couldn't believe it. I could only assume he must have put a lot of money on the race. I met people afterwards who said they had done very well at the bookies. I wasn't the favourite, so the odds were good. All of that made beating Carl seem even better. It was a really great night for just about everyone except Carl Lewis and his small group of supporters.

I find that I remain pumped up for quite a while after a race, particularly if I have won. On the other hand, if I don't win, I am instantly deflated. With a boxer, you can batter him as much as you want but, if he wins, he can put up his arms and he doesn't feel a thing. If you batter him and he loses, he really feels the pain.

Sometimes the lap of honour can give you problems because, after the buzz has gone, you feel the effects of running a whole lap. But I don't agree with the theory that once you cross the line, that's it, you should be completely finished, having given everything. If you've put a lot into it, why do you want to feel bad? You want to experience pleasure more than anything else.

Sometimes I feel that if I had needed to go quicker, then I could have done. On the other hand you may have run, say, 10.2 seconds, put everything into it – and only just won. In which case, you are in trouble. You think 'Damn. Is that all?' You always have to feel you can go quicker. There has got to be 'the next time'. But if you try too hard, then it's going to be hard work. If you just go with the flow, everything will be fine.

What isn't so good from the winning athlete's point of view is having a microphone stuck in your face immediately after the race is over. Okay, reporters need an interview and sometimes you don't mind. But there are other occasions when you may be on your knees or bending over. In comes the microphone followed, quite often, by a really stupid question. Because the adrenalin is still pumping, the answer can be quite rude.

You need time to calm down, especially if you have just lost the race. The last thing you want to see is a camera. You are angry with yourself because you have lost and you can lash out without thinking of the consequences. It's like cornering an animal. There is no danger as long as the animal can run away but, if surrounded, it will hit out at random because the feeling is that there is nothing to lose. Interviewers don't understand that. In fact, I sometimes think they don't care; just so long as the interview is done, then it doesn't matter how.

There is a huge release of emotion for the athlete, a great relief. If there has been hassle of any sort, then the lap of honour really lifts you. It's a very, very nice feeling, particularly if you have won against the odds.

Usually, I will no longer be interested in the running of that race. I may want to watch a video, just to see if there is anything I can learn, but otherwise, the race is history. There is no time to dwell on it; there is nothing that can be done to change the result. The next race is all that matters.

Having said that, I want to look back on all that I have done and enjoy it when I retire. Until then, I am only interested in what lies ahead. You can help it to be a better future, but you can't make it a better past.

After a big meeting I am drained, emotionally, spiritually and physically. It takes everything out of you. There are interviews, this has to be done, that has to be done – you get dragged in all directions before falling into bed in the early hours. The following morning, more interviews; you have to be obliging all the time. It takes its toll, particularly if, say, there is a 200-metre race to be run the next day. Once again, your reputation is on the line; get beaten in the 200 and straightaway questions are being asked. Even when you win the Olympics there will always be someone ready to attack your position.

The Gateshead race was actually the second challenge I had received that year. When I had been winter training in Australia, a coach challenged me to race one of his athletes for $5,000, which was about £2,500. I laughed in his face because the man was being so stupid. But the Australian press kept running the story and the coach wrote me letters saying he was not going to give up until I had accepted his challenge.

Eventually I said 'Okay. Put up your house. You may think $5,000 is a lot of money but that's not the point. If you really want me to race, if you really believe your athlete can beat me, then put your house up and $50,000. Then we will have a challenge and I will give your house to charity.' Not surprisingly, the race didn't come off. But his athlete was in the Gateshead race and I'm told that not even the Australian commentator mentioned his name. It said a lot about the athlete's part in that event.

In a way, I found it sad that Carl's career had come to this. He was a great athlete, one of the greatest of all time. He was as near to perfection in technique as you will ever find. And the way he could dominate everything – the 100, the 200 and the long jump – made him unique.

I think a lot of him as an athlete but I thought he was wrong to say the things he did about me and I never expected this from Carl. When he was at his peak, there was no need to resort to such tactics. Carl was Carl, a brilliant runner and that's all there was to it. He seemed to find it hard to accept that he was mortal, just like the rest of us. Every dog has its day and he found it difficult to let go, to concede that he would not always be the best.

Running world-class times over such a long period eventually had to take its toll on his body. When you have been as good as Carl Lewis, there should be no need to have a go at another athlete which, in my opinion, is what he did. Gateshead was a case in point.

Even though I had beaten Carl, I had to remember that this was not the World Championships. I did not see Carl as the major factor. I had to get my feet back on the ground and concentrate on the forthcoming championship in Stuttgart. But first, I had to deal with a press conference the day after Gateshead.

This race had been like the heavyweight boxing championship of the world, thanks to the hype from the press. Without them, Gateshead wouldn't have been anything. *Today* newspaper was one of the sponsors and yet it joined in the post-race chorus of 'Why were Linford Christie and Carl Lewis paid so much money to run this race?' I had never said how much I received and I had no intention of telling anyone once the race was over. In fact, I remember very little about the press conference because I wasn't with it. It was a mixture of mental exhaustion, elation and the thought that I had work to do.

I finished a close second to Leroy Burrell in Zurich but Leroy hadn't made the American team for the World Championships, which was frustrating for me. Even though I had beaten Leroy in Barcelona, I knew that if I won in Stuttgart there would be the usual claim that if Leroy had been present, he would have beaten me. And the irony was that, after missing the Olympics the year before, Carl Lewis was in this race.

I did my usual routine of building up by running 10.4 seconds in the first round, then 10.00 in the second. Andre Cason, meanwhile, ran 10.04 seconds – in the first round! The crowd was responding and I went out to watch. I was interested in seeing what Carl was going to do more than anything else. I knew he would want to run flat out and if he wasn't faster than Andre in his heat, then Carl would be finished. Carl likes to dominate throughout, show who's boss. Lo and behold, he was not as fast as Cason – and that was the end of Carl.

I ran 10.00 seconds in my second round and Andre Cason went down to 9.96 seconds – 9.96! I ran that to win Barcelona and this guy was just ripping those times out with no trouble at all! I ran 9.97 seconds in my semi-final. As I walked through the tunnel, I heard the crowd roar; Andre Cason had run 9.94 seconds! He had taken something like 0.05 seconds off his personal best. Shit! This was going to be some final . . .

I began my preparations. I had a massage, did some stretching. I took my top off and I was walking around the warm-up area. Carl was standing there with his coach and he looked at me. I could roughly lip-read what he was saying: 'Effing hell . . . look at that', or something along those lines. It confirmed what I had been thinking earlier on; Carl would not be a problem. He had seen the shape I was in, and that was it.

Athletics is all about confidence. You need to go out there and think 'I'm going to win'. Once you are self-assured, it is amazing what you can do. He who dares, wins; it's that kind of thing.

My attitude is that you've got to try. When I was at college, I seemed to be able to do things which nobody else would either contemplate or get away with if they tried. People begin to think, 'well, if he's got the balls to do that, then he must be okay', and your confidence grows even further as a result.

When I go to the blocks, I realize that other athletes are scared of me. I am scared of them too, but you have to make them believe that they are more scared of you than you are of them. That's where the confidence comes in. Sometimes I know I'm not on form but I will walk out there and do my drills and runs, really strut my stuff. It works. As Carl Lewis implied, I'm a pretty impressive sight and I make sure I use that. I am always in shape. I'm lucky to have the kind of metabolism I've got, the physical structure. But it's no good having that if you can't put it to good use.

I have no need to run my mouth off, since rivals are aware of my reputation. It is like being the fastest gun in the west. Others know that if they want to shoot you down, they have to be on top form – but they don't want to take that chance just in case they aren't quick enough. There are some, however, who want to come out and fight and that seemed to be the way of it with Andre Cason in Stuttgart.

Andre was running . . . bang! bang! bang! . . . down this warm-up track and doing some really fast starts. He was about to do a run and, to avoid some people, I walked in his lane. He looked up, saw me – and stepped across into another lane.

As soon as he did that, I knew that I was going to beat him. If he had walked in my lane at that particular moment leading up to a major final, I would not have changed lane. I would have run straight into him.

Even so, I still needed a little bit of reassurance from Ron. Andre had run 9.94 seconds but, if I could run my personal best of 9.92, then I would win. Ron agreed. 'What's more,' he said, 'this is new territory for Cason. You have run those times before so you know what you are capable of. Cason doesn't know how fast he can run.'

I felt more relaxed and that was helped by the crowd, who seemed to be behind me. They knew it was going to be a good race and there was a chance of a European win instead of an American victory. The others were jumping around. I was standing still, looking straight down the line. I didn't blink. All I wanted to do was wait for the gun – and go like hell.

The pressure got to Andre. He made one of his slow starts. He began to come back to me. Andre covered 60 metres in 6.43

seconds; I was on 6.45 and still going strong. I crossed the line in 9.87, just missing the world record. Cason was second on 9.92, Mitchell third with 9.99 – and Carl fourth in 10.02. That gave me great pleasure. Fourth is the worst position of the lot. So near and yet so far.

When we crossed the line, the first thing I did was look for Mandy, Ron, Philip and Bernie. During the rounds, they had been hiding from me. They knew I would be looking out for them but they didn't want to break my concentration – that's what I call friends. I saw them in the middle of these wild scenes of celebration. People had painted their faces with the colours of the Union Jack; there were life-size Linford Christie cutouts. Everyone went to town. My sponsors, Puma, gave me a T-shirt which had 'Biggest, Baddest, Best' written on it. I felt really, really happy.

In fact, this gave me more pleasure than actually winning the Olympic Games because it was such a relief after the pressure of the previous few months. I felt I had answered the critics. If Carl Lewis had not been there, they would have questioned my win. But Carl Lewis was there. With the exception of Leroy Burrell (and I had beaten him the previous year), anybody who was anybody had started that race.

That was it. I had won everything there was to win in athletics.

After the race, Andre Cason said to me, 'Listen, let's forget all the bickering and everything else. Let's be friends.' I really appreciated that and we did a lap of honour together. Carl didn't say a thing to me. But he tried to join the lap of honour – and the crowd booed him. That really put him in his place and it was sad that had to happen. If he had not shown such disrespect, I don't think the crowd would have treated him that way.

I decided I wasn't going to run the 200 metres, I was just too tired. But I did take part in the relay and we finished second. The Americans, who won, broke the world record and we smashed the European record which had been held by the French. And, once again, we didn't listen to Frank Dick; we ran the team the way we thought best. This was to be one of my last problems with Frank.

It had become his habit not to say who would be on the relay team. He would run maybe eight athletes on the individual promise that they would be on the team. Then, when they weren't picked, they would be so disappointed. I was always trying to persuade Frank to let everyone know beforehand. He could inform the four who he intended to pick and tell the rest that they were reserves. They would be there on the understanding that the four fastest guys would be on the team.

But he wouldn't do that. He was making everyone run around like cart-horses and then, at the last minute, he would drop them. The team that would eventually run was Jackson, Jarrett, Regis and myself. We were the fastest guys. Jason John, Toby Box and Darren Braithwaite were running really well but Frank didn't want to tell them who would be on the team because he wanted to call a press conference and make a big announcement which, in truth, no one really cared about that much.

I was getting ready to run when Jason John said he had heard from Frank that I didn't want him on the team because I wanted Colin instead. Of course, that had nothing to do with it. Frank simply hadn't told Jason that he had already decided on the team. And this was from the so-called director of coaching, who was supposed to keep peace and harmony within the team.

The difficulty was, we wanted Jason to run in the rounds because Colin had to run the hurdles. After this incident, however, Jason didn't want to run because he felt he was being messed around. So we had a problem. I told Jason the decision had to be his, but he should think of it this way: if Great Britain failed to put out a team, who did he think Frank Dick would blame? The press would come to Jason for an explanation. He decided he would run.

We would never have beaten the Americans, the best team won. Second, with a European record, was as good as we could have hoped for. But we never saw Frank afterwards. He resigned at the end of 1994 and, as you might guess, that was no big loss as far as I was concerned, on a personal basis. But what would bother me far more in 1994 would be the fuss which would lead to the removal of Andy Norman.

Chapter 14

THE ANDY NORMAN AFFAIR

There are two reasons why I stay away from home; one is that I have to train and the other is that I have to race. It sounds simple but I have to explain that so many times to people who believe I go to Australia and Florida to sun myself while other British athletes are at home, struggling in the winter cold.

The fact is that because the climate is warmer, I want to train. I train twice as hard when I'm abroad than when I'm at home, not through choice, but because that's the effect of the heat. If it's cold, muscles don't want to perform as well as they would in a more favourable climate. If Ron asks me to run 21 seconds when I am in England, then I will end up running 21.5 or 22 instead of 21 seconds flat. But, when I'm away, I'll be able to run 21, or maybe 20.9. I recover more quickly and the quality of the work is much better because the muscles are more relaxed and responsive.

Working in the heat also cuts down the chance of injury. If it is cold, then it is necessary to warm up for longer. But, of course, the tendency is to avoid that because all you want to do is go on to the track and get the session over. The other problem with winter training in England is the constant distractions as sponsors and various people ask you to do this and do that. Going to Australia means being out of reach when it comes to making appearances and attending functions.

It's not that I'm work-shy. Quite the contrary, because the training is intense. If I am spending the day in the gym I will arrive at about 10 a.m. and carry on until at least 3 p.m. I can remember one occasion in Australia when we did not leave the track until around 6 p.m. The weather was so good, we wanted to do just that bit more.

There is no substitute for being at home but, by having a group of us rent apartments, it helps being together. We all have the same goals and, under circumstances like that, we train harder than usual because everyone wants to be the best. There is a huge desire to improve. Everyone pushes themselves to the maximum and there is always an element of competition.

For example, we were doing sit-ups in the gym one day. Frankie Fredericks reached the target of 250 – and then did another fifty. Not to be left out, someone else made it 100 more. And so it went on until we had done something like 600 sit-ups. That had not been the original intention. In fact, it is very unlikely that any athlete would do that sort of thing on their own. On another occasion, Colin and I were doing cleans – an exercise which works the whole body as you pick up weights from the floor and raise them to chest height; a pretty difficult exercise if you don't know how to do it. We decided to have a competition to see who could do the most until we dropped. That sort of thing really helps because, when two or more athletes train together, it brings out the competitive edge and drives them on.

We train in the middle of the day, when it is hot. People think we are crazy but we do it because working in the heat burns off a lot of fat and, at that time of day, there are no distractions. The track and the gym are usually deserted; we can concentrate solely on what we want to do.

By the time the work is finished, all we want to do is go back to the apartment, eat and go to bed. Now and again we will go to the movies but that is just about the only outside enjoyment we have. There are no parties or anything like that. The cinema is relaxing. If there was a different movie each day, we would go to an early show and then go home and sleep. There is nothing else to do apart from thinking about training the next day. Sometimes there is the excitement of going to the supermarket to buy food!

Before Mandy and I had the luxury of a washing machine in the house, I used to take our clothes to the local launderette, wash them, fold them and take them home. People talk about 'New Man' and that sort of rubbish. What does that mean? I've been washing, cooking, cleaning and ironing for as long as I can remember. When we are training, I have to do that much more because we change our kit every day and, of course, we eat a lot.

I tend to do the cooking when we are in Australia. We rent apartments in a modern block overlooking the sea in a suburb of Sydney. I cook not because it is particularly relaxing – in fact, it's actually quite stressful at times! – but because I want to eat properly. If I don't eat well then I can't train effectively. I make sure of having one main meal each day, so I may as well cook for everyone while I'm at it.

I was busy in the kitchen during Christmas 1993. I was training as usual in Australia, this time with Colin Jackson, Mark McKoy and a few others. Colin's mum and dad flew to

Sydney and Mandy also joined us for Christmas. That made it seem more like home, even if the traditional feeling is hard to find when the temperature is 30°C.

Mark McKoy is a really nice guy. I've never seen him get upset or angry; sometimes I think he's too cool for his own good! Nothing seems to get to him. No matter what time of day you catch him, he's always the same, always helpful. He trained with Ben Johnson in the early days before switching to work with Colin. His running improved almost straight away.

Mark has a lot of experience. Not only is he an excellent hurdler, he is also a very good 100-metre runner too. He has run times that few people have equalled – which is unusual. Hurdlers frequently run good 200-metre races but Mark is fast over 60 metres as well as 100. He's very competitive even though he's so laid back. All round, he's an ideal guy to go training with. We get on very well and that goes back to the Canadian team in Seoul in 1988, when we really hit it off.

I left Australia earlier than usual in order to take part in the indoor season, starting with a GB v Russia meeting in Glasgow. For the first time ever, Colin and I were to compete against each other in the 60 metres. Colin is a much better starter than me and I was a little apprehensive about it because I had not done any starts.

My work rate and his work rate were totally different; he was prepared for the indoor season and I wasn't. I had been training as normal, whereas Colin concentrated on weights and short-sprint work. He was always going to be that bit sharper than me. Even so, I just caught him on the line and that win gave me a lot of confidence.

We raced each other again in a match against the USA. I won by the same margin but, this time, our times had come down – mine from 6.56 to 6.53 seconds as I got into my running more and more.

The following week I lost the 60 metres AAA title to Michael Rosswess. I slipped from my blocks but we both ran the same time – 6.56 seconds – and the photo finish proved to be very controversial. They gave the result to Michael but a few people said that it should have been the other way round. In my view, when the race is that close, it's not worth arguing. However, the result meant that this was the first time I had been beaten by a Briton over 60 metres in six years.

The 60 metres is all about getting out of the blocks and hanging on. Usually, it favours the smaller athletes because they can get going more quickly. And yet I do pretty well in the 60; don't ask me why . . .

On a 60-metre track, you have to anticipate stopping in the small amount of room available. In other words, if the 60 metres was held on a 100-metre track, you would run a lot quicker because there would be 40 metres and more in which to stop. But, on a 60-metre track, there is usually only 10 metres or perhaps a bank on which to pull up. There is something psychological about the fact that there is potential danger ahead; you begin to slow without realizing it. Also, if you make a bad start there is no time to recover.

A couple of weeks later, we raced again and sorted things out; I won and Michael was fourth. A week after that, I ran 6.48 seconds in Karlsruhe to establish a new European record. I was ranked number one in the world over 60 metres. Overall, it had been a very good indoor season; I was ready to tackle the European outdoor circuit.

The actual travelling does not really bother me, I see it as part and parcel of the job. Of course, Spain one day, Austria the next conjures up exciting flights and luxury hotels when, in reality, it's not like that at all. The living quarters I described in Barcelona were the extreme of generally poor conditions for athletes when on the road. Usually, it is two to a room and some of the rooms are so small that you couldn't swing a cat's tail, never mind the cat.

The hotels are arranged by the organisers, so there is no choice. Well, there is if you want to spend the money and stay elsewhere but it is the duty of the organisers to provide food and accommodation. As for sightseeing . . .

A typical schedule could mean travelling on Monday, racing on Tuesday, flying to the next venue on Wednesday, racing on Thursday, moving on again on Friday, running on Saturday before boarding the plane for somewhere else on Sunday. I am lucky in so far as I get to visit so many different countries. But what do I know about them? I couldn't tell you anything about places such as Zurich and Berlin because I never get the chance to see them properly.

Once in a while there may be a free day but, even then, nobody wants to walk very far for fear of perhaps taking too much out of their legs. Running is our business, it's a serious thing. If there is time available, I will go to the track and perhaps do a little bit of training but, otherwise, free time is spent in the hotel room and struggling to eat pretty awful food. It is far from glamorous. But I have to say that the European-based athletes are the lucky ones because it is possible sometimes to fly in, do an event and return home. The Americans may have to stay in Europe for two months before they get the chance to go back home.

I started off the outdoor season with a win in the 100 metres in Seville on 5 June, followed by another victory in Nuremberg five days later, before flying straight back to England for the AAA Championships in Sheffield.

A win there with a wind-assisted 9.91 seconds gave me my seventh AAA title to equal the record set by McDonald Bailey in the 1950s. There was quite a fuss about that, but running is totally different now; much, much more competitive. It meant more to me to win the sprint double when I ran in the 100 and 200 metres at the European Cup meeting in Birmingham two weeks later – I believe I was the only man at the time to have won it twice. I was also part of the winning relay team, and that helped Britain qualify for the World Cup at Crystal Palace later in the year. Behind the scenes, however, there had been one or two problems with the relay.

We didn't have a very good team because a number of people decided they didn't want to do this meeting. My argument was that any top British athlete should not hesitate in competing for their country. They were complaining that the programme was too hectic but that didn't wash with me because nobody had a tougher schedule than mine. Each time I race, I am up against three of the top five sprinters in the world. I turned out for the European Cup; in my view, everyone else should have done the same. I made a noise about it.

My argument was that the people who didn't want to help Britain qualify for the World Cup would be the first to want to run at Crystal Palace once we had qualified. I don't agree with that. My feeling was that whoever helped the team qualify should be given the first opportunity to run on the day.

It was the distance runners who were moaning about it the most. They said I don't know what it is like to run three 1,500 metres or three 10,000 metres in a few months. Maybe so, but I was prepared to bet that if there was money available they would suddenly find the time to help Britain qualify. Anyway, the men had a good enough team to get through and the women qualified for the first time.

By the time we got to the next meeting in Linz on 4 July, the qualifying argument had died down and a new dispute arose when they changed the starter for the final of the 100 metres. The starter during the heats had given us a decent length of time, once he had called 'set', to get up from the kneeling position. In the final, everything changed; there was virtually no time on the hold at all. Frankie Fredericks and I were really annoyed about it, we felt cheated. I finished third and it was the first time ever I had run slower in the final – in decent conditions – then I had in the heats. I ran 10.01 seconds in the heats and 10.03 in the final. That's not the way it works but it was just one of those things.

A few days later, Leroy Burrell broke the world 100-metre record in Lausanne; he ran 9.85 seconds. I was commentating for the BBC at the time. It was something I had been asked to do because I was not competing. I didn't mind because it meant I would be talking about something I know. I must admit, I find it pretty easy to commentate because I have been there and done it. The usual commentators can only say what they think might be going on and, to be honest with you, I sometimes cringe when I listen to the things they say. You know it is rubbish. So, I'm quite happy to go to the studio and talk about how I see things. And, when Leroy ran that time, I had to admit that I couldn't believe it.

The race looked pretty easy but I gave Leroy full credit; he had run really well. Then he said he had just stepped off the plane from the United States. In which case, if he could run like that under the circumstances, then he must be capable of doing a 9.80.

I often think that Leroy is more talented than he realizes. He is strong, he is young and he has so much ability. I think, in the past, he allowed himself to live in the shadow of Carl Lewis. Leroy did not believe in himself, he did not feel that he was a great athlete in his own right. People may say he knows he is good – but knowing and believing are different.

I think that an on-form Burrell is dangerous; very, very dangerous. I rate him highly because, if he hits it right on the day, he's going to be pretty tough to beat. I'm always aware of Leroy although, at the time, I wasn't particularly worried about the new record. I looked at it this way: my best had been 9.87 seconds and if Leroy had pushed the world record out of my reach with, say, a 9.80 seconds then, okay, he's The Man. But I felt his new record of 9.85 seconds was attainable.

The world record has never really been something I go for. My aim has always been championship medals; they can't take those away from you whereas someone is always going to run faster and beat your record. Leroy may have become the world record holder, but he would have swapped it for my Olympic or World Championship gold medals.

All of a sudden, war had been declared. When Leroy announced on television that he was 'ready to race Linford', the hype started all over again. I had been through all of this with Carl Lewis. Now Leroy was taking his turn. Suddenly I was washed up, too old; my status was under threat. Leroy went on to say that I wasn't the best and yet the first person he wanted to race was me. He claimed he would race me for nothing.

I ignored him. I would race Leroy when I was ready, I would call the shots. I'm sure Leroy was thinking of the possible financial benefits but I would be blowed if he was going to make money out of me in that way. In order to gain true recognition in the world, he needed me. He would have to wait. His challenge fell on deaf ears and, in any case, I was thinking about the European Championships and the Commonwealth Games later in the year.

Part of my preparation is to take part in as many races as I can. When offered the chance to run the 100 yards in Edinburgh, I took it and duly won. Apart from establishing a new British record, taking part in a 100-yard race made a change for me and the public. I'm sure they get fed up watching the 100 metres, the 200 metres or whatever, day in, day out.

I don't think enough thought is given to entertaining the public. It would be nice, say, to run the 150 metres, just to break the monotony. If you have twenty races of 100 metres and win them all, it becomes tedious. The spectators incline towards the other runners because you become boring. I try to break up my programme if possible, just to do something different. In this case, it was nice to have another record in the book.

It was not so pleasant, around this time, to find heavy discussion about Andy Norman in the British press. His name had been linked to the death of Cliff Temple, a reputable coach as well as athletics correspondent for *The Sunday Times*.

I respected Cliff. He avoided the sleaze reporting employed by some of the athletics journalists. Being a coach, he understood how athletes felt. He knew the business and he did a lot of work with youngsters. He was okay.

Cliff had one or two run-ins with Andy and he also had some personal problems. The press suggested heavily that it was Andy Norman who caused Cliff to commit suicide. I still think it was wrong that they should blame Andy for what happened. He may have been a factor, he may not. I can't say because I don't know all the facts. But I will say that Andy should not have been portrayed as the sole reason for the tragedy.

Ultimately, the pressure from the media led to Andy losing his job as promotions officer for the BAF.

As in every case like this, the person at the centre of the controversy gets the universal cold shoulder. As far as I was concerned, Andy had a problem with the federation and with the media. But he did not have a problem with me. So why should I cut him off? A lot of athletes felt the same way. We continued to show a bit of loyalty to Andy by supporting him at a difficult time. He appears to be a very hard person, but he actually went through a lot.

The press said he hounded Cliff Temple to death but now the media were hounding Andy. If Andy had committed suicide, who would have taken the blame for that? Two rights don't make a wrong; not even Cliff Temple would have wished to see that. The last thing anyone wants is to be blamed for someone else's death. I couldn't give Andy any help as such, but the least I could do was sit down and listen; hopefully, that would make him feel a bit better.

There were all sorts of stories. One said that Sally Gunnell had left Andy because she wanted to distance herself from him and the story then went on to suggest that Colin and I had parted company with Andy because we didn't want to pay him commission. By trying to make Sally look good at our expense, it seemed to me that some of the articles were bordering on racism. I could think of no other reason for writing in such a provocative manner.

Andy took care of my races until the beginning of 1995. Most of us stuck with him as a way of saying thanks and showing our appreciation. He looked after the top athletes and, through his contacts, got us invited to meetings. I didn't have an agent. Andy told me when to run, when not to run, what meetings to go to and when to train. When I first started getting near the British record, it was Andy, along with Ron, who chose my races. It worked every time.

He made sure that the athletes were paid and that we were not ripped off. He arranged warm-weather training camps so that we could prepare properly for major championships. We paid him back by winning medals. We won medals for our country but very few people realized how much of that was due to Andy Norman.

I have known Andy for a long time. He was one of the biggest names in athletics when I first started and I would not be where I am now without his help in the beginning. He was very hard, but fair. He did not suffer fools gladly but, at the same time, you knew that if you did right by him then he would respond. We had our ups and downs but there has never been anything I have taken personally.

He gave me races which others would never have allowed me to do. The trip to Finland, which I mentioned earlier, is a very good example. I ran well there and that did a lot for my confidence. Andy guessed that would happen. He went out of his way to give me encouragement and he always had faith in me. I don't have anything bad to say about him.

I thought it was wrong of the BAF to dismiss him without first finding a replacement capable of handling the job. You shouldn't throw away the blueprint without taking a copy but that's what they did. They were trying to build a house without any plans.

The athletes suffered as a result because the people who tried to do his job didn't understand what was going on. Andy was a very clever person but he kept a lot of the knowledge in his head. There was nothing for his successors to go on.

If he was involved with a meeting and there was not enough money to go round, Andy could persuade athletes to run for nothing. There are very few people around who can pull that kind of favour. The organization of the meeting would go like clockwork, he was very good at his job. In my view, the people taking his place seem to be inefficient. It's just that they can't replace Andy Norman.

I am sure the BAF would not agree, but I thought they handled the Norman case very badly. First of all, it had nothing to do with the BAF, it was a problem between Andy and the press. The media wanted rid of Andy, so they brought the BAF into it which, in turn, meant the athletes became involved. Our job is to go out and perform on the track, but we were dragged into the politics of it all, and that was wrong.

Once entangled, the BAF should have made a swift decision. But the longer they left it, the worse it got. It was like a fire which started off smoking and was then fanned into a huge blaze, consuming everything. The BAF should have said 'We will have an internal inquiry and a decision will be made.' But the decision was left so long that it just built up more momentum. In the end, the BAF left themselves with no choice but to do what they did.

I think it is true to say that British athletics was showing signs of needing a change. But I think this happened at the wrong time. The BAF should have got rid of Andy Norman because they wanted to, not because they were made to. Some of the administrators have become so far removed from the sport that they have not got a clue about how the athletes feel. They understand very little about what is going on. Athletics has changed so quickly that these people are out of touch.

To be honest, the various federations hardly affect me now. I run because I want to run, whereas in the past I did everything they wanted me to do. Of course, they can take sanctions against me if I bring the sport into disrepute. That is how it should be because I am not above the sport. They have a right to do that but, on the other hand, if an athlete has done nothing wrong then I do not believe the sport's administrators should have full freedom to make the athlete do something he or she has no wish to do.

I can't think of one specific area which needs to be addressed if athletics is to be improved. There are a number of things, starting with the need to listen more often to what the athletes themselves have to say. The people who run our sport do not realize how important the athletes really are. It has been said that the officials are the most important people in the sport because, without them, there would be no athletics. In my view, you can get officials from more or less anywhere but good athletes are hard to find. The athletes themselves do not recognize their own importance, how much power they actually have. Every year there is more moaning and groaning about this not being right and that not being right but nobody is willing to do anything about it. Everybody is looking after themselves. 'United we stand, divided we fall' sums it up. We are falling because there is no unity among the athletes.

The majority of athletes worldwide agree with me, but many of them are afraid to speak up because the sport gives them a living. Money has ruined the sport. I can remember the days when there was no money in athletics. If you look at the top administrators, many of them were running in the days when there was no money in the sport. Now the majority of the young, up-and-coming athletes are doing it for the money. Circumstances have changed. Andy Norman was one of the few administrators who fully understood that.

Chapter 15

FAME EXCEEDS FORTUNE

Athletes do not get paid for running in the Olympic Games. They do not receive a penny for competing in the World Championships, the Commonwealth Games or any of the major championships, both indoors and outdoors. People are still surprised by that even though, in the case of the Olympics, much is made of the amateur status of the athletes – despite the fact that money plays such a big part.

A case has been put for athletes to be paid for the World Championships and I understand that argument runs to the Olympics as well. I don't believe an athlete should be paid to run in an Olympic Games because it is the pinnacle of his or her career. Everyone wants to be an Olympic champion.

The spin-off which comes from that is vast, provided the athlete is marketed correctly. A number of gold medal winners fail to capitalize on their success. On the other hand, there is a widespread belief that, once the medal goes round your neck, you are automatically rolling in money.

People see me on a television chat show and assume I am paid a fortune. The going rate, when I appeared on *Wogan* a few years ago, was around £150. Nice to have, but hardly the road to enormous wealth. The most frustrating part is continually having to explain this, almost defensively, to people who do not understand.

I have no complaints because I have been used to this ever since I started competing. Puma would help me with my running kit but I had no sponsor. The only help I had came in 1986, just after I had won the European Indoor Championship. I thought the money would pour in after that. But there was nothing. I was unemployed and depending on help from Mandy and my parents. Determined to do something, I phoned Capital Radio in London and spoke to their Helpline. They couldn't believe this was an athlete calling and asking for financial assistance. Like everyone else, they thought I had piles of money in the bank; it was a typical case of fame exceeding fortune.

I did an interview and a man called Peter Canham heard it on his car radio. He got in touch and offered help. I told him that what I needed most was transport – so Peter bought me my very first decent car, a Nissan Sunny. I had that car for years. He would service it and look after it. Eventually, Peter sold me the car for a written-down price. I gave it to Mandy and she had it for years before we sold it. Even though I am no longer in touch with Peter, I will always remember him. How can you forget someone who does you such a good turn?

Mandy had been using her secretarial skills to write letters for me to various prospective sponsors. We put together a portfolio by photocopying press cuttings and presenting everything in a plastic folder. We produced between fifty and 100 of these and sent them off to various companies. Usually, there was no response. Only a few bothered to reply, saying 'sorry, we can't help'. Our approach was probably not perfect, in which case what we really needed was to have the folders returned because all of this cost money which I could have used elsewhere!

For most athletes, that situation never changes. There are only a handful who actually make a living from the sport. A lot depends on the event. If you are the world's number one shot-putter, you make very little money; and if you are the number one shot-putter in Britain, you make nothing.

Fortunately for me, the 100 metres is the event which attracts the most attention. It receives more publicity than any other; everyone wants to see the fastest man in the world. So, off the back of that, the athlete will find a shoe company or a clothing manufacturer willing to pay to have the athlete use their products. Promoters will pay to have the best athletes take part in their meetings, since the big names attract big crowds. But apart from those sources, the athlete has to rely on outside commercial sponsors – adverts and so on – to make money. There is no other way.

Sometimes, the promoters of events will offer bonuses if the athlete runs inside a certain time or breaks a record. If it is a world record, that will mean a lot to the promoter because everyone will then want to run on what is deemed to be a fast track.

Promoters will pay bonus money to anyone who beats me or Colin. I have no problem with that because it gives the others something to aim for. Some athletes have said that everyone should be paid the same but receive bonuses for first, second and third. That's nonsense. The people who say that are usually past their best, not earning much and they want a share, as if by right. You have to earn it. I believe that the sprint is the most difficult event because of the consistently strong competition.

Why should I be paid the same amount as someone who is not under the same pressure as me?

There have been attempts in the past to form some kind of union. It's totally impossible because there is no unity among athletes, which is a pity. If we worked together, we could realize our strength and run the show. Certainly, I would want to make sure that athletes are paid better than they are now. I truly believe it is wrong that the athletes at the bottom should receive nothing at all. I once suggested that the top athletes take a £1,000 pay cut. That way, there would be enough money in the kitty to pay everyone something, no matter how small. People thought I was mad. But I meant it. It's a disgrace that the youngsters, the potential stars of tomorrow, are not paid a penny.

The BAF have grants, medical schemes and so on, but I do not take any of their money. I pay my own way for two reasons. One is that if I don't use the money on offer for, say, a flight to the training centre in Tallahassee, then somebody else more desperate than me can use that money. And two, I would prefer to pay for a flight to Germany for treatment rather than make use of the BOA medical centre. If something goes wrong, I can go back and kick up a fuss. If it's free treatment, then I can't. If I pay, then I expect to have the best. My health is more important than any financial considerations. And if, by turning down the money, other athletes below me can benefit, then so much the better.

I tell up-and-coming athletes to try to make sure that they are paid when they begin to make a name, to try and ensure they have something other than a Great Britain tracksuit at the end of their career to show that they have been on the team. There is no point in complaining that I am making too much; I tell them to go out and earn money for themselves. It is people like Sally Gunnell, Colin Jackson, John Regis and myself who make athletics watchable, put bums on seats and persuade sponsors to support the sport.

Newspapers like to speculate on just how much I earn. There was a lot of talk about money at the time of the race against Carl Lewis in Gateshead. The figure of £100,000 kept surfacing but at no stage did I confirm or deny it. There were complaints that £100,000 was far too much money. Assuming the figure was correct, £100,000 is next to nothing when compared to Nigel Mansell's eight-figure annual income in recent years or the sums earned by heavyweight boxers.

I did say that the figure concerned was not enough. That was not said through greed, simply as a comparison with other leading sportsmen. The figure soon comes down once the tax man takes his forty per cent, and commission and other fees are paid. But the exact details are my business. Anything in the press is pure speculation.

I have read that I turned down $12 million for running or for playing NFL football in the United States. I have never had an offer like that but these stories get printed and create completely the wrong impression. My name has appeared in the list of high-money earners; I never deny it, I never agree. My earnings are nobody's business but my own. Not even my father knows the figures involved, we never discuss that.

Fortunately, I have job satisfaction and I now get paid decent money for doing my job. I didn't make a thing until after I had won the European Championship in 1986, when I began to pick up sponsorship and promotional deals. It went on from there. My marketability increased with success which got better and better each year. There was no drop-off point, the progression has been consistent and I have kept building to the stage where I have become one of the best-known sportsmen in Britain.

I am one of the lucky ones. There are a lot of athletes worse off than me and I can see no reason for rubbing in how much I earn. That would be inconsiderate and flash. I can remember just how it was to be earning very little money.

I have made the most of my position. I was supported by Toyota for a few years and that allowed me to drive a Supra sports car. Now I am sponsored by Mercedes-Benz and they have given me a beautiful 600 coupé. I also had a Mercedes which I won at the World Championships in Stuttgart. Mandy drives that car now.

I invest my money wisely. There are others in the sport who earn less than me but you wouldn't believe it because of the way they throw it around. Andy Norman used to say to me, 'save your money', and that's something that I am pretty good at. That is the reason why I am in this position. It is not the fact that I earn a lot of money, it is because of how I look after what I've got.

As with most sports, the window for earning the maximum amount of money is not particularly large. In fact, compared to many sports, the athletics window does not open very wide and it's double-glazed! But I have made some good investments along the way and, if anything happened and I had to stop tomorrow, I would be able to manage – for a while, at least!

The amount we earn does not, under any circumstances, compensate for the job we do. We have to start at an early age and put in a lot of time training – three to six hours a day – for which, of course, we do not get paid. If I do not run, I don't get paid. It's as simple as that. If I slip outside the top three in the world, the sponsors will not be interested.

With Leroy Burrell having set that new world record in July 1994, my standing was being questioned once more. As I said before, I was confident I could beat 9.85 seconds but that did not allow for the return of a familiar injury.

During an invitation meeting at Crystal Palace, I was leading at sixty metres when I pulled my hamstring. Every time I went to surge, I was in so much pain that I had to stop. The newspapers went to town. I had been beaten by Jon Drummond, I had been whipped. I made no excuses; if you line up for a race, you are fit. I lost because I was injured.

Jon Drummond must be one of the funniest guys in world athletics. He's one of the very few athletes with personality. He accepts that he may never become one of the greatest athletes in the world but he goes out to enjoy himself and entertain. You like him or loathe him. I like him, we get on well. He knows how to work the crowd – and they respond. He does clownish things and there are times when you definitely need that.

The Goodwill Games followed soon after that but, because of the hamstring problem, I couldn't run. During the press conference after the 100 metres there, Carl and Leroy were asked about Linford Christie and the fact that he was injured. They said, 'Linford who?'

They could throw words around as much as they liked but they knew that I had beaten them in all of the major championships for the previous three or four years. They thought they were very funny. I didn't respond publicly because it gives people the opportunity to kick your butt. My main concern was to be fit for the European Championships and the Commonwealth Games which were following in fairly quick succession. I was determined to remind them exactly who Linford Christie was.

An X-ray on the hamstring showed that it was torn, which was worrying because that meant the recovery would take four weeks and I had only three weeks before the next championship. I went to Germany for treatment from Dr Muller-Wohlfhart and he really worked on me. My back had also been seizing up, but he sorted me out.

I started the build-up with Ron in Monte Carlo. There was so much temptation to push hard but I began by running slowly, just taking my time. The hamstring felt stronger; better and better and better. We increased the speed and the work rate to the point where I felt I was strong enough to run in a meeting in Monte Carlo. Ron said no. I was biting my nails in frustration because I really, really wanted to run. But missing that race was good for me, it brought the hunger back.

When I missed the Goodwill Games, David Miller wrote in *The Times* that I didn't run because I was afraid of being beaten by Leroy Burrell. Miller questioned the severity of my hamstring injury, the inference being that there was nothing wrong with me; I was scared of Leroy Burrell, and that's all there was to it.

I was just dying to race. In the European Championships semi-finals, I ran 10.08 seconds. Once I did that, I knew I would win because nobody else in Helsinki would get close. Do a time like that in the heats and everyone panics. And the competition had been unsettled already by the fact that I had simply turned up.

There had been rumours that I was going to miss the championships. Some stories even suggested that I was out for the season. I worked as normal and I had arrived a few days before the championships were due to start. As soon as a few of my rivals walked in – Panic Zone! Damn! He's here! Let's go back to second place. They thought they would be promoted because of my absence.

I duly won against a Norwegian and a Russian. It was not a

great entry and I was not overwhelmed by my time. I knew I was going to win anyway – which is not to be disrespectful. My aim was to win but I knew it was no use being European champion if I couldn't be the best in the world. I couldn't wait to beat the Americans.

In the meantime, we had to deal with having Solomon Wariso banned after he had been found positive. That was the signal for the tabloid newspapers to send out their so-called top writers and, once again, we were being scrutinized from every angle. One of the newspapers latched on to the fact that Solomon had apparently said the illegal substance had come from the training camp in Tallahassee, so therefore I was responsible for bringing it into Britain.

When you are successful, you have to expect that kind of thing. The only way to look at it was that I would be a nobody if they didn't write about me and, in any case, having the newspapers talk about me took the pressure off someone else. Even so, it can become very annoying.

During the championships I had been sitting in the stand watching the high jump. Dalton Grant did not jump as well as he could and, in my capacity as team captain, I went across to find out if he was okay. The next thing I knew there were stories in the press that one of the British officials had said I was not allowed on to the infield. None of the officials admitted to having said it later on, but the newspapers were saying that I could have got Dalton disqualified. I don't know how they reached that conclusion because Dalton was already out of the competition. If I could not go on to the field as team captain and console one of my fellow athletes who had just competed below par according to his standard, then what could I do?

If it was wrong, I wouldn't have done it. I was told there was no offence committed. The way it was reported was ridiculous. And there was more to come after the relay.

John Regis was injured and Darren Braithwaite was brought in as a replacement. Tony Jarrett gave Darren the baton and, when Darren went to run, he hit his leg and dropped out. It was a mistake anyone could make. I was waiting for the baton and, when I saw everyone else running past, I just shook my head and walked off.

The press descended on me, asking what had happened. I said they must have seen more than me. When asked what I was going to do about it, I said I had no comment. Now, according to the media, I was being arrogant towards my fellow athletes because they had made a mistake! I suppose if I had smiled, that would have been construed as not giving a damn.

Of course I was disappointed! According to the times, we should have won. Instead, we had lost a gold medal and it went without saying the guy who made the mistake was going to be upset. There was no point in me having a go at him because that would have made him feel even worse. It was a no-win situation in every sense. It was a case of putting it behind us and looking forward to the Commonwealth Games in Victoria.

Most of the team went out early to Canada but Colin and I chose not to join them because we didn't want problems with jet lag. The danger in going out too early is that jet lag sets in after about four days and we didn't want to be a part of that. In any case, I needed to run more races in Europe because I was not yet fully fit. Zurich in August would be perfect.

With the exception of Frankie Fredericks, the top sixteen sprinters in the world were at Zurich. There was the usual talk of The Fastest Man in the World, particularly as I would be running against Leroy Burrell. Not many people gave me a chance. I won my heat, run in the pouring rain.

There was a dispute before the final because Andre Cason and Leroy Burrell had run the same time, but they gave Andre the final place. Leroy's people complained and, to my amazement, they decided by flicking a coin. Leroy won. Leroy was not fit, so they should not have made such fuss. But I was glad he had made it. I was really worked up for this race. While nobody really thought I would win, at the same time I knew my name would be mud if I lost. When the chips are down, I can pull it off.

I ran 10.05 seconds to win in the rain – but I don't remember being wet. The crowd went mad. They were shouting and chanting 'Christie! Christie!' They loved it because I think this was the first time that a non-American had won Zurich. Brugger, the promoter, said he had thought Carl Lewis was one of the most popular sprinters ever to come to Zurich, but apparently Carl had nothing on this.

Carl should have been in the race but he said he had drunk some bad water when he was in Russia and he was sick. With or without Carl, the Americans were not pleased with the result. Leroy left straight away, he didn't pass 'Go', he didn't collect his $200. He just went home. Joe Douglas, Leroy's agent, said I was not the fastest sprinter in the world. But I was the fastest wet-weather sprinter because I came from England, where it is always wet and always cold. That, according to Joe Douglas, was the reason I had won! I didn't bother to ask him how I had managed to beat the Americans to the gold medal in Barcelona.

I had finally had my say. Everyone knew that whoever wins Zurich usually ends up being number one. Two days after

Zurich, I won again in Brussels before flying out to Victoria. As far as I was concerned, I was going to win – no problem.

I won my first round but, in the other heats, athletes whose previous best times had been in the region of 10.3 and 10.4 seconds were suddenly doing 10.1. Frankie Fredericks in particular was on song. I said to him, 'What are you guys trying to do to me? Are you trying to make me panic or something?'

In the second round, I made my mark by equalling my Commonwealth Games record. That sent up the warning signals. Frankie had been running in different heats and his times were always a fraction slower. But I was beginning to think that he was going to be The Man.

Frankie remains an untapped talent; he is still comparatively new to the sport and, in some ways, he is waiting to get out. Frankie is not that interested in athletics. He's doing it now because he is enjoying it but he doesn't put in one hundred per cent effort. Even so, I think that one day he will shock a few people.

I think he wants to win but I don't think it means as much to Frankie as it means to some of us. He has got other plans. He has his head firmly screwed on; he knows what he wants to be. But I think if he ever becomes really hungry, we're going to be in a lot of trouble. I think he has got the ability to be one of the fastest 200-metre runners of all time.

I have trained with him and really enjoyed it, he is one of the nicest people you could meet. Really genuine. I see a lot of me in Frankie – it's just that Frankie is a bit quieter! But I didn't underestimate him in Victoria.

The following day I ran 9.98 seconds, which broke the Games record. The over-zealous Canadians decided they wanted to test me just before I ran in the final. I told them that they really couldn't do that because I was due to run in a couple of hours' time. They had a word with our team management and agreed that a test after the final would not be a problem.

I won the final with a time of 9.91 seconds but, instead of Frankie finishing second, it was a guy from Sierra Leone by the name of Dove Edwin. He ran a lifetime best of 10.02 seconds. I was very pleased with my time and did my lap of honour. Dove Edwin, meanwhile, was really playing to the crowd and the media. Here was the big athlete with all his sponsors taking on the little guy with no money.

It was a sports fairy story, even though one race does not make a champion. They were gushing over Dove Edwin and gave him a special medal, saying he was the spirit of the games, the epitome of what athletics and amateurism is all about. Dove Edwin was cashing in for all he was worth. Someone said they would rather wait until after the results of the drug tests were known. Sure enough, Dove Edwin was tested positive. The whole thing was a bad joke.

Once the 100 metres was over, I returned to Europe. This had always been my plan; it was on a schedule which my office had given to the press many months before. But now I was slated for going home, for chasing dollars and turning my back on a city and games which had built their advertising around me. I was getting annoyed because, if they had wanted to use me to publicize the games, then perhaps they should have contacted me first so that we could have come to some sort of arrangement.

I was accused of not wanting to run in the 200 metres when, in fact, I had offered to run some time before. When told I would not be required, I had stopped training with the 200 in mind and therefore felt I couldn't run when they changed their minds at the last minute. That was interpreted as being begged to run and turning them down flat.

Also, the business of being British team captain wasn't relevant. This was the Commonwealth Games where the English, Welsh, Scottish and Irish teams run under their own colours; the British team didn't come into it. I don't know what it was about the summer of 1994, but it seemed I could do nothing right.

I travelled to Rieti in Italy at the end of August, where I was beaten in the 100 metres by Jon Drummond. It was very revealing because I believed I could simply step off the plane from Canada and run, just like the Americans do. I had felt fine during the warm-up but, when the gun went, my mind was off the blocks quickly enough but my body refused to follow. One or two Americans had been watching the race on television and, as soon as they saw my start, they knew immediately what the trouble was. I had always assumed it was easy to fly across the Atlantic and start racing. Now I knew different.

In fact, it took me ages to recover. I went to Berlin and Paris and was beaten by Dennis Mitchell each time. I lost by no more than a dip on the line. Usually, when I win, there is a gap between me and the second place man but, during these races, I would get to sixty metres ready to pick up and go, and I just couldn't do it.

There had been too many championships – European Cup, World Cup, European Championship, Commonwealth Games – in 1994. Although I was in good shape, apart from the injury, it was one of those years where my mind needed a rest. I tended to run without really thinking about what I was doing. I was trying to tick over. I had been doing too much.

I established a British record of 14.97 seconds for the 150 metres in Sheffield and, by now, my legs felt as though they were hanging off me. I had had enough but decided, as team captain, I should turn out for the World Cup at Crystal Palace in

September. It was freezing cold but a win in the 100 metres gave me my third consecutive World Cup title, which made it very worthwhile, along with being part of the winning 4 × 100 relay team.

On the final night, we returned to the hotel and I was playing pool when the phone rang. It was a girl I had not heard from for a long time and I couldn't understand why she would want to call at three in the morning. We had met while I had been training in Lanzarote. She had said she was a dancer and wanted to train with us. She was there all the time and stayed in our apartment for about two weeks. We fed her and looked after her. We became friends. That was it.

I had spoken to her several times since. She had problems with her boyfriend in Greece and I had acted as a sort of counsellor. When she phoned the hotel, I said I would call her back at a more convenient time. When we got in touch eventually, she kept asking me, 'When I slept with you, did it mean anything?' I thought, 'What are you talking about?' I was obviously very suspicious. I rang Sue Barrett on another phone and placed the receivers so that Sue could hear the conversation.

The girl said she had been offered £10,000 to do a story on me because we had slept together. She wanted to know what I was going to do about it – meaning, how much more are you willing to pay to stop me? I said I wasn't into blackmail and told her to do what she had to do and, most likely, our solicitors would meet one day.

I told Mandy immediately about the conversation so that it would reduce the shock if anything reached print. A Sunday newspaper carried the story but, if they paid this girl £10,000 for the story, they were robbed. It was sheer fantasy about how we were going to share our lives together and rubbish like that. Apparently, I had asked her to come away with me to the training camps. Not even Mandy is allowed to come to the training camps.

Money was obviously the motive. I can't imagine she was paid more than £2,000. I felt betrayed and annoyed because the story caused some friction between Mandy and me. The only positive thing to come out of it was the claim that I was good in bed. How she knew that, I don't know, but it was better than saying that I was no good at all!

I didn't feel good for anything when I went to Japan for my final race of the season. I had caught flu, probably as a result of that bitterly cold night at Crystal Palace, but I somehow managed to win. This was seen as the final test over who should be number one, and that win put me ahead of Dennis Mitchell, four wins to three.

I was not alone in being surprised when an athletics magazine which considers itself to be the bible of the sport ranked Dennis Mitchell first in the 100 metres. They used some strange criteria which didn't take account of the fact that I had won Zurich. They concentrated on the statistic that Dennis had won more grand prix meetings – but that was only because he had entered more than me. It seemed to me as though the magazine could not recognize the fact that a non-American was number one, something which the rest of the world seemed to agree on.

Everyone was out of step but America and it was slightly ironic that Mandy and I should decide to go to the United States for a six-week holiday. It had been a very long season and, for once, I thought I deserved a very long rest.

Chapter 16

A PRICE ON PRIVACY

Mandy and I value the little time we have together. Holidaying in America gave us more privacy than being in Britain. I don't want to give the wrong impression because I have no problem with being a public figure and, if it's not a vain thing to say, one of the best-known sportspeople in the country.

Some personalities find difficulty in coping with their fame. For me, it's not a problem to be liked or appreciated. To be honest with you, I've never found it difficult dealing with the public. I sign autographs because it is the only opportunity people have to come up and say 'Hi!' or 'Thank you for all the pleasure you've given us.' That is very, very rewarding and if anyone in the public eye says they are not affected by that then they are not being honest with themselves.

I enjoy what I'm doing, but it's even better to know that, along the way, I'm also giving pleasure to a lot of people. When you hear them scream out your name and sometimes go hysterical, you know it's all worthwhile. If you can put a smile on one person's face, then that is an achievement as far as I'm concerned. It is greater than all the money in the world. That's what I'm out there for.

Obviously, there are drawbacks. It is not easy to do something routine such as going shopping. I can do it but it takes a lot longer. Once people get over the shock of seeing me in Safeway or Tesco or the corner shop, they seem to think it is something special because a number of people in my position would not be seen in places like that. When I meet people in the shops, their first reaction is usually 'Hey! What are you doing here?' I tell them I have to eat, I'm no different from anybody else. I do exactly as they do, the only difference is I run a little better than most people – and that's it. I've never given it a second thought. I'm very down-to-earth, I've never tried to be anything that I'm not, or say that I am better than anyone else just because I happen to be good at what I do. There are times when, to be honest, I would prefer to be left alone, for example, when I am out with family or friends. I take the opportunity to get away when it comes and the holiday in America was a good example of that.

Anyway, what else can I do? Being recognized is part and parcel of my job. I have to accept that. The fans put money in my pocket, they allow me to be in the position I am in. As with any sportsperson, if the public does not come to watch, then I am nothing.

When Carl Lewis came to Gateshead, he had bodyguards and escorts. I couldn't understand that. I don't want people to keep me away from the public, I feel I am a part of them. When I meet people in the street, they will invariably have seen me on television. I have been in their front room and they seem to accept me immediately as part of their family with a 'Hey! How're you going mate?' – that sort of thing.

I'm not saying I'm happy about it on every occasion. There are times when I want to be off-duty and there are times when I might not be in the mood. But, if someone asks nicely, I will always sign an autograph or whatever. At the end of the day, it is all the public can get from you. It's not too much to ask.

I am particularly conscious of the role sportspeople in particular have to play in the lives of children. I'm like the Pied Piper when it comes to kids. They are so much easier to deal with than adults; they are up front and that is the way I prefer to be. If kids say they like you, then they really do. If they say they don't, then you know all about it. I can cope with that very easily.

I don't like the expression 'role model' but there is no doubt that the kids look up to us, more so than ever now that there is so much leisure time available. We have to give them all the encouragement and support to do well in everything and teach them that it is always possible to achieve if you work at it. It is important, because they are the next generation. It is part of the responsibility we take on.

I think kids are a gift. I have three children outside my relationship with Mandy. I see the eldest quite often but not the other two, because that is the way my relationship with their mother worked out. Kids are not stupid. The last thing I wanted was to have them worry because their mum and dad were squabbling and bickering. There is no point in telling them not to fight when, as parents, we go out and do exactly that. When the kids get older and are capable of fully understanding why their parents are not together, I will tell them everything.

I have always refused to talk in public about my kids because they must be allowed to get on with their own lives. I don't want them to have to live under the constant threat of being

29 Wearing the flag after my win in the 100 metres at the European Championships, Stuttgart, 1986. This was to cause much controversy, but I felt a great sense of pride.
30 Britain won the European Cup for the first time in Gateshead in 1989, and I was chosen to collect the cup for the team – the best thing to happen to me that year!

31 The 100-metres final at the World Championships in Tokyo, 1991, when six people finished in under 10 seconds. Carl Lewis set a new world record of 9.86 seconds. I ran 9.92 seconds and finished fourth!

32 On the rostrum recieving my medal at the Barcelona Olympics, 1992. There was definitely a lump in my throat, but I was determined not to cry.

33 Making it look so easy ... Beating Carl Lewis (*left*) and Jon Drummond (*right*) in Gateshead, 1992 – a win that gave me great pleasure.

34 Biggest, Baddest, Best: a flying win in 9.87 seconds at the 1992 World Championships in Stuttgart.

35 Crowded out but quite alone, I get on with my race preparations, oblivious to everyone around me.

36 A close-run thing: Denis Mitchell and I get the same time in the 100 metres in Lausanne, 1995.

37 Powering through to win against Carl Lewis in the 100 metres in Paris, 1995.

38 Saying it with flowers – and a big smile. I always look this happy when I've won!

39 Being congratulated by Jon Drummond on my win in Paris.
40 After the race . . . providing the quotes.

41 Answering questions from the media in Paris.
42 A chance to be with Mandy as we wait to see how John Regis gets on in the 200 metres in Paris.

43 End of my World Championships, 1995. I finish the 100-metre final in Gothenburg with a torn hamstring. Frankie Fredericks offers some words of comfort.

44 Returning to form. Beating Jon Drummond to the line in Zurich, 1995.

subjected to either unnecessary scrutiny by the press or the thought they can't fend for themselves. I want to let them fight their own battles. I would never encourage them to do athletics. If it is something they choose to do, then they will do it.

There is time to think about things like that when I am away from home, particularly during the warm-weather training sessions in the off-season. In the British winter of 1994–5, I returned to Australia. I wanted to avoid the hassle of Christmas shopping and running around doing the things which would interfere with my training; I thought I might as well fly to the warmth and get some real work in.

I have finally built up a rapport with the Australians, especially in Sydney, after having been there so often. They looked after me very well, Keith Connor and his wife Jane cooking for me; it was almost like being at home. Besides that, training in Australia has gone well for me since 1992. It worked at the beginning of the year I was to win the Olympics; it worked before the World Championships in 1993; it worked in 1994. I could see no reason why 1995 should be any different.

Frankie Fredericks came to Sydney to train and we learned a lot from each other, but it was not the same as having Colin Jackson and Mark McKoy at Narrabeen and practising starts together. The ideal situation would have been for the four of us to work as a group. Having said that, I trained well and learned a lot more about 200-metre running which, of course, is Frankie's event.

I took part in some local races in Australia and found I was in very good shape, running 10.48 seconds in atrocious conditions – wind and rain – in Adelaide, then a windy 10.02 seconds in the final in Perth. I was pleased with that and what made me even more chuffed was that Adrian Patrick, a young athlete from Slough who was working with Ron and me in Australia for the first time, ran two 200-metre races and won them both. It showed that, all round, the training had gone very well.

Now I had the taste for some serious running and I wanted to continue measuring myself against the competition and make final preparations for the season in Europe. I accepted an invitation to run in a 60-metre race in Japan, which seemed reasonable because Japan and Australia are not that far apart. After a bad start, I ran 6.60 seconds to win in a photo finish. It was my first indoor race of the season and some of the other guys I was racing against had recently been competing. Although the time wasn't that great – the track was not a tremendously fast one – winning did me the world of good. I felt ready to go back home, see Mandy again – briefly as it would turn out – and get straight into the start of the 1995 indoor season.

I arrived in Britain on a Thursday, flew to Scotland the next day and raced on the Saturday. I ran 6.56 seconds which, at the time, was the second-fastest indoor 60 metres in the world. Again, my start had not been that good but my pick-up was strong. I knew then that I was bound to run a lot faster in matches which were due to follow in a few days' time although, to be honest, I could not have dreamed of the way things would work out.

I didn't get off to a particularly good start – in every sense – because I was not particularly happy with my time set on a poor track in Vienna. That same night, I left for the next meeting in Liévin, in northern France, not really knowing what to expect. I actually had to fly to Brussels, where my luggage failed to turn up. We had a lot of trouble finding out what had happened after such a short flight. The airline people said they knew where it was but the problem would be retrieving the bags with all my running gear in time for me to compete. My luggage arrived just a few hours before the start.

John Regis had been running well and had previously broken the British 200-metres record with 20.48 seconds. He and Frankie Fredericks were both in Liévin. Everyone wants to run in Liévin because it is a big track, fast with good bends. When you have a track like that, the competition is always going to be good – and John was claiming he was ready to set a new world indoor 200-metre record.

I consider John to be a good athlete – a lot better than he realizes. He is very wide, a powerhouse! He is a 200- and 400-metre runner and yet he runs the 100 and 200 metres. I think he needs to believe in himself a lot more. If he has a bad race, it bothers him – which shouldn't be necessary most of the time.

When we had a problem with the BAF in 1995, it was the first time we saw the full depth of John's character as he stood up for what he believed in. A lot of people think that John and I don't get on but I've got to know him a lot better over the past few years and the more I've got to know him, the more I like him. He's a very strong character, not afraid to say what he thinks. He's good company, a good laugh. You could be with him all day and never have a dull moment. At Liévin, he was on very good form.

I raced in the 60 metres, winning in a European record of 6.47 seconds. I was trying to get into the 200-metre race but it was difficult at first because so many potential runners were present. Eventually, on the day, I was told I could run.

John had the choice of lanes because he was the fastest. He picked lane four. Frankie had lane five, so they gave me lane six. Normally I would favour lane six in any case because it is on the outside, which suits my long legs; it gives me a little more room to get going.

John was watching Frankie, Frankie was watching John – and I sailed round the outside. John said he thought I was going to fade after 150 metres, but I just kept going. I was putting into practice the various bits of technique I had learned while training with Frankie. I won – and broke the world record!

The first feeling was that I had beaten John and Frankie, the number one and the number two. Then, when I saw the time – 20.25 – I went wild. I was ecstatic. I really hadn't expected this, particularly breaking a world record. I was so happy and, at the same time, I was exhausted. It meant all the hard work in Australia had paid off and I had made history into the bargain. I was the first British sprinter in thirty-five years – since Peter Radford, in fact – to hold the world record, so I was pretty happy with that.

I felt, to be honest, that I could go much quicker. I had been cautious because I didn't want to run as hard as normal and then fade. It was a brilliant feeling. But that was about to change.

A few days later, I took part in an invitation match in Birmingham. I was beaten by Darren Braithwaite, the first British runner to beat me over 60 metres for God knows how long. He ran really well and it was a class field. Now and again, you have to get beaten. Sometimes you can become complacent and begin to believe that you are invincible. A defeat provides the necessary kick up the butt.

The next meeting was in Stockholm and all I could think about was beating Darren, just to square things up and put it behind me. I won my heats, Darren won his. As soon as I had overtaken Darren in the final, I thought I had done enough. Then the Canadian, Donovan Bailey, pipped me on the line. It was my fault. I can hardly claim it was inexperience. Ron had always said that if you run the 100 metres, you run 101 metres; if it is a 60-metre race, you run 61 metres. In Stockholm, I ran 58 metres and Donovan came through and beat me.

I returned home to decide what I needed to do next. I felt I was running really tight, I was not relaxed enough. My technique had gone out of the window because, during this time, I had not been training. I was withdrawing performance from the bank but I was not putting anything back in. Also, I was getting tired because I had not given myself a chance to rest properly ever since returning from Australia. I knew I had work to do.

At the time, it was announced that I would run in the World Indoor Championships. Before that, there would be one more meeting at Sindelfingen in Germany. It seemed the best thing would be to do some training, teach my body how to run again, regain technique and confidence, and go to Germany and give it a shot. I ran 6.49 seconds; a time which, so far that year, had only been beaten by me. It seemed pretty good.

Even so, I felt I was just too tired to run three more races in the World Indoor Championships. I told the BAF that I wasn't going to go and explained why. They said they were going to announce a team that day, but they would give me until the end of the week. John Regis had been injured in Stockholm and they were giving him until the Friday to get ready. They said they would do the same for me; perhaps I would feel rested by then.

When I finally decided I wasn't going to go, I informed the federation again. They said they would pick Solomon Wariso instead and made the announcement. Then all hell broke loose in the newspapers. The gist of it was that I shouldn't have pulled out. Not all of them took that line but some said I was being selfish again and thinking only about myself. 'Was this the way for a British captain to act?'

I have given over ten years of my life to British athletics. I have competed in conditions when other athletes refused to run for their country; I have made personal sacrifices which I would not expect the press to know about. But, if they were going to criticize, then they should at least have given a balanced view and checked their facts.

Then the IAAF weighed in. Christopher Winner, who was the spokesman for the IAAF, said I had acted in a manner unbecoming of a champion. The Americans – Michael Johnson, Leroy Burrell and others – had not turned up. That seemed to be acceptable. Perhaps Winner was speaking not for the Federation, but for himself.

Dr Primo Nebiolo, President of the IAAF, said he was going to ask me to run. By that stage, I had already decided that I would go to Barcelona and spectate; it would make a change to be able to actually sit down and watch athletics rather than take part. It is something I never get the chance to do. For once, I was going to think of myself and not run.

I couldn't understand what all the fuss was about, much of it caused by unconsidered observations to the media. I paid my own way but there were suggestions that the IAAF had paid for my room in one of the best hotels in Barcelona. The fact was that Sue Barrett and I also had to have meetings with various promoters about my outdoor season; that was one of the reasons why I decided to go to Spain.

I had thought about going back to Australia to continue with my training but according to Colin, who had recently been in Sydney, the weather was not ideal. There was the option of the British training camp at Tallahassee but I felt that would be overcrowded since it was now April and everyone would be busy preparing for the season.

I had just bought a house in Tampa and I decided to go to

Florida instead. It made a lot of sense because, apart from the investment, living in my own house would save on hotel bills. There is a track I can use and, of course, the weather is usually perfect. I was joined by Ron, Colin, Adrian, Mark McKoy and Marcia Richardson, another young sprinter who works with Ron and me. While we were there, Bruny Surin, the world indoor and Canadian 100-metre champion, joined in. It made a very good group.

I have to admit I was giving thought to retiring. The Barcelona business, coming after the fuss which had been kicked up over the Commonwealth Games the previous year, made me wonder why I needed the aggravation. I am not contracted to anyone; I run when I want to run.

Then, without warning, I began to wonder if I would be able to run at all. I had been training really well but, one morning in Tampa, I woke up to find that the bone in the toe next to the big one on my left foot was so sore I could not walk, jog or do anything.

It was the same problem I had before – but with the other foot. I had been in really good shape and this just got me down. There is no obvious remedy for it. I had to miss two weeks' training and I was becoming upset because, if someone had asked me if I thought I had been close to the world record, I would have said yes. I could tell training had been going well when Bruny went to his first race and ran a windy 9.92. I thought 'Good grief' because I had been beating Bruny and that news depressed me. But there was nothing I could do about it.

Mandy had returned to England but the other athletes were still in Tampa. I couldn't do much so I resorted to weights, putting on extra muscle. I went home for a short while and returned to Florida for about ten days with my physio, Dominic Hickey. He worked on my foot every day even though, ideally,

I should have rested. But when you have problems like that, what else can you do? I had made my commitments and I had to keep on working even though I couldn't train properly. I had to overdose on painkillers in order to keep going. I wanted to race.

I went to St Denis in France, which happened to be the next race on the calendar, and decided I would start by running the 200 metres because that would help build up my strength. I lost to Frankie Fredericks but, considering I had an injury, I felt well within myself. I was running faster times than previously and it was inevitable I was going to get even quicker because this was not my usual event. But the headlines were all about Christie losing. My club asked me to run at Crystal Palace and I accepted. I won the 100 metres and lost the 200. There was no mention of the 100 at all; the stories seemed to be about me being beaten in the 200.

I think I ran five races and I lost four of them. In Rome, I finished third in the 200 metres with 20.53 seconds. That was a reasonable time for me and it showed that training had indeed been going quite well. Some of the Americans I had been competing against were bound to have been a lot sharper because they had been getting ready for the American Championships. I wasn't supposed to be running fast in June because if I had been, I knew it would be almost impossible to keep my momentum up until the World Championships in August. I may have been criticized for losing, but I knew what I was doing.

Meanwhile, I kept hearing that Jimmy Greaves had made some comment on a television programme which had been taken to suggest that I was taking drugs. Apparently Liz McColgan had said there was no out-of-season testing. That was rubbish because we had been tested in Tampa, which was definitely out of season! When athletes start off the season beating people and then lose by the time the championships come along, the implication is often that these later winners must be taking drugs. It is such a stupid thing to say. It only means some people peak and get it just right. That's what Ron and I always try to do.

Jimmy Greaves, I am told, had asked why it was that someone not running very well in their early twenties had all of a sudden started to run better than before in their early thirties. The inference from his remarks was that there was something fishy going on.

I went on the programme *Sport in Question* with Chris Eubank and the journalist, Patrick Collins, because I saw it as a chance to put the record straight. My first impression was that they were out to nail Chris Eubank, because they began talking about his tax problem. In my opinion, that had nothing to do with anybody but Chris Eubank. It was a personal matter which he would have to sort out. And the questions went on from there.

I was to become so frustrated that I wanted to bang somebody's head. The public knows that I am trying to run as fast and as well as I can. The media seem only to want to pull down, to discredit, any successful British person, any successful sportsperson. Each time we argued this on the programme, the journalist would argue that it was some other tabloid, some other headline writer who was doing this.

During the course of the debate, I said, 'Let's see what happens in the papers when I retire and don't go to the 1996 Olympics'.

I was really angry with the way the programme was going, and with Jimmy Greaves' interventions, but I counted to ten to compose myself. I was very happy with the audience's reaction to my stand.

Ian St John then asked me again about my comment on retiring. It was later suggested that I had boxed myself in, but that was not the case – what I had said was exactly how I felt. We talked about it during a programme break and I said that when you stop enjoying what you are doing, then it is time to get out. In athletics it is one man against everybody else, unlike football, where there are ten other guys who can help you out.

You need to have a clear mind in athletics. You need to enjoy what you are doing and you need to be allowed to take whatever chances you can, to capitalize on every little moment. A little slip, you blink, it's over. What bothers me is that very often people who voice opinions about athletics know absolutely nothing about the sport. I had tried to make the point on the programme that the media should be part of an overall British team, should be supportive and proud of British athletes who are out there flying the flag for Britain. Other countries' media support their athletes but the British media do not seem to agree with this.

I was happy enough with what I had said on television that night. I had been thinking about retiring for a while, to be honest. I had sat down some time before the programme and looked at my sister's baby. He was two years old and beginning to be really naughty; changing every day. It occurred to me that I had missed out on all that. There are so many things that have happened in my family that I feel I have missed out on because I have been so caught up in my own little world. I have been doing all this and that, much of it for my country, when I have not been able to be a part of the lives of my immediate family. Retirement had to come one day.

When I was up and coming, I said that all I wanted to do was to be the best in the world for one year; that would satisfy me. I have been the best for three years, I have achieved everything beyond my wildest dreams. I didn't feel I had anything to prove to anybody. Someone will always come along who is faster than I am, someone will come along one day and beat me. But that will not change the fact that I have been the best.

That was the thinking behind what I said on *Sport in Question*. I didn't see anything wrong with that but, the next day, journalists came to my house and reporters turned up at the track where I was training. As far as I was concerned, if I didn't want to go to the Olympics then I wouldn't go. It seemed pretty straightforward to me but, by now, the whole issue was out of control. It is hard to be the centre of that sort of media circus when you're trying to train, to get your head round your next race. Unless you have been in the middle of a bunch of journalists and cameramen, it is hard to understand how oppressive it is.

Along with all of this, we were also having a problem with the BAF. In effect, the federation wanted me to take a pay cut. They had given other athletes pay rises, but they forgot that athletes talk among themselves. They had offered Colin a rise over what he had earned in 1994. Why then should I take a cut? It was a matter of principle and I refused.

Ian Stewart had been negotiating on behalf of the BAF with Sue about appearances in Britain. Certain figures appeared in the press and these details had to have come from the BAF. The line was that I had been asking for too much money when there was no cash available because they had been using what they had for the benefit of athletics.

My view on this was that I recalled so-called development races, which are supposed to help up-and-coming athletes, and those who were invited to take part were told they had to pay their own way. There was a girl in our group, a mother of two kids, and she had been invited by the BAF to run in a race in

Gateshead. But they told her she had to pay her own fare and accommodation. Where did they expect her to get the money from? This was supposed to be a development event. And besides, when they ran a development race at Crystal Palace an hour before the main programme was due to commence, there were no spectators.

Then the BAF decided that John Regis had been overpaid during the previous two years and they were going to make a cutback. Here was the guy who had run the fastest 200-metre time in the world, the Commonwealth silver medallist. The view was that John was not showing form. But John's contract had been based on the form being shown at the time: in fact the contracts for all the athletes had been signed before the season had started. So why the attempts to renegotiate with John?

We pointed out that if the people at the BAF were saying they were saving money in order to give it to the up-and-coming athletes in the form of training grants or whatever, then we would accept that. There would not be a problem. But they weren't doing that. So we refused to run.

The argument was put forward that there was not enough money coming into the sport from sponsorship. My view was they had four or five people handling the job that Any Norman had done on his own, all drawing salaries. If there isn't enough money in the sport then surely, as well as asking the athletes, the BAF itself should be making savings. And I believe administrative costs and salaries should be cut before those of athletes.

In another instance, the BAF sent two people to Sacramento to sign the top Americans – and some who were not so good. And yet we had people in Britain who were running just as well but couldn't get a lane. Why give the money abroad when the whole idea was supposed to be about developing the athletes in our own country? It is the top athletes who put backsides on seats. It is the big events that enable us all to develop the younger athletes.

I have paid for athletes' medical treatment with my own money. I have been funding warm-weather training and various other activities when the federation hasn't been doing so. I may have been earning the money, but I have been putting it back into the sport. I took two young athletes to Australia for warm-weather training. I have sent other athletes to Germany for medical treatment because the federation refused to pay for them. The BAF will give you £100 for physiotherapy, but once an athlete called me because she needed a scan and she couldn't afford it. This was one of our top athletes, running for Britain. I promised I would find someone and then paid out of my own pocket. This is the sort of thing the federation is supposed to be doing for our athletes.

I wouldn't normally advertise the fact that I help in this way but it is difficult not to feel frustrated when some of the sports writers claimed I was turning my back on Britain when I didn't run at home.

The problems with the BAF meant, for example, that we missed the Gateshead meet. In the past, athletes have been accused of not being able to stick together but this was the first time that we had been united. None of us would run without the other. If John Regis wasn't going to run, then I wasn't going to run. If Colin wasn't going to run, John wasn't going to run, and vice versa. It did not start as a personal issue but some people in the federation began to take it that way.

We had bills to pay. We had commitments. We had to get ready for the championships, so we signed a deal to run in Paris, where I won the 100 metres. We competed in a few more events and, not long after, there was the meet at Crystal Palace, a so-called Grand Prix One event which would require a good entry if the meeting was to keep its status. By now the BAF was starting to panic because a lot of agents, coaches and athletes were backing us.

The BAF wanted me to run, but I had already competed in the 100 and 200 metres in Lausanne. There was no way I was going to run, because I was tired. A number of people were saying that they thought I should run because it was not good for British athletics if I didn't. As far as I was concerned, the BAF should have realized that, long before engaging in a very strange negotiation. It was as if someone offered, say, £1 to do a job and you responded by saying it was worth £2. It is then up to the other party to say whether or not they can afford £2. The BAF responded by doing the equivalent of reducing the original offer to 50p! That's no way to do business. It seemed like they were trying their luck.

Then the BAF found £12,000 – and offered all of it to Colin, presumably in the hope that he would accept it. The rest of us would have got nothing. For the first time we stuck together, although everything in the newspapers simply referred to Christie, Christie, Christie. I was prepared for that.

We agreed with the BAF to go to Crystal Palace and wave to the crowd, mingle and visit the hospitality centres. My memories of Crystal Palace go back a long way but at the end of the day a venue is a venue. It's the crowd that makes it. We made our appearance but the meeting seemed to be lacking a bit of excitement. Apart from Colin, John and me, Sally Gunnell was also on the sidelines, though in her case through injury. And still the written debate continued. The strange thing is that I have never met anyone who actually agrees with what is written in the papers. For instance, I think a lot of the ethnic minorities buy tabloids and yet, if you ask them, they will say the tabloids are racist! I can't understand that because if they did not buy such papers they would not survive. The readers should have control, not the editors.

But as far as I was concerned, during that period in the summer of 1995, the media were completely out of control.

Chapter 17

MUM

My mother was sixty-six. She had been ill for some time but nobody expected her to go.

The Bible says three score years and ten but some people die young, others seem to live on borrowed time. I think it would have been much worse for my mum if she had had to bury one of us. That would have been far more difficult for her to cope with than the difficulties we had in coming to terms with her death in June 1995.

The way I look at it now is that she has gone to a place where she doesn't have to worry about pain or being in hospital. That helps me to get over it. We cried. But how much can you cry? It is very, very sad and that is all there is to it.

My dad and I had been to visit her in hospital on the Monday. She was talking to the specialist about how much she was improving and we were trying to find out if anything more could be done for her. She was diabetic, and then she had suffered a stroke. There was not a lot more they could do but she seemed to be getting better.

I spoke to my dad the following morning and he said he thought she was going to go. He was so sure because he had seen the signs and symptoms and he said that she wouldn't make it. But you kid yourself. You say, 'of course she will be all right'.

I decided that I didn't want to wait around for my mum to die. I needed to occupy my mind, so I went to Nuremberg to compete. I know that's what she would have wanted me to do. Mum always said, 'Go out and run. That's what you want to do.' I knew that made her happy, even though originally she had not been that keen on me becoming an athlete. Black people tended to think that sport only came about when you had nothing better to do. It seemed to me when I was young that boxing was the only sport in which a black man was 'allowed' to take part.

I went to Germany, spoke to my dad, and he said he would ring me back later if anything happened. We were having breakfast the following morning when dad rang. I can't remember exactly what he said, it was like a dream. He said something about coming home. I told him not to tell me any more. I knew what had happened because I had that feeling; something strange, something you automatically know.

I was with Colin, John and a few others. We had been sitting around having a laugh but, as soon as they saw my face, they knew instantly. Nobody knew what to say. I kept asking them to talk to me. John said he had a cold and Colin said he had tonsillitis. I didn't want to break down in front of them because it wouldn't have been fair. I think it had affected them enough as it was. I went home, feeling totally numb.

The family did everything together, which was a good thing because everybody wanted to play a part. It was our last chance to pay our respects and we just wanted to make everything the best. As it happened, my sister and aunt were coming over from America in any case, but they didn't know my mother had gone. Now it was up to me to tell Lucia. She was my older sister and trying to break the news to her was really strange.

I felt that I was the best person to do it because Lucia and I are very close. My aunt kept saying, 'That's life' and I wondered why she was telling me. Then I realized that, somehow, she knew. I was talking to my sister on the journey from the airport and she was saying she wanted to be in the house in Acton, which is close to the hospital, so that she could go and see mum. I asked her, if push came to shove and the worst happened, would she be able to cope? She said she would cry, but she would be able to handle it. I asked how she thought auntie would cope with it and she said she would wail, scream the place down and go into hysterics but she would be able to calm her down because she would cry, but generally be a lot calmer.

So I said, 'Okay, you would be able to cope. Give me your hand.' She held my hand and I told her mum was dead. She went into hysterics. I said, 'I thought you told me you could cope. Here you are having hysterics on me.'

I was trying to play the man. I felt I had to be strong for everybody else which is good in one sense but, in another, it wasn't, because it meant I had to keep everything bottled up inside. I told my sister she would have to be quiet or else she would make me cry. If everyone broke down at once, we would have a problem; there would be no one to hold anyone else up. She calmed down.

I told my aunt and she said that she already knew. She was crying and she said she just had a feeling. My little nephew in America had said to my aunt before she left, 'Tell me the truth.

230

Is grandma dead?' He didn't know anything about it – but he just had this feeling.

I went to get my dad and it was rough because, the day before, I was supposed to go to the morgue to see my mum but for some reason the newspapers found out she had died and that I would be at the hospital. We didn't want any commotion because, at times like that, anything could have happened. I rang the hospital and they told me that one or two people were still hanging around but the rest of the reporters had gone. I was at my parents' house when the phone rang. Dad picked it up and then slammed the receiver down. That was very unlike my dad. I asked what had happened. He said that a reporter had asked if he could take a picture of the body.

What can you say? What can you think? I asked if he had got a name, but he hadn't given himself time to ask. It was too much to take in.

Eventually, we all went down to see my mum. My dad was pretty strong about it; he was bearing up better than we were. The whole family was there and we decided to get together and organize things. Everyone wanted to do something but, at the end of the day, my dad's well-being was more important than anything else. We made him play a major role. We put our ideas togther but he said how he wanted mum to look and what he wanted her to wear. It had to be the way he wanted it. They had been married for thirty-five years.

I was trying to imagine how he must have felt, but I couldn't. I was thinking that if you had a long-term partner and you had just broken up, that would be a terrible emptiness. But there would always be the hope that you could get back together. Dad would not have that consolation. My mum had been his first girlfriend. They were childhood sweethearts.

It made me realize that you will always wish you had spent

one more day, said one more thing. There will always be an emptiness and I don't think there can be anything worse. Now there is no one to tell secrets to.

Chapter 18

WATER, WATER, EVERYWHERE

Immediately after the funeral, I didn't know if I would want to compete. I didn't know what state of mind I was going to be in. Emotion hits everyone in a different way but I knew I was going to be low. However, I did not want to sit down and become depressed; it was tough enough as it was.

The European Cup Final was in Lille immediately afterwards. I spoke to Malcolm Arnold and he said Darren Braithwaite could cover for me if necessary. He said it would not be a problem, I could leave it until the very last minute to see how I felt.

The funeral was on a Friday and the meeting was due to be held on the Saturday and Sunday. Late Friday night, I felt that I needed to get away and do something. I got up really early on Saturday and caught the Eurostar from Waterloo. John Brown, the sports administration officer for the BAF, is a really great guy. He met me at Lille and, to be honest, I was glad I went. I could sense the excitement in what was a very young team. The athletes were saying they were glad I was there; it was giving their confidence a lift and that alone made the trip more than worthwhile.

On the morning of the competition, I was knackered, but it was more emotional than physical. On the first day, I won the 100 metres; on the second day I won the 200 — both in record times. It wasn't a release of emotion as such because I don't believe in mixing home life with work. The two are quite separate and I was running, doing my job.

I joined Colin and Ron in Lanzarote for a week's training. It was a case of getting down to business but Colin and I spent some time reminiscing. We were saying how there doesn't appear to be as much fun in athletics — or any other sport — any more. It didn't take us long to remember some of the more outrageous incidents we had been involved in.

The girls are just as bad as the men when it comes to playing tricks but the one we both remembered occurred in Seoul. Colin and I were rooming next door to Sally Gunnell and Kim Hagger. We managed to get a key and sneak into their room, where we hid and waited for the girls to return. We let them sit and talk for a while before suddenly jumping out. They *screamed*! It was around midnight and Joan Allison, the team manager, ran out of her room dressed only in a little negligee, shouting 'What's up! What's up!' Then she saw me and Colin — and *she* screamed!

The best year was probably 1989 when there were no major championships. It was just one grand prix after another. We used to play basketball, volleyball, badminton — anything, really. Board games were very popular too. But the trouble was, people took them incredibly seriously and changed the rules as they went along. Everyone wanted to *win*. Water fights played a major part. The only people who didn't get wet were Colin, me and Daley Thompson. Daley would look at you and say, very quietly, 'Don't even think about it . . .'

The girls were outrageous. They would use baby lotion and washing-up liquid so that you would skid all over the place. Myrtle Augee, a shot-putter, would be at the forefront and you didn't argue with her. Simmone Jacobs was the smallest – but she was the ringleader. She would set everyone up, tease you and lure you into trouble. The problem was, there was no way the boys could tease the girls.

Dalton Grant tried that when we were in Split in 1990. But he didn't reckon with Myrtle. She got togther with Sharon Gibson, the javelin thrower, Sharon Andrews and a few others. They got Dalton in a room, locked the door and held him down. They pulled down his pants, and wrote on his bum and drew little faces with lipstick. All he said was, 'Please don't tell anybody!' As you can see, the story got out . . .

The girls were across the corridor from each other. Colin and I had to pass by each time we went to our room, which was at the end of the corridor. You had to *run*. One day, I had just been to the physio and I only had my underpants on. I was passing through and Simmone came from nowhere, grabbed me and started shouting 'Girls! Girls! Girls!'. She was holding the waist of my underpants and I was running like mad. She wouldn't let go! She eventually had to give up when we reached a sharp corner!

It was in Split that they threw me into the water jump at the end of the event. I was *soaked*. I went back to the room to take a shower. As I started to wash, the water turned pitch black. It was so bad that I immediately accused Colin of giving me trick soap – but it was the water. It had looked okay in the water jump but, in actual fact it was absolutely filthy.

The water fights would become so serious that we would dress up in wet suits and chase each other down the corridors.

Our reputation was such that it backfired on Colin on one occasion. I had pushed him into the entry to one of the girls' rooms and locked the outside door. The girls, thinking he was coming to soak them, had immediately locked the inner door. There was hardly any room in between – and Colin was stuck there all night. He had to sleep, all scrunched up, on a floor that was wet from a previous water fight. Fortunately, he had finished competing. I went down to the room in the morning, unlocked the door – and there he was! I didn't realize the girls had refused to let him in.

We once kidnapped Tessa Sanderson in Lanzarote, filled the bath with cold water and chucked her in. But she got her own back one evening when Colin and I decided to invite the girls to dinner. There were three of them – Di, the physio, Lesley-Ann Skeete and Tessa. Colin went up to their room to borrow some plates. When he got to the bottom of the stairs, somebody said something. Colin looked up. The girls had a big dustbin liner – to this day, I don't know how they managed to lift it – full of water. I saw it all. Colin was too shocked to move. He held on to the plates because the water came down with such a force. Then they threw the bag at him. And he didn't drop a single plate.

Colin and I agreed that we don't seem to have fun like that any more. There is too much pressure and not enough play. One of the last free-for-alls I can remember was at the Commonwealth Games in Edinburgh. We began by throwing bread rolls and eggs at the Australians. Then they started to *boil* eggs and throw them, along with tins of drink; anything that came to hand, really.

There was no chance of that happening when we went to Paris for a one-day meeting in July 1995. As I was explaining earlier, the British meetings should have been on the schedule but we decided we could not sit around and wait for the BAF. We just had to make other arrangements.

Paris was a bit of a worry because it would be my first proper race as such in the new season, in that it would be the first time I would meet the Americans. There were a lot of big names and I knew the Americans, because they had been competing more often, would be a little bit sharper, despite my training having gone well. I was nervous about it. But I won. It was very satisfying because I am not keen on one-off races. If you have a problem, that's it; whereas, if you make a mistake during a heat in the championships, there is always the opportunity to put it right. The next meeting in Lausanne would be a case in point.

I just fell asleep in the blocks. One of the guys on the outside, Mike Marsh, had a false start. You can tell. He moved and you automatically expect him to be called back. But they let it go this time. Everyone moved before I did but I still ran a season's best (10.03 seconds) and finished fourth. I was happy, considering the way it had gone. I had been way down and yet I had managed to come through some pretty good people.

When you don't run well and you don't know what's wrong, that's when you've got problems. When you don't win and you know what you've done wrong, especially something which you can easily rectify, that is not a problem. I had also taken part in the 200 metres – more or less to see how it would go – and I had finished third behind Michael Johnson and Frankie Fredricks. My times were good and I was pretty pleased with that too, all things considered.

I was confident going into the AAA Championships but events

in Birmingham were to take a different turn which seemed to twist the knife even further in my preparations for the World Championships in Gothenburg.

I had been having fun with Darren Campbell. He kept saying he was going to beat me in the heats. I said that was fine by me because I was going to take my time and concentrate on qualifying.

I was running comfortably within myself when, about half-way through the 100 metres, I began to have trouble with my left knee. Each time I picked up my knee, it hurt like hell. I eased up and people went past me. There was no alternative because, if I had continued at the same pace, I would not have made it to Gothenburg. I had already qualified for the World Championships with a time established in an earlier event but that would have been of no use if I had to pull out of Gothenburg because of injury. Dominic, my physio, started work on my leg straight away.

I needed another run because I needed to make sure the knee was fine; I was due to run in Padua the following day and I didn't want to go to Italy without knowing more about my condition.

Malcolm Arnold asked the officials if I could run and they said it was impossible. I gave it one last shot by putting my case to the track referee, Maureen Smith. I understood that I couldn't run in the semi-finals because that would preclude someone who had beaten me in the previous round. But Maureen said they would try and put me in the final as a guest runner. I was happy with that.

They have ten or twelve lanes on the home straight at the Alexander Stadium and there were only eight runners in the final. Therefore, I could have lane nine which would mean that everyone entitled to run in the final would not be affected.

Then Michael Rosswess dropped out, so I was moved to lane eight. The only stipulation was that if I won the race, I would not be the AAA champion. I said that was fine; I just wanted to run.

I won the race – and there was a big fuss about it. The organizers had been helping me prepare for the World Championships but one journalist in particular was hellbent on stirring things up. He had obtained an athlete's pass from somewhere and got himself into the warm-up area where the press are not allowed. He was interviewing young athletes and trying to persuade them that they should complain, even though these guys had nothing to do with the 100 metres.

The business of me running in the final was being referred to as a fiasco. I was talking about it some time later with a few American athletes and they couldn't see the problem. As long as you don't jeopardize another runner's chances, then it seemed to make sense to let me run.

It was argued in the press that I had been given special treatment. I don't deny that. I would like to think that any medal prospect for a major championship would be helped in the same way at an event in their home country. When Donovan Bailey ran a 9.91 seconds in Canada, there were silly headlines such as, 'You're Don For, Linford'. Presumably somebody was pretty pleased with that, but it was hardly encouraging for an athlete preparing to represent Britain in the World Championships.

The British press didn't say much when we went to Oslo and Donovan failed to make the final. The British reporters stood in the background at the press conference and let the foreign journalists ask the questions. One writer, who didn't even come to the press conference, made excuses in his newspaper for Donovan by saying he had travelled a long way and was therefore not on the pace. That was probably true, but you have to wonder where the newspaper's priorities lie.

Each instance I have quoted is only a small example in isolation but, collectively, and over a period of time, these things wear me down. But not enough to prevent me from being the fastest in the heats and first in the final.

Oslo is famous for its strawberries, a fact we know well because of a traditional strawberry party each year. The strawberries are better than those you find at Wimbledon; they are so big and sweet I reckon they must put sugar on the roots. The strawberry party is a form of press conference, but an informal one with everyone wandering around, eating and chatting. I talked to a lot of journalists and did pieces with writers from *Sports Illustrated* and other magazines and publications from abroad; I don't seem to have any problems with them at all.

Back in Sheffield, I set the fastest ever time – 14.74, wind assisted – in the 150 metres, an event which made a pleasant change as well as providing good training for both the 100 and the 200 metres, which I planned to run in Gothenburg.

In the background, however, politics played their usual part although I did appreciate it when Ian Stewart, of the BAF, apologised to Sue and me. Talking about the dispute between 'Nuff' Respect and the BAF over our participation in the British meets, Ian said he had discovered that the leaks about details of the negotiations had been coming from somewhere within the BAF office.

Meanwhile, I knew that there was every likelihood that I would be dope tested again. Sure enough, I was selected, although they would not allow me to go straight away. They had one toilet with about ten athletes waiting. It was completely inadequate but I eventually took the test with no further problems.

The subject of testing came up when I returned to the hotel to be interviewed by the *World in Action* programme. They said they were looking at testing in competition and there was something about the IAAF and the Sports Council not having my home address, which meant they couldn't spring an unexpected test on me. I said they had tested me three times at random and they had the number of my mobile phone, which I always carry with me.

The suggestion was that I wasn't available for testing. At the time, I had been tested seventeen times over a considerable period. At least three of them were with no notice and one of them was in the middle of a training session in Tampa. They were able to find me there without any difficulty. So long as they have a contact number – not even an address – there is no problem. I have always made sure that is the case, but the television programme didn't seem to want to know about that.

To be honest with you, I could have been forgiven for forgetting where I lived because, the day after Sheffield, I went to Monte Carlo for final preparations for the World Championships. I didn't take part in the meeting there on the night I arrived but went along to the gala, held immediately afterwards. It was an amazing show. It would also be the last chance I would get to relax before Gothenburg, just over a week later. Trouble was to strike during the first day of training.

I set out to do six 100-metre runs. On the fourth run, I felt a strain in my hamstring. I stopped running and started panicking. Time was short. My physio was with me and we tried massages; everything we could. The following day, I flew to Munich to see Dr Muller-Wohlfhart, who I thought would be the best person to deal with this. I was there for a couple of days but, apart from a little jogging, I couldn't train properly.

I returned to Monaco on the Saturday and began training,

doing more and more each day but nowhere near my normal level of preparation. I should have been doing endless block starts and so on but there was no way I could even think about that. I was simply trying to see if I could run. Period. I thought I could – but it would be a case of keeping my fingers crossed.

I had one night at home before flying to Sweden and settling into the athletes' village. It was like all other villages; no air conditioning, beds that were too small, seven guys sharing two bathrooms. But this was worse than usual because there was a fifteen-minute walk down the street from the dormitory to the dining hall, an arrangement which left athletes open to the press and the public. It was the same deal when getting from the village to the track. This is not the kind of thing you need when preparing for a world championship.

For example, once you had finished competing and needed to get your clothes, it was necessary to climb stairs, pass the TV and media people and walk down another flight of stairs. It was a hopeless arrangement, particularly for the runners at the end of the marathon. They were exhausted. Most of them could barely walk and yet they had to do this. Some even had to walk backwards down the stairs because they were hurting so much. Apart from the obvious inconvenience, this also represented a security risk. I think they felt that nothing could happen in Sweden. They thought that about Munich in 1972.

During the pre-event press conference someone asked, inevitably perhaps, about my son, Merric, having recently become a father. Judging by the sensational coverage given to this in the papers during the previous week, I must have been the only thirty-five-year-old grandfather in the world. I said that I didn't think private life had anything to do with athletics, certainly not before a championship – and that's why I was in Gothenburg. I was very happy to talk about that. I was very confident that, barring injury, I would run really well.

During the two heats, I was surprised how easy things felt despite the fact that I had not trained properly for over a week. I honestly felt that I was going to win.

The semi-finals were the next day, Sunday. Looking back, I probably had too many races in too short a space of time because my semi-final took its toll. I was vying for the lead, just beginning to surge through and make my move, when I felt a strain in my hamstring. It was like cramp, in that the muscle went into a ball. I knew immediately that I had to relax; if I had continued to push, I would have ripped my hamstring.

I finished fourth and just qualified for the final in three hours' time. I did everything I could; massages, gentle running, more massages. All I wanted to do was run – even if it meant falling over at fifty metres. I wanted to be out there because I believe you have to go down fighting.

Deep down, though, I knew that I wasn't going to finish. I thought the hamstring would go halfway through the final. But, if they wanted my title, I was not prepared to hand it over, just like that. I couldn't sit back and take the easy option of withdrawing.

I was in lane one. I honestly can't remember the last time I ran in lane one! But I knew I would have to make the maximum out of everything from the word go. I could no longer rely on my surge at half distance. I had one of my best starts in a long time and I was hanging in there. But I could feel the hamstring all the way. I made it to the finish; sixth place in 10.12 seconds – on one leg! It left me wondering what I could have done had I been really fit.

As soon as I crossed the line, I dropped to the floor and the medical guys were very quick to apply ice to my hamstring. As

I lay there, all I could think initially was, 'My God, that hurts!' The hamstring was throbbing; it was incredibly painful.

Then, all sorts of things came into my head. I had let down a lot of people. I had been expected to go out there and run really well, to boost the confidence of the team. I hadn't done that. I felt miserable.

In one respect, it had been a stupid thing to do because I had made my injury a little bit worse. But, saying that, I had taken part. The alternative had been to miss out and then go to Zurich and compete ten days later. Then I would have looked back at Donovan Bailey's winning time and thought, '9.97 seconds. Damn! Maybe if I had been there, maybe my leg wouldn't have gone.' I *had* run. Okay, I lost. But I could do no more.

On the Monday, I still felt miserable, but I tried not to think about it. The 1995 100-metre World Championship was history. There was nothing I could do. Any athlete, any sportsperson, cannot look back. You may learn from experience but you must always look forward. I began to focus on getting fit again, ready for the next race.

An ultrasound scan at a hospital in Gothenburg found a slight tear in the outer tendon. It was small, but with a bit of bleeding. I had some treatment and, on the Tuesday, flew to a specialist organized by the promoters of the Weltklasse in Zurich. My own specialist, Dr Muller-Wohlfhart, was away at the time. The only certainty was that I would not rush this recovery.

Before I left Sweden, in an interview with Brendan Foster, the question of the 1996 Olympics came up again. But I am not tempted at all. My preparations for the World Championships had been far from ideal. Apart from the family bereavement, the media focus had done nothing to help. There is no chance of a reconsideration at the moment because I don't want to go through all of that again. I wanted to forget the pressure and get on with my life. I still wanted to compete but Gothenburg was my last championship. It was a shame that I had not been able to concentrate on it fully.

They have some very good people at the Institute of Sport in Zurich and they gave me the best treatment they could. The doctor was surprised at how well the injury responded. The press assumed that I had gone to Munich and, when they discovered that I had not seen Muller-Wohlfhart, one or two people tracked me down to Zurich. I did my best to avoid them because I wanted to concentrate fully on getting fit again and, in any case, there was nothing to say at that point.

On the way back to Gothenburg, a reporter from Reuters stopped me at Zurich airport and asked if we could talk. I said, no, I had no wish to say anything.

At Passport Control there was a photographer from Reuters. I told him we didn't want any pictures taken but he kept trying. I had my x-rays in my hand and I put them up to my face so that he couldn't take pictures. We passed through and went to the lounge.

When the flight was called, we had gone through the last security check before boarding the plane – and suddenly, there was a click of a camera. It was the same Reuters photographer. I was really surprised to see him there because, as far as I was concerned, he should have been regarded as a security risk.

I said to him, 'Didn't I ask you not to take my picture? Why can't you respect that?' I decided to try and take the camera off him, expose the film and hand the camera back. I got hold of the camera and he began to run. It was so funny because he was a very big guy!

The security guard told the photographer to go, and he ran

off up the stairs. I told the ground staff collecting boarding passes that I thought, in view of terrorist attacks and so on, it was wrong that a photographer should be wandering round. I was told that someone had given him a pass when, in fact, he shouldn't have had one and a complaint would be filed about it. I got on the plane and that was the end of it as far as I was concerned.

When we reached Gothenburg, the press wanted to know what the doctors had said about my injury. I explained that I had a tear in my right hamstring and a cartilage problem in my left knee. Then someone said, 'We heard that you beat up a guy in Zurich'.

I thought he was joking and told him so.

The next day, I heard that every single British national newspaper had written the story that I had attacked the photographer, and that three armed security guards had to pull me off! I just couldn't believe it. One of the papers even went as far as to say that I had been walking through the airport with a redhead. Sue Barrett is far from being a redhead. None of the writers had been there and yet they had published this story – but each version was slightly different.

One said I had grabbed the photographer by his lapel and tried to take his camera. If I had done that, I would have needed to use two hands in order to get the camera, which was around his neck. Unless, of course, I dragged the camera – which was pretty big – down and pulled his neck off. All I did was hold on to the camera for a second or two. As for three armed security guards, if there had been three such guards in that area, then how come the photographer had got that far in the first place?

The fact that it was Reuters somehow made the story correct and all the newspapers had rushed to publish. It made me think that if someone told the press they had seen Linford Christie flying across the sky with wings, it would be accepted as the truth.

One way or another, the championships were dogged with scandal – not least being the story which broke alleging that I neglected my kids. The truth was that Yvonne Oliver, the mother of the twins, Liam and Korel, had wanted more money. So, we agreed that a solicitor should draw up a contract stipulating that I would pay her an amount each year. She did her sums, claimed for private school fees and mortgage repayments, and reached a figure, which I pay annually. What she does with that sum is up to her but the kids do not go to private school and she has not bought a house. It is not the sort of thing that I would want to see brought out in public because that is Yvonne's business. But suddenly, all of the details were in the press.

The papers made a big deal about the fact that DNA tests had been taken in order to prove that I was the father of the twins. We had gone our separate ways before then and, naturally, I was suspicious of any such claim about fatherhood until a test proved otherwise.

I pay a considerable sum each year. I don't mind that, so long as the kids are being looked after. But, because she was claiming social security, I was, to use her words in the papers, 'a tight-fisted bastard'. She is also alleged to have said that she didn't want to talk to me because, if she saw me, she would attack me. Yet she turns up where I train because the kids go there. She goes jogging; she sees me. She is quite bitter and it seems to me that all of this was making the story more attractive to the press. When I subsequently started legal action, Yvonne claimed not to have said any of these things.

Judith Osborne, Merric's mother, was also quoted in the

newspapers but she told me that she didn't say anything to the press about her situation and whether or not she is on social security. If that's true, then the newspapers went ahead and made up the story. They jumped on it. Yet I don't think I'm the only person to have children without being married . . .

The papers also took the opportunity to use bits of an interview I had given to a magazine a few years before. I had made the point that the authorities chased fathers all the time and I agree that, in some cases, that is necessary. But it takes two to tango. If a woman is willing to sleep with a man, then it is a fifty-fifty thing. If the woman says she wants the child and the father says he doesn't, what happens then? What if the couple have split up? Most men can have kids but not every man can play the role of a father. A father is a person who lives with the child, someone who is there all the time. From that point of view, I wasn't a father.

The papers said I had criticized single mothers. That's not the case. I respect single mothers – many of the women I know are single mothers – and I appreciate that it is not easy bringing a child up on your own. The point I was making was that the CSA goes after men when, in fact, they should be also be going after the women in some cases. They should look into what is happening to the money the father is giving to the mother to help take care of the child. Sometimes the mother has a new partner and that maintenance money is being spent on the whole household and not just the child.

It is not for me to knock single mothers; I don't know what it feels like. But the onus should not just be on the father. If you can't afford to bring a child into the world, then don't do it. Obviously, both partners should take precautions but, if accidents happen, then I believe that both people should be equally responsible. After all, conception does not usually occur under duress.

I found it upsetting that the newspapers should single out bits of the story and take the view that I was not interested at all in children. Of course, all of this had been promoted by the news that I had become a grandfather.

An anonymous caller had been in touch with the newspapers and told them that Linford Christie's son had become a father at the age of sixteen. Judith told me and, when she did, I was annoyed. I wanted to know why Merric had not taken precautions. It wasn't as if I hadn't talked to him about it.

Ours has never been a father-and-son relationship in the true sense because I was not living with Merric as he grew up. But I had tried to become friends with him; it was the logical thing to do. We had talked about women as men do, and I had told him that it was his life, but whatever he did he should use condoms.

Of course I had been through the same thing with his mother. I was nineteen at the time and things were different; condoms did not seem to us to be as acceptable or essential as they are now. In any case, I am supporting him, so how is he going to support his child? My dad used to tell me that if I slept with a woman, then I obviously thought I was a man. So therefore I should act like one and be able to support a child. In my view, it was no different for Merric.

Regarding the story about Merric bringing the baby to the gym for me to see for the first time; that was not true at all. Two weeks after the story had been printed in the papers, I still had not seen the baby because, of course, I had not been around. The newspapers just made up that part. The day Judith told me about the baby, I was on my way to Monte Carlo to train.

I can deal with the press. But Merric can't. They followed

him, hounded him, knocked on the door, talked through the letter box, persuaded him that if he didn't co-operate, they would take pictures and run the story anyway. So he decided he might as well make some money out of it.

I advised him not to do that. I said that once he had taken money, his life would never be his own. Then he told me he was going on a breakfast television show. I asked him if, when he got all his GCSEs, he had been on television because he was Linford Christie's son? Of course not. So it was because he had become a father, he was my son – and he was black. It was a way of saying, 'There's another black man out there having kids and not being able to support them.' Merric could have the highest degree in the land and they were not going to call him on to television for that. They were not, as he might think, making him a star.

It made me sad; you try to explain and kids don't understand. They think it's an easy life out there, they don't realize it is a dog-eat-dog world.

I had discovered some time before that these things always seem to come to light in the press just as I am preparing for a championship – hardly ideal circumstances under which to tackle the high point of your year. I was a British athlete looking for medals for my country but the papers always see that as the time to go to great lengths to make some damning revelation.

When I returned to Gothenburg, I thought it best to train and just get myself back together. But all the aggravation made me realize that I was risking injury and that it was not worth it. In the midst of all of this condemnation, I thought, 'Fair enough; I'll look after myself from here on and just do what I want to do.' I was still injured so, rather than risk causing further damage, I decided not to run the 4 × 100 relay. I concentrated on training, increasing the workload bit by bit each day.

By the time I reached Zurich at the beginning of the following week, I was feeling better and better. At first we thought I would have to miss the Grand Prix meeting on the Wednesday night. But, on the day before, I trained with Frankie Fredericks and found that I really, really wanted to run.

It just felt so good to be on the track. It's hard to explain; you have got to be an athlete to understand what I'm trying to say. Its like being a keen driver and you haven't been able to get behind the wheel for some time. Yet you can see everyone else rushing by and you are just bursting to drive again. I was dying to test my leg and I felt I was in a position to do that. After consultation with the doctor and with Ron, we decided that I should at least run the 100-metre heats.

The doctor said the torn hamstring was actually the result of a cartilage problem in my left knee. I had been favouring my right leg and the hamstring had been taking all of the strain. It proved that you have got to be really, really careful after an injury because, if you come back too soon and favour the other leg, you will have a problem there too.

I didn't want to go out if I couldn't do myself justice. Looking back, I didn't feel it had been the real me in Gothenburg; the acute disappointment still lingered. At sixty metres in the final, I had been in front at the point where I normally make my move. Had I been fit, they would not have seen me. I wanted to make sure I could do myself some kind of justice in Zurich.

It would be a matter of whether or not the leg was going to hold up. As we settled into the blocks for the heat, the starter was much much too quick with the 'set'. I put up my hand to let him know that I wasn't ready – not good for everyone's nerves but I had to be settled in properly. I was ready, however, when we got away first time on the gun.

I didn't push hard because the first two would go through from each of the three heats, plus the two fastest losers overall. My main concern was to qualify. I had to concentrate more than normal on my technique because at times like that, if the technique is not right, then the injury can return.

I won my heat and was surprised to see 10.09 come up on the scoreboard. I had been in good shape in the past and struggled to run that sort of time! But concern remained over the injury holding up during the final.

There was an hour to wait and I went to see the doctor laid on by the organizers. He checked me over, asked how I felt and said I should take some more painkillers. I didn't do anything further because I had done a long and careful warm-up with Colin Jackson in an indoor area which not many athletes seemed to know about. It is an ideal place, away from the crowds and warm enough to allow you to work up a good sweat, so that when you come out you feel ready to run. That feeling was still there when we were called forward for the final. After the disappointment of Gothenburg, there was a lot at stake here.

I had been given lane six, which surprised me a little because my winning time in the heat had been one of the best so far. Ato Boldon was on my right in lane seven, Jon Drummond on my left in lane five. I really wanted to be next to Donovan Bailey in lane four because he was the guy I thought I was going to have to beat. I wanted to be able to see exactly when he would make his move. If I could get out before him and he began to come back at me, then I would know when to change up to another gear. But, by being in lane six, I would have to use Drummond and Boldon. They were quick starters; if I was in front of them, then I would probably be okay.

Drummond got out the fastest – but that is reaction time only. The blocks are pressured and those times just show who moved first; what happens after that is a different story.

Ron and I had been discussing Donovan's starts. Ron said he had watched the tape of the final in Gothenburg and he had begun to realize that Donovan must be strong to have beaten everyone because his start had not been good. I had noticed that too in previous meetings; it was a case of knowing as much as you can about your enemies. It all came down to the fact that, if I could get out of the blocks ahead of him, then he would have no answer to my surge at sixty metres. Provided my leg held out.

It all went to plan. The start was not one of my best but I was ahead at sixty metres and I didn't really need a surge. It was easy. There are times when you run and you have to fight. On this occasion, I wasn't really fighting at all, I was quite relaxed. I won in 10.03 seconds. Donovan was second and Jon Drummond third.

For me, it was a relief more than anything else. I had got through the race with the minimum amount of discomfort. However, I was to know all about it the following morning; my hamstring was really throbbing and the cartilage in my left knee was sore – but then it was always going to be like that unless I had an operation, and I wasn't keen on that idea. The main thing was that I would be able to go back to Monte Carlo and train rather than having to go for special treatment and deal with a lot of pain.

At the press conference after the race, I was asked what this win meant to me. I said it had proved that I was the best guy on the night – but that it had come ten days too late. *C'est la vie.*

There was no ill-feeling between Donovan and me. We have known each other for a long time and we get on quite well. Competing against Donovan is different from racing against Carl Lewis and most of the Americans. Donovan doesn't talk rubbish. If the other athletes don't talk smack, then I won't wind them up either. That's the way it is with Donovan; we go out and race, it's a more relaxed atmosphere. When Carl was around, there was so much nonsense being talked that I just wanted to pummel him into the ground. It meant there was nothing like the good atmosphere we had in Zurich on 16 August 1995.

I still love running. Circumstances at Zurich had been ideal because there had been no pressure to compete. I had done a lot of promotion work for the organizers and they paid for all of my medical treatment. They had been really good; I had been paid to be there and yet they said I didn't have to run unless I really felt I could. It was the perfect way to come back from injury.

After the final, I was advised that I should not run too many races in quick succession. That meant I would miss the meeting in Gateshead a week later and I was criticized for that by the British press. But it was my decision; it had nothing to do with money. I had to do what was right for my health and fitness from here on.

I had run Zurich because I had wanted to. I had the urge to run. It's very difficult to sit on the sidelines and watch, you just want to be out there. If I hadn't taken part, I would never have known that 10.03 was possible. That time equalled my season's best – and it had been into a headwind. As I have said before, a minus wind affects the bigger athlete more than the little guy. Having run 10.03 in a minus wind, I knew I had a sub-10-second time in me somewhere.

This was the second year in succession that I had won Zurich. The atmosphere was fantastic; it always is. It is good because you are part of your public. The packed enclosures are really close. There are no barriers in the way, no fighting or hooliganism. It is a family occasion and people in the crowd feel that they are contributing to your effort. It is a tremendous feeling for everyone, athletes included.

The *Weltklasse* (part of the so-called Golden Four; Oslo, Zurich, Brussels and Berlin) provides more than four hours of solid entertainment. It is extremely well organized and puts meetings such as Crystal Palace into the second division. Places such as Zurich pay the money and the athletes of all nationalities come to entertain. Records get broken. Everybody wants to compete in Zurich.

If the athletes are looked after, they will return next year. Even if the promoter doesn't have much money, the athletes will come for less if the meeting is as good as Zurich. The food is good – at some of the other meetings struggling on low budgets, the food is so bad that we go out for a pizza – and I don't particularly like pizza! The accommodation is comfortable and we feel well looked after.

The Golden Four pay well; $7,000 for a win, plus appearance money and bonuses. In London, you have to run 10 seconds flat to earn £800! Under those circumstances on 16 August, I would have run my backside off and risked injury – and got nothing for it! Break the world record in Zurich and you get $50,000. That's a lot of money!

I am on a contract with the Golden Four. There are so many bonuses you can pick up – for winning, for finishing second and third, for setting a time that puts you in the world ranking, for breaking your national record. There are bonuses for everything! Of course, the fact that athletes should want to make the most of such an opportunity was wrong in the eyes of some members of the media.

Immediately after the World Championships, there had been suggestions in one or two of the newspapers that athletes had been saving themselves in Gothenburg in order to set a world record in Zurich and make a lot of money. People who write that sort of thing do not understand the first thing about athletics.

The World Championships are not about times; they are about winning. So, obviously, the athletes went to win. That was what they wanted to do. With no time bonuses or anything like that, they did enough to win. What is wrong with that? The thing some writers forget is that no athlete likes to *lose*.

However, there were some interesting points made about changing the structure of the prize funding. I think, for instance, that prize money should be paid in the World Championships. But not the Olympics, because it is prestigious to be an Olympic champion; it is priceless in many respects.

The World Championships come every two years and the time has come to pay athletes to perform. Giving them a car is, by comparison with the money earned elsewhere, worth very little. Man cannot live by bread alone and I don't think the IAAF understands that. The World Championships had been an anticlimax, certainly not as good as Stuttgart in 1993, and the reason was that the athletes were very, very tired.

You cannot keep performing, year in, year out. In 1994 we had the Commonwealth Games, European Championships and the Europa Cup; you can't keep going at that rate. We are human beings yet we are treated as if we are mechanical; they wind us up and we go out there and perform, zombie-like.

Every year they put more and more meetings on the calendar. If they want us to perform, perform, perform, they are going to have to start paying us. They tried to say that if we didn't go to the World Championships they would ban us from the Olympic Games. That's how bad it has become.

If there was £100,000 paid for winning in the World Championships, then the athletes wouldn't do the small meetings which pay a couple of thousand. Athletes have no other means of living, so they have to do all the minor events and, as a result, you get low-key World Championships such as Gothenburg. That is no way to run world athletics.

Chapter 19

WHERE TO FROM HERE?

I have often wondered just what I will do when I retire. My initial reaction is that I will stay at home. Simple as that. I would finally have the chance to take Mandy to some of the places where I have been, but never really had the opportunity to look at properly. I have always thought that I would like to do a world cruise but Ron insists it is not a good idea. Apparently he once went on a cruise and put on two stones. The only certainty is that I will take a long holiday.

After that? Perhaps I will think more about poetry, which is something I have been good at since my school days. I write quite a bit, it's just a knack. Mandy is pretty good, too. I don't know why or how it happened, but it is something that we both enjoy. I find it very easy. If, say, I am in a hotel room, it is no problem to sit down and compose a few verses. I have filled many books and written for Mandy. Nothing has been published; I'm not sure I want to go into that just yet. I have written about the sport, about love, about things you would never expect. It really is fun.

Then again, perhaps I could help Mandy set up a business. She is brilliant at interior design work and was responsible for choosing the decor at our new house in Florida. It will be really nice to have a more settled life together. Obviously, we have talked about children and that's one of the things we're looking forward to. It's a gift to be able to have kids and I am in a position to give my children all the things they need – but without spoiling them.

I consider myself blessed to have found someone like Mandy because athletes must be the hardest people to live with. When we are injured, we are a pain! I try not to bring my work home with me and that is one of the reasons why Mandy and I have managed to stay togther for so long. There are occasions when we talk about athletics but, even if someone at the track annoys me, I don't bring it home with me.

When it comes to business, I may become more involved with the day-to-day running of 'Nuff' Respect, but my feeling now is that I would prefer not to be involved with athletics. I will admit, however, that I could be drawn into working with young athletes. I see that some of the training and advice they receive is not of much use. It is not that the coaches concerned are of poor quality, it is just that I think I have a great deal more experience and feel I could do a better job.

I know what is going through the athlete's mind and I'm sure I would make a good coach. In fact, there are times when I feel that I would love to do it, but then I recall the politics and that makes me think again. I've had some very good times in the sport but I have also been through some very trying circumstances. I don't feel I would want to be a part of that unless the sport changes dramatically.

I've heard athletes say 'When I get into the management and become involved in the sport's administration, I'm going to change things'. And what happens? When they move into management they become even worse than their predecessors. I really don't want that to happen to me. I have my own way of doing things and it would cause certain clashes. If I am to coach, then I would want to be the best coach in the world. But I don't think that is possible because certain people would stand in my way and say, 'I'm your boss; now you do what I say'.

I remember meeting an administrator who had one of our former athletes working under him. He took great pleasure in telling me that he was the athlete's boss and generally running the guy down. It was obvious that the athlete needed money and had to put up with such treatment. Hopefully I will never need to do that.

I am aware, however, that I can communicate well with athletes. When Bruny Surin, one of the world's top ten sprinters, came to Tampa to train with me, we discovered that some of the points I was making were completely new to Bruny. He asked if I had thought about coaching when I retired; he reckoned I would be good. Frankie Fredericks has said much the same thing.

I have always had ideas of my own. I look at my body and ask what, exactly, do I want from it and what is the best way of achieving that. I have always listened to other people and taken everything in. My weight training, for example, developed solely from ideas picked up from others and adjusted to suit what I need. I have found that when training in a group in Australia or wherever, I am asked about the best way to tackle work in the gym. I help people when I can but I never feel that is enough because, of course, I have to get on with my own training. But it gives me a very good feeling if positive results come from athletes who have acted on my advice. At times like that I think, 'Yes, maybe I could be a coach'.

Perhaps this is the wrong time to make a decision about my future. It could be that, after a period away from the sport, I might get a hunger for it and change my mind. I would like to be able to do something for athletics but, right now, I want to get away. Ten years of top-level competition has brought me everything, both good and bad.

I can honestly say that I don't look back with regret on any part of my career; I am satisfied with everything I have achieved and there have been no major disappointments. Things have not always gone the way I wanted them to go – but that didn't mean huge disappointment. The popular expression is that 'life's a bitch'. But life is only a bitch when things are going badly wrong and I don't think I can really say that.

I love life. My career on the track has been good to me; I've had a minimal amount of injuries. There is not one thing that I would want to change. Of course, I made mistakes along the way but you learn from mistakes. They are a necessary part of life. Generally, the good things have outweighed the not so good by a very long way. I wouldn't swap any of it. I've had the opportunity to travel and meet people I would not otherwise have had the chance to become acquainted with. Some remain really good friends.

One or two have become enemies but I don't hate any of them as people; it's their attitude more than anything else. I am often told that the main reason I have problems with the media is because I am good. If being average and of no interest is the only way to stop the hassle, then I would always want to be the best.

I would be very happy to think that I had given hope to a lot of people. I believe I have demonstrated that with hard work, dedication and a few sacrifices, you can achieve anything you want. It is all about self belief. The saying 'how can you discover the ocean if you are afraid to leave the shore?' sums it up.

My only regret is that my grandmother was not alive to see some of the things I achieved; I know she would have been so proud. My mother was aware of everything, of course, and that helps to give me a sense of belonging. In many ways, my achievements will help keep them both alive in my memory.

I have been asked, if given the chance to do it all again, I would start my running career earlier than I did. The answer is no. I came into athletics at the right time, just as the sport was reaching a peak. I was in the middle of quite an era. I've been with the best, I've been with the worst, I've been with the inbetweens. I've seen them come and I've seen them go. I've been in athletics when there was no money at all; I'm still involved at a time when things are changing quickly from the financial point of view. Overall, it could not have been better. If I had started earlier, I would have finished earlier. So I would not change anything. I believe that it was God's way. It has been in His hands; my athletics career has been part of my destiny and I thank God that I was able to fulfil it.

I was considering earlier where I go from here but, really, that is not for me to decide. Only God knows what the future holds for me. There is a line from a song which goes, 'I don't know about tomorrow. I just live from day to day.' That's the way I look at it.

I'm an impulsive person and I think that is the best way to be; just enjoy life and get on with it because there is too much to worry about otherwise. If you thought you were going to be run over by a bus tomorrow, you would never leave your house, never mind crossing the road. We are all in God's hands.

I find it sad that religion no longer seems to play such an important part in family life; certainly not as much as it did when I was a child in Jamaica. There seems to be a general decline in standards all round and, as I said in an earlier chapter, we are hardly set a good example in this country by high-ranking officials and members of Parliament.

It is also very clear to me that racism, especially in Britain, has become institutionalized. That's how I honestly see it. I try to put myself in a position where it does not affect me too much but it is inevitable that we should have problems when more than one race or creed try to live togther. In Britain, racism is ingrained so cleverly that you can't do anything about it. If you are black and complain, the first thing they say is that you have a chip on your shoulder. There is no way round it. I know it exists; I know I am black, I don't have to go out and shout about it.

I try, in my own way, to show that something can be done – not just for black people but for all races. I try to put a smile on faces across the world and I am in a position to do that because I am known more or less everywhere. I talk to everybody. In my small way, I would like to think that I bring nations together thanks to my achievements on the track. I don't go out there and say I'm running for black people; I'm running for everyone.

I am a working-class person even though I've heard it said that I am otherwise. I am just a normal guy who happens to be able to run a bit faster than everyone else. People who have come to know me during the past four or five years don't necessarily appreciate what has gone on before. I've worked my way up. It's been hard and I've never gone for the easy way out. I hope that kids can take something from that and realize that if it is easy, it's not worth having.

I like to talk about respect. As a black child, one of the first things my parents taught me was respect. I learned to respect my elders; I learned to respect other people; I learned to respect another person's possessions.

I get knocked for that now. The British media say I am searching for respect and they have a problem with the fact that our company is called 'Nuff' Respect. Respect is a value, and it is no longer taught in Britain. As a black kid, I was told all about good manners. Britain is in the state it is now because those values don't seem to exist any more.

I hope that somewhere along the way, this book will help people. I hope that the book will mean different things to different people. I don't mean to be blasphemous or presumptuous in any way but I think of this book as being like the Bible in that it will be widely read and there will be different interpretations placed upon it.

It should tell you that there is a way which seems right unto every man. I hope that there is a little bit in the book that has appealed to everybody. But I want to share my achievements. I may be a champion, but I don't profess to win everything. The time is going to come when I won't win anything at all. But I am a fighter and I think that is the best part of it. People are behind me, not just because I go out and win, but because I fight.

I don't always accept the saying that it's not the winning, it's the taking part which counts. Winning is pretty important but you can't be criticized if you fight, even if you don't win. Not everyone can be a champion – but everyone can try.

I am comfortable with what I've done; your conscience sets you free. There is the saying that on the day of judgment, every man shall give an account of himself to God. It's not your parents who will give the account, nor your friends. Everyone is responsible for how they live their life on this earth, but it would be too easy if everyone did exactly what they wanted to do and nothing else. I do believe that, one day, each of us will be asked to give an account.

Because I am an athlete, people say I should be a role model. I never felt comfortable with that. *All* adults should be role models. We should set standards for the kids, but it should not be one rule for them and one rule for us; I think we are all guilty of that.

I've gone down in history, whether I like it or not. People will look back and see the name Linford Christie. To me, it is a legacy for my children, and for my grandchildren. They can say they had someone in their family who achieved and I really hope it gives them a sense of purpose, something to aim for in their own lives.

From my point of view, I will be able to remember the happy times, recall the good races, tell my kids about them, enjoy what I have done. But, I won't be doing any of that until I have totally finished with athletics and, as I said at the beginning of the chapter, I can't be sure exactly when that will be.

When I do, I know I will miss the camaraderie, and I would like to think the feeling will be mutual. When I was in Zurich, one of the young women athletes from another country said she really enjoyed being in my company. I was staying at the same hotel as everyone else – unlike some of the top names who had moved away to a bigger and better place – and she was saying that she wished the other athletes had stayed in the same hotel, because that sort of thing rubs off. I have always believed that if you win a medal, you should stay with the team, because success breeds success. I have stuck by that and I'd like to think I will be missed because if it.

I will always remember the saying, which was permanently attached to the notice board of my school in Jamaica, 'When a great writer comes to write against your name, he writes not how you won or lost, but how you played the game.'

This book tells you how I played my game. I can't say what the judgment will be but, to be honest with you, I will have no complaints if people remember me as one of the best sprinters in the world. Nothing will ever change that.

INDEX